Dragon Rule

BOOK FIVE OF THE AGE OF FIRE

E. E. KNIGHT

A ROC BOOK

ROC
Published by New American Library, a division of
Penguin Group (USA) Inc., 375 Hudson Street,
New York, New York 10014, USA
Penguin Group (Canada), 90 Eglinton Avenue East, Suite 700, Toronto,
Ontario M4P 2Y3, Canada (a division of Pearson Penguin Canada Inc.)
Penguin Books Ltd., 80 Strand, London WC2R 0RL, England
Penguin Ireland, 25 St. Stephen's Green, Dublin 2,
Ireland (a division of Penguin Books Ltd.)
Penguin Group (Australia), 250 Camberwell Road, Camberwell, Victoria 3124,
Australia (a division of Pearson Australia Group Pty. Ltd.)
Penguin Books India Pvt. Ltd., 11 Community Centre, Panchsheel Park,
New Delhi - 110 017, India
Penguin Group (NZ), 67 Apollo Drive, Rosedale, Auckland 0632,
New Zealand (a division of Pearson New Zealand Ltd.)
Penguin Books (South Africa) (Pty.) Ltd., 24 Sturdee Avenue,
Rosebank, Johannesburg 2196, South Africa

Penguin Books Ltd., Registered Offices:
80 Strand, London WC2R 0RL, England

Published by Roc, an imprint of New American Library, a division of Penguin
Group (USA) Inc. Previously published in a Roc trade paperback edition.

First Roc Mass Market Printing, July 2012
10 9 8 7 6 5 4 3 2 1

PUBLISHER'S NOTE
This is a work of fiction. Names, characters, places, and incidents either are the
product of the author's imagination or are used fictitiously, and any resem-
blance to actual persons, living or dead, business establishments, events, or
locales is entirely coincidental.

The publisher does not have any control over and does not assume any responsibility for author or third-party Web sites or their content.

TO THE MEMORY OF SAM,
MY FAITHFUL ALLY IN GOOD TIMES AND IN BAD

Contents

THE SADDLE VALE

AIRCASTLE

BARBARIAN LANDS

INLAND OCEAN

PROTECTORATE

RED MOUNTAINS

SWEEP OF THE IRONRIDERS

GROWTH
OF THE
DRAGON
EMPIRE

OLD UPLANDS

SWAYPORT

PROTECTORATE OF HYPATIA

FALMER RIVER

DISPUTED LANDS

PROTECTORATE
OF CHIOZ

PROTECTORATE
OF OSSUM

PETTY PRINCIPALITIES

Map by
Thomas
Manning

THE LAVADOME

BOOK ONE

Faiths

"INTENT AND RESULT ARE TWO ALLIES WHO RARELY MEET."

—*Aphorism engraved on the south wall
of the Hypatian Directory*

Chapter 1

The Copper dragon, Tyr of Worlds Upper and Lower, Exalted Protector of the Grand Alliance, tried not to show the pain.

The velvet darkness of the warm air over the Inland Ocean might have been that of summer instead of late autumn. The oceanic currents near the nighted shore swirled with the balm of the shallower waters of the delta country to the south. Heat rising from the phosphorescent waters, alive with tiny glowing creatures riding the warmth, caressed his wings and underbelly as he flew.

He couldn't remember the last time he enjoyed such a perfect night for flying.

Not that there was time to enjoy an idyll. The moon had vanished below the horizon; it was time for hard flying to Swayport, rocky fastness of the Pirate Lords on the Western Shores of the Inland Ocean. The soft air, seemingly made to beckon young dragons into the sky to chase and turn and embrace at last as mates, was cut instead by wings bound for war.

Healthy wings with intact joints, that is. The Copper dragon's pinioned right wing was held together by cable and gear, and tonight the contraption that allowed him to fly chafed and pinched. Terrible time to come up wingfelled, with a battle to be fought.

He'd been trying for the last hour not to think about the rising pain in his wing, but a raw nerve under torn flesh would not be ignored. The pain was like an arrow tearing through his joint at each reverse of the wing. The topstroke and bottom both brought stabbing agony, alike as twins.

Having given up not thinking about the pain, he fell back to his second line of defense, as one of his captains might have put it. He tried not showing it, to keep his appearance to the other dragons in the flight line that of a Tyr eager for battle in the coming red dawn.

If the second line fell, he would just have to grimace, squint, fall back on his final cave-redoubt: showing the pain but keeping his place at the point of the long arc of battle-arrayed dragons, forty-one veterans aloft. They rode laden with fur-tufted soldiers with scrimshawed whalebone lensholders protecting their eyes against the wind and woolen scarves warming the breath entering their windburned noses. A proud Tyr at the head of his warriors, he'd rather have his wing give out and spin to his death into the sea than take one of the easier positions behind.

The throbbing came from his bad midwing joint, of course. Severed by a vicious human called the Dragonblade when he was but a hatchling, he could only fly with the aid of an artificial joint his clever, dwarf-trained thrall Rayg had created. Hearing of the long journey he proposed to undertake, Rayg had crafted him a new one. So superior—thanks to the work of the best dwarfs money could rent—was his new design in execution that after a short test flight the Copper pronounced it a brilliant improvement on the older model and ordered a feast in Rayg's name. His wing had a much more natural motion now. He could fly farther with less effort.

Except his leathery wing skin had not yet toughened to the task of the new brace.

The Copper blamed himself for not taking the time for conditioning flights. Both he and Rayg had been distracted by other matters: the Copper with his plans for war against the pirates, Rayg with his numerous projects. Rayg had been behaving lately like a man with his brain aflame with genius to the point the Copper imagined smoke coming from his ears. Plans for improvements to the Lavadome and everything from dragon-saddles to food storage silos covered Rayg's laboratory walls like intricately layered paper of a wasp nest.

The Copper, bound to his roving battlecourt watching training runs for the suppression of the Pirate

Lords, had only taken to the air for brief periods of exercise before his daily consultations and messaging.

Now he was paying for it in blood, pain, and torn flesh. *What's a little skin off my wing? If only Nilrasha, my Queen, could see how gracefully I fly. Faster, without the constant lurching course corrections . . .*

He promised himself a long, restful visit to his mate's eyrie if the war against the Pirate Lords proved victorious.

Of course, if things went ill with the Pirate Lords, he might still join Nilrasha as an exile rather than as a conquering Tyr. Feeling ran hot in the Lavadome against this war, which would benefit none but their allied human provinces in the Upper World.

Dragons bleed for Hypatia's need!

Some young, freshly fledged dragons had sung outside his private air gallery, before being chased away by his guard. He hadn't objected to the opinioneering so much as being awakened after a long night's work.

Of course, he'd tried diplomacy. The Hypatians sent emissaries with demands that their former colonies of Swayport cease molesting their shipping and interfering with the fishing fleets. They'd returned with a tale of laughter and ridicule.

The Pirate Lords claimed not to fear dragons, presenting trophies of a victory against the Wizard's Dragonriders twoscore years back, when dragons who had assaulted their fortress fell before its gates.

He wondered if the pirates had considered that dragons flighting under rein and rider fought very differently from dragons directed by their own commanders and Tyr. They showed no sign of it in their brag and bluster.

Thinking didn't help with the pain. So much flying. He regretted not accompanying the surfwater forces, but a Tyr's place when going to war was at the head of his Aerial Host. Even at the cost of some pain. But the hurt did bring one benefit. It put him in a foul mood. Nothing like pain and the smell of blood to fill the firebladder and set it quivering. He was ready for battle.

Lights twinkled on the horizon. Swayport at last!

The Copper's sharp eyes picked out the outlines of the port. From his position, a good score of dragonlengths above the water with the rocky coast to the west and the gentle Inland Ocean night to the east, Swayport as seen from the air resembled a reclining cat facing out toward the ocean, its spine in a gentle curve creating a sheltered bay. Against its belly was the port itself, a long crescent of sand beach, protected by a barren bar exposed at low tide. The cat's dangerous—to rodents, anyway—*sii* were stuck out as a series of rocks perilous to mariners approaching from the north, its long tail a wave-breaking sandbar to the south.

A rocky bluff at the cat's head held an ancient sloping fortress of double walls and three towers with its own wharf between the forelimbs. The fortress had been built an age ago by the Hypatian Empire at the height of its wealth and power, and the wharf was intended so that the defenders might be resupplied by sea if the rest of the landward settlement fell.

The town of the Pirate Lords proper had not been so solidly built. A tangle of streets and structures of wood and stone rose to the temple domes on the cat's haunches. The Pirate Lords no longer worshipped the gods of their forefathers there; instead the temples sheltered gambling and drink and slave-auctions, the usual low pursuits of men who lived by fighting and pillage.

He'd promised to hand them back to the Hypatians with only minor scorching.

Swayport, and six other colonies on this coast like it, had long since declared their independence from the old Hypatian order. In the best of times there was trade across the Inland Ocean, at other times war, and chafing between rival fishing fleets and trading lines in every season—even the storm-months at the death of the year, when ships driven into opposing ports seeking shelter from storms were charged outrageous harbor fees or had their cargoes seized.

The Copper had listened to weary hours of it from Hypatian shipowners and the whaling guild until he thought he'd dream of nothing but the price of lamp oil and salted fish for the rest of his life, before making his decision to end the pirate menace.

Well, if men couldn't settle their differences, he'd force a peace. As the Hypatians were his allies, though sometimes they were hard to distinguish from unusually quarrelsome thralls, he'd see the disputes resolved in their favor.

He had two advantages, and he intended to use them. The first was a pretext for war that had all Hypatia seething. One of the great merchant lines—they flew a flag with blue and yellow and a fish design; the Copper couldn't remember the name—had one of its deepwater trade boats blown off course and into the hands of a commerce-raider, who brought it back to Swayport.

Such a matter could usually be resolved with paying a small ransom, but this ship held the merchant line's owner and family, a man of influence as wide as his belt size and deep as his purse. They put his crew to work cutting paving stones and his family in the fortress and sent the youngest son of the line back to the Hypatian Directory with a ransom demand.

The Copper, when told the tale by one of the Directory's many skilled tongues, growled that if it was one of his own dragon families from the Lavadome, he'd be descaled if he'd pay anything with drakes and dragonelles locked up in some dungeon with excrement running down between the walls.

With that Hypatia begged for assistance in a war to humble the Pirate Lords.

His other advantage was knowledge of Swayport and its fortress, now ever so much closer on the horizon. But the moon would reappear soon—was it yet looming on the southeastern horizon? It musn't be allowed to frame the oncoming dragons like a shadow-puppet light.

The far-off battlements formed a false horizon

against the stars. The old works must be massive, at least the size of Imperial Rock in the Lavadome, though perhaps not quite so high.

Swayport had been attacked a generation ago by the thrall-dragons from that fog-shrouded island to the north that his gray brother skulked upon, back in the days of Wrimere Wyrmaster, the Wizard of the Isle of Ice. One of the human veterans of his Aerial Host, now a proud and battle-scarred Captain, had been involved in the attack.

The attack had failed strategically because the men of Swayport had learned dragon-fighting from the dwarfs, and filled the towers overlooking their harbor with war machines that fired aerial harpoons. His sister Wistala had shown him one, a souvenir of one of her own battles, when she gave a tutorial to the Firemaids about aboveground hominid fortifications and defenses. The Copper still shuddered at the memory: it was a horrible barbed thing the length of a spear, full of spurs that went in easily but wouldn't come out without destruction to muscle, blood vessel, and organ. He'd rather take an arrow through the eye and die at once.

Worse, the dwarfs and men like the Pirate Lords attached long chains or weights to the harpoons. The chains might catch on rooftop or tree branch and yank the harpoon out with crippling damage; the weights caused even the strongest dragon to come to earth eventually, where he'd remain, ground-bound and vulnerable, until the metal could be broken.

According to Wistala, such a device had been the death of their father.

The Copper, trying to forget his wing for a few more beats by thinking back on his conversations with the captains, both dragon and human, remembered, too, the strategic blunder the dragons-slavers had made. A scouting rider had passed over the town and took it upon himself to demand food and drink for himself and his mount. When refused, the fool angered and started burning small craft in the harbor before flying off with his dragon hungrier than ever.

With Swayport alarmed, when the dragon-slavers returned, they found a populace ready for battle. After some skirmishing, cooler heads prevailed and the dragon-slavers decided the battle wouldn't be worth whatever could be gleaned from a poor series of villages and a fishing port.

Now Swayport was thriving and prosperous, in part thanks to their resistance to the dragon-slavers. Refugees from wars elsewhere had settled under the protection of the old Hypatian colonial fortress that had seen off the dragons once.

The Copper could now make out the outlines of the craggy fortress atop the cat's-head bluff. The towers made it look like the cat was wearing a crown, or perhaps had grown an extra docked ear. He glanced at his wing. It was leaking blood and throbbed, but he'd made it through the night at the head of his dragons. He'd brought the dragons to war, at the place and time arranged. The rest was up to his commanders.

The Copper swung his tail down three times.

With that, the six biggest and most ancient dragons of the Aerial Host struggled to gain altitude. The men tied and strapped on the broad dragon-backs, clad only in warm riding-furs with a few light blades, shifted position so they were boots-down, looking like storm-wrecked sailors clinging to the sides of an over-turned boat.

The Copper's Griffaran Guard closed up around him, ready to protect their Tyr in battle.

The colorful *griffaran* were more feather-skulled bird than noble dragoncrest, but they were fellow egg layers and ancient allies of the Dragons of the Lava-dome. Though lazy and playful and argumentative around their own nests, those who dedicated them-selves to the Tyr found ample mental stimulation keep-ing watch and guarding the Imperial family, and in return the dragons kept egg raiders away from their nests and brought delicious dried fruits and salted nuts from far away, or had their thralls bake oily seed-crackers the avians preferred above all other foods. They had long talons and powerful beaks that could tear through dragon-scale, and as they were rarely called upon to fight thought the constant stream of tasty tidbits, shiny decor, and soft nest-bedding the Im-perial family gave in exchange for their service ample compensation.

Night-fishing birds cried an alarm to their kin as they passed, but Swayport itself still slept. Only a few lights glimmered in town and fortress.

A swift-winged dragonelle broke off from the rest of the formation and headed for the sandbar. There were some flat-bottomed Hypatian river barges there in the surf outside it. Not the most seaworthy craft, but the Firemaids had managed to swim them up from the ruins of the old elven city loaded with Hypatian soldiers. Supposedly the scions of some of the great old military families of Hypatia, they looked more like a rabble in half-polished rust to the Copper, but they'd do for keeping order after the attack and going down some of the smaller, darker holes with the aid of slender young drakes and drakka swimming beside the barges.

The barges' arrival, just off the sandbar, had precipitated the flight of the Aerial Host.

Ignoring the pain in his wing, the Copper sped up as though eager to come to grips.

Tide wasn't in their favor. The sandbar to the south had several flooded passages across it, but with the tide out, the barges couldn't be pulled through. They'd have to be emptied, dragged across the shallow by the dragonelles, and then filled again.

Well, if that was the worst thing to go wrong in the war with the Pirate Lords, he would take it.

A blue-white light on one of the boats in the harbor danced across the deck, then ran up the rigging. A signal of some sort.

The Aerial Host had been spotted. Or perhaps the dragons coming across the sandbar had become tangled in someone's lobster pots.

The Copper checked to see that his man-laden veterans were on the way to the fortress towers, two heading for each, and then stiffened his wings and went into a glide toward the signaling ship.

He picked out a yellow and blue banner atop the tallest mast. So they had a guard on the captured Hypatian ship ready to signal at an attempt to retake the craft.

The Copper ran his tongue along the inside of his teeth in satisfaction. *Much more than that is on its way, oh pirate sailor.* But now the *foua* pulsing in his firebladder would have to be directed at some other target.

He shot over the captured ship and swung with his tail. Lines sang as rigging parted and he felt a satisfying *krrack!* as his tail broke salt-dried timber. But when he glanced behind, the man climbing the mast still hung there, waving his burning blue light in circles. Sparks from it rained down toward the bay in brilliant parabolas only to die like fireflies.

Little man, think you'll escape me?

The Copper folded his hurt wing—sweet relief!—in a quick diving turn and—

A mass shot under him *kunk-twaaang!* followed by chattering chain.

Clever men! They put a dragon-harpoon on the boat. Of course everyone knew the Hypatians had dragon allies; it was a sensible precaution.

"Get them—at the war machine!" he called to his Griffaran Guard, who banked to flank him with their usual effortless grace. *Griffaran* could literally fly circles around a dragon.

Two circled, misunderstood his order—the unfamiliar dwarfish-based word translated into Parl translated into the accents of dragontongue and then hurled at a pair of anxious users of a patois of dragontongue and birdspeech in the night was a recipe for confusion but two others darted for the forged shell of the harpoon-thrower in its reinforced pinioned mount.

The *griffaran* landed atop the device and tore into the men working cranks on the machine like fresh calf meat. Pieces flew messily in all directions.

The Copper saw men at the tail—or rather stern, the tail end of ships were called *sterns*—aiming another war machine at the dragons cutting across the bay. All this nautical terminology suggested secret knowledge as obscure as any of the studies of the sages on Ankelene Hill, but it was part of the marvel of all the devices hominids invented to compensate for physical, mental, and moral weaknesses.

He forgot the man in the rigging, folded his wings, and landed on the deck—shattering rail, machine, and men. A few good stomps and the whole mess went overside, weighed down by heavy chains and weights.

Good riddance.

Ship fighting wasn't without its hazards. He felt several painful splinters in his *sii* and *saa* and he had lines and nets tangled in his scale. His *griff* rattled in vexation.

"My Tyr!" HeBellereth, his scarred old Commander of the Aerial Host, called. "Are you injured?"

The Copper straightened his neck to trumpet:

"The towers! The gate! Never mind me. Keep to the plan! That fortress must be taken."

The moon peeped the top sliver of its great white eye over the Inland Ocean. By it the Copper could see the barges coursing across the bay, pulled by churning pairs of Firemaids with leather-wrapped cables in their mouths.

The smell of salt—salt from the blood, salt from the water, salt from his own rended flesh—brought the night to brilliant life. He'd rarely felt more alive. The pain of his sore wing was forgotten in triumph as he watched his laden dragons alight atop the shielded towers of the fortress.

Men dropped off the hovering dragons and onto the battlements the way squirrels fell out of a tail-swiped tree. As planned, they seized the deadly war machines in the towers before they could be loaded and readied.

A mass roared out of the night. The Copper couldn't react until it was upon him, so intent was he in watching the human warriors of his Aerial Host.

It struck him and the deck of the ship with such force the ship flopped over on its side. The ship's timbers groaned in protest.

It was a dragon. Not one of his own, no *laudi* marked its wings as testament to worthiness to serve in the Aerial Host, no white stripe painted on the side of its flank and crest for the night attack showed him as friend. Nor was it a dragonelle.

A black dragon, and a huge one at that, climbed out

of the mass of lines and wood, dragging it like a water dog emerging from seaweed.

This dragon hadn't grown up in the Lavadome, and fed on stringy lightsick cattle and fatty pork. Its limbs and haunches and back ridge were meaty, and nine long horns had been left to grow riotous and wild into a barbed thatch, a barbaric look when compared to the polished horns of his own dragons.

"They said I'd be able to spot the leader with the birds and all," the great dragon said thickly, speaking Drakine as though it were a foreign tongue.

The Copper scrabbled up onto the side of the tipped ship, fighting lines that tried to pull him under. The two dragons' joint weight sent it rolling again and the Copper felt the snaps of masts transmit through the hull.

His Griffaran Guards fluttered about like anxious nectar feeders. The black dragon batted one away with the tip of a massive wing.

Griff flanking his jawline rattling of their own accord, the Copper tasted the air around the stranger. He reeked of whale blubber.

"I take it these are your men?"

The black ignored him and lunged forward, mouth agape. Their weight upset the ship, and they both slid into the bay before the diving *griffaran* could sink their claws into the stranger's flanks. The big black struck him like an avalanche. Only the water, slowing his enemy's limbs, kept him from being opened at the inner joint of his left *saa*.

A digging, rending grip caught him across the back. Not since he'd fought old King Gan in his bats' cave did he feel such power. The only chance the Copper had was to make it to the surface where his guard could hit the big stranger from all sides. He pressed with his legs and broke the grip, losing more skin and scale in the process.

Whoever the stranger was, he hadn't spent his youth in endless trials against other dragons. For all his strength, he fought rather clumsily, used to letting his size exhaust his prey. He should have coiled with his tail to secure his hold from the other direction.

The Copper lunged out of the water and the *griffaran* swooped down to meet him, letting out alarmed cries. A dragonelle circled above, crying out, but his ears had little but his only pounding pulse in them and he couldn't distinguish her words.

He was halfway out, using the crusty creatures covering the bottom of the overturned ship for purchase, when the black's head broke water. The black took a deep breath and shot a warning gout of flame at the frantic *griffaran*.

He dove again and the Copper felt teeth clamp around his tail. The Copper dug in *sii* and *saa*, but the black swam like one of the great whales beneath the overturned ship, and once again the hull rolled as he was dragged under.

The Copper became doubly entangled in rope and wreckage. A powerful mass closed around him, and the black hauled him to the surface, its neck wrapped around his.

They came out, tresses of rope and broken wood hanging about their crests and horns.

"Call off your dragons," the black gasped.

Strong, but not in very good fighting trim.

He tried to feel around with his *saa* for somewhere to gut, but the black had his legs about them like the coils of King Gan.

"Before I say anything, I'll have your name," the Copper grunted.

"My name's Shadowcatch the Black, from the Isle of Ice," the dragon said.

His brother's island? Had the reclusive wretch sent assassins? Madness, especially since his drakes and drakka—or had they fledged?—were promising young members of the Drakwatch and Firemaidens.

Two of his veteran dragons, having lost the heavy load of troops, now circled low overhead.

"My Tyr?" one called.

"Answer with aught but a recall of your wings, and I'll tear your head off," Shadowcatch said.

Not an intelligent dragon at all, more bulk than brain. Did the brute think he could just bellow and have the soldiers now landing on Swayport's beaches and advancing behind flame-spewing dragonelles return to their craft? Fire burned bright at a seawall protecting the town and in one of the towers of the looming fortress, an orange torch sending reflective flame across the comfortably warm waters of the bay. A little foggy, the Copper reckoned some of the warmth came from the two opponents' mingled blood.

The Copper struggled in vain. He thwacked the brute's head with his tail, but that great tangled crest warded off the weak blow; all they did was spin.

A broken mast floated among the wreckage, tangled in place like the rest of them by rigging lines.

"Even if I pass the word, it will be some time before I can recall all my forces. The moon will be halfway up." The Copper flailed about with his tail, managed to strike the mast. He got some semblance of a grip with his tail, for once in his life grateful that his *sii* had been maimed in the hatchling fight rather than his tail.

"Just do it," Shadowcatch said.

"As you say," the Copper said, doing his best to get a better view of his opponent.

He reached with his tail, found a grip. With all his remaining strength he pulled the splintered end of the mast hard toward him, striking the black in the thinner scale of the neck where the tight coils of his own left the scales raised and turned at a vulnerable angle.

The black bellowed, gave one final tremendous pull—the Copper was sure his spine would snap under the pressure, leaving him to be pulled under by the deadweight of his hindquarters—and reared up to bite.

A pair of *griffaran* clawed at the black's head, not going for his eyes but wrapping their talons around his thatch of horns. Flapping together, they pulled him out of biting range; dragon jaws are strong, their necks less so, and a third member of the Guard whipped under his chin and clawed at his throat, going for the pulsing neck-hearts.

Shadowcatch released the Copper and used weight and momentum to topple back into the water. One of the *griffaran* released his hold and flapped away; his companion was caught under the black's mighty crest and struck water hard.

Water roiled and the Copper bobbed in the black's wake.

"He's heading out to sea!" the Firemaiden above called.

"Leave him," the Copper gasped. He pushed the sodden, dead-eyed bird up onto the wallowing hulk of the ship. The Copper bent his ear to it, heard a faint pulse. Not sure what to do, the Copper tapped it a couple of times with his snout and gave his guard a lick on the display crest between the eyes. The bird was a veteran of many battles; he had painted marks on his beak. The Copper felt he should know his name—Mishi or something like that. Suddenly the bird-reptile's pulse strengthened and the *griffaran* blinked.

"Thank you, my Tyr-awk!" it squawked, taking a deep breath and preening out sodden feathers.

The rest of the Griffaran Guard made a colorful, taloned tornado above his head as the Copper gladly left the wrecked ship and coursed for the beach, limbs tight to his sides and body writhing like a snake's. The whole waterfront was alive with flame and cries.

The Copper pulled himself up onto the beach and shivered, chilled. He must have lost a good deal of blood between the wing and his fights. He made a pretense of issuing orders as reports came in—the overall direction of the battle could be better handled by He-Bellereth.

Someone brought him a dead horse and he managed a few mouthfuls. Digestion warmed him, and he brought the rest of the meal and propped it atop the chimney of a burning building facing the seawall so it might toast and smoke. He'd lost his taste for raw mammal flesh long ago.

He took to the air, rather tiredly and painfully, his Griffaran Guard trailing him so close they looked like a colorful extension to his tail.

HeBellereth had done a dragonlike job of directing the fight. Some fires raged below, small fast ships that might be used to put crews into the larger ships burned and a few houses wore hats of flame. The Aerial Host had spared the warehouses and workshops, fishing boats and big-bellied merchant craft. The wealth of Swayport remained intact.

Discipline. His dragons knew better than to burn a city. Reducing flimsy human dwellings to splintered fuelwood and charcoal with flame and tailswipe might be fine fun, but it wasn't the way of the Tyr's dragons as Protectors of the Grand Alliance. Burning homes meant the exposed humans would sicken and die, a loss of valuable thrall capital.

Alley fighting sputtered below, brief shouts and clashes that faded into chases in and out of urban gardens, tiny side doors, or narrow staircases.

The Copper dipped first his right wingtip, then his

left, ignoring the newly revived pain as he sought a better look.

A young human led one of the storming columns off—at least he seemed young insofar as the Copper could judge things. He was fencepost-thin and thickly furred; his thick and shining mane flowed out from beneath helm—even the best older human warrior tended to go a bit thin as they aged. He was a whirlwhind, tearing doors off their hinges, upsetting carts placed to block streets leading to the cliffside fortress, hurling javelins uphill at the fleeing Swayport archers two full dragonlengths and more when he wasn't leaving crumpled foes like dropped bundles in his wake with swings of a battle-ax.

The Copper marked that he wore the furs and goggles of one of the Aerial Host. He thought he knew most of the men, but this tall, thin fellow was new to him.

The storming columns converged. Though the gates had been bashed open by tailswipe and dropped stones, the Swayport soldiery had made a barricade of the rubble, broken timber, and bent metal. The Hypatian soldiers faltered here, and were flung back by desperate spear fighting and pressed shields.

The young human picked up a fallen Hypatian banner, leaped upon the pedestal of a broken statue in the paved plaza before the citadel's gates, and swirled the banner. He called to one of the Aerial Host crossbowmen behind, who touched arrow to smoldering match and sent a sparkling signal-bolt into the Swayport crowd at the gate.

The Copper marked that one of the attacking dragons passed low. The dragon altered course, swooped for the gate, and executed a neat spin to dodge a harpoon fired from some concealed war machine in the fortress.

Alert fellow to mark the signal and attack so quickly. He'd get a new *laudi* dyed to his wing for that.

The dragon landed atop the rubble and turned into a biting, clawing fury. Swayport soldiers were tossed through the air or fled the the dragon's fighting madness. The dragon leaped into the sky again as missiles rained down from the tower. A boulder struck him hard across the back and he fell.

The lanky young human, howling the *raaaaah!* battle cry of the Aerial Host, ran forward, armed only with the Hypatian banner. Soldiers of the Lavadome and Hypatia streamed behind.

The Copper watched in satisfaction as the storming column flowed over and through the gates, axmen foremost to break down doors. The mass of men divided, flowing off into riven portals and up the fortresses' ladders and stairs to reinforce the men still fighting at the tower tops.

With that he watched the sun come up, while the wounded and the booty-laden returned to the waiting barges.

The resistance, what there was of it, was broken-backed by the time the last tower fell, threatened by his Aerial Host men who'd been dropped onto the higher levels and spry young drakka climbing the sides and fighting drakes from below—with the usual competition for glories and honors and tallies of bitten-off heads between the males and females, of course.

Many of the Pirate Lords had run away by secret paths, only to be rounded up by hunting Firemaids, but a few stewards and captains remained to plead with the dragons to leave the rest of the city unburned— for a city it was, a much more impressive one than the old maps based on memories of his aged warrior showed.

They'd won a rich prize indeed. The Copper had half-formed plans to carry off the valuables and leave nothing but piles of broken stones as a warning to others who might defy his emissaries, but his Hypatian allies must have their colony back.

The Copper snorted when he learned the Pirate Lords had hired three dragons to guard the skies above their cities, only to have two take flight when they looked up and saw the array of approaching dragons. The Copper wondered if the dragons had been paid in advance for their services. Only the black, cursing, took wing toward their foes.

They held a celebration, and a memorial service, the next night in the conquered fortress. The men enjoyed wines from half a world away; the dragons feasted on skewers of organ meats discreetly collected from the dead and sliced into unrecognizable hunks. The men of the Aerial Host were rather hardened to dragon tastes and appetites, but surrendered potentates of Swayport might be provoked into foolish violence.

It had been a terribly busy day for the Tyr and he was eager to fly back to Hypatia—and his mate in her fastness—but the proprieties had to be observed. Under the broken battlements the dragons gathered, awards were announced and names and deeds read into the Song of the Aerial Host that would describe the war against the Pirate Lords, as soon as a fitting one could be composed by one of the more talented dragons.

The fallen young dragon who had answered the signal-bolt at the gate was broken-backed and unconscious. HeBellereth judged he'd never fly again, or even open his eyes to receive his justly won *laudi*. His rider, as was the custom for the fallen in foreign lands, dispatched him with a quick spear thrust under the right *sii*.

The humans then lowered the head and opened the neck-heart.

"Only one loss. FeMissanith, an Ankelene who fought like a Skotl. Sorry to lose him. We don't have many Ankelenes in the host, and he was a good example to others. Until the end. Young and foolish, alighting like that in the thick of them."

"I recall a young and reckless dragon serving in the Bant with me. Chance favored him, he recovered from his wounds, and he rose high." The Copper nudged HeBellereth.

"Seems a waste to let all that dragon blood be spilled for nothing," HeBellereth's signalman-rider drawled.

"Quiet, now," HeBellereth drawled. HeBellereth, who always bristled and sparked before a fight, spoke rather slowly and thickly afterward as he attended to his duties. The rest he could leave to his lieutenants, but he always looked after the hurt and fallen before consuming a barrel of wine and some marrow bones and sleeping the strain off.

"He's right," the Copper said. "Our men deserve a victory toast of dragon blood. They'll need it for the work of loading compensation. Save us from having to open a vein."

Someone snorted. The idea of bleeding the honored dead rankled, but the Copper needed his men's and the Hypatians' energy for the work of setting Swayport in order ahead, and dragon-blood would do the trick. Besides, hadn't their allies just feasted on human corpses? "Speaking of victory toasts, I'll offer my own blood to that young human who led the storming column in from the sea. I didn't know him."

The Copper hoped he had enough to spare. But he'd always had a strong constitution and was used to veins being tapped by his bats.

"That's old Gunfer's son," HeBellereth said. "He was the first human boy born to the new Aerial Host after you became Tyr. Gunfer's too old to do much but sharpen weapons and fix buckles before we fly into battle and tend wounds after; his years take him back to the glory days of that cursed Wizard on his isle.

Threading dragons with rein-rings indeed." HeBellereth snorted.

"One more thing, HeBellereth. Make sure he gets a golden storming stripe upon his wing before his body is burned."

"I'll paint it myself, my Tyr," his rider said in a choking voice, cleaning the merciful spearpoint with his own silken scarf.

There'd have to be a new promotion from the Drakwatch into the Aerial Host. HeBellereth had mentioned, more than once, a likely young dragon, newly fledged. His brother AuRon's son AuSurath the Red had strength and wit and skill and followed orders well, even if it meant hanging back rather than being foremost in seeking glory in battle. Most reds flamed first and answered questions after. But something in him rebelled at putting one of AuRon's into the Aerial Host.

Always too suspicious, he told himself. *Well, that's how you've managed to stay alive all these years*, he argued back to himself.

He could think about it later.

A few of the dragons shifted uncomfortably as the human dragonriders gathered around FeMissanith for the victory toast from the dead hero's neck. The Copper silenced them with a glare as he personally filled the first tankard and handed it to the human captain of the Aerial Host, a one-armed fellow the Copper always thought of as "Blaze" because of his red-veined nose and ruddy, windburned skin.

The second came out of his own *sii* at the elbow

joint, one of the favorite spots for his "gargoyles" to sup. He gave that to the young human, Gundar, son of Gunfer.

The young human drank it in one lusty downing. Red overflow ran out either side of his mouth, and when he put down the cup his almost hairless face suddenly had a new beard and a mustache.

The Copper watched captured Swayport men gathering wood for the pyre. One of the Aerial Host kept a watchful eye on them, lest they try to dig out a tooth or claw.

It had been often pointed out to the Copper that odds and ends of dead dragons were worth a great deal in trade in the Upper World. Even his Hypatian allies, canny merchants all, had suggested it.

It was one thing to collect dropped scales for sale in the Upper World. Harvesting bones and teeth, hearts and livers and sinews for alchemists and craftdwarfs gave him a ghoulish shudder. No, he'd never allow *that*.

Once an Ankelene named CuRemom had approached him in the throne room. CuRemom, probably urged on by some dwarftrader, had calculated what a year's dead dragons would be worth to the Imperial Treasury if properly harvested, bottled, ground, and dried. Hominid witch doctors and physicians counted dragon bits as the most potent of medicines and magics. He'd even tried it on a corpse of a dragon killed in an illegal duel, weighing each part and saying how long it had taken to properly preserve. The Copper did his best to forget the sum mentioned. He'd given the slinker a fuller appreciation for his Tyr's disapproval of corpse-robbing by hard words and harder pokes with the tip of his tail.

CuRemom had slunk out, promising to make amends.

The Copper watched Gundar, invigorated by the blood, dance a jig. He looked to his father, stout and squinty, clapping along from the throng. The father was short and fair and the son tall and dark.

"Fine pup you have there, Gunfer," the Copper said. Now the youth was whirling, his whipping hair blurring with his face as he spun.

"M-My T-Tyr?" Gunfer said, kneeling at the address. He trembled a little at being recognized.

Humans! He'd never once simply reached out and eaten a thrall, and he wasn't about to start now. Wasn't he famous for decreeing an end to the summary devouring of the Lavadome's thralls?

"Your boy. I marked him carrying the Hypatian banner through the gate at the head of the storming column. You should be proud."

"Yes, my Tyr. First boy born after you took charge, so to speak."

"Yes, I've heard. He's grown up strong, even without the sun and rain of the Upper World."

"Aye, little secret of ours, passed down from the Isle, you know. For the long winters. His mother, she worked in the nursing halls during all the fighting with the demen. Lots of blood being sloshed about as broken scales were pulled out and wounds sewn up, especially during the fighting in the star cave."

The strangest of all the hominid races, the demen were pointy and thick-skinned, almost as though they were carrying their armor with them like a lobster. They were vassals of the Dragon Empire now, contributing the Tyr's own Demen Legion.

In the air above them a young dragon and dragonelle flew circles around the city in celebration. A Hypatian banner flew in the highest battlement of the Pirate Lord fortress. His human allies had reclaimed their own. It was soon joined by the woven scale and knotwork pattern of the Grand Alliance. Some Hypatians and an Ankelene had labored hard over the design and presented it to him in great solemnity. The Copper didn't have the heart to tell them he thought it looked like goat tracks, but then he wasn't of an artistic bent.

"She drank dragon blood every day while nursing, and mixed it in with his gruel when he started eating on his own. Turned him into a little hellion, but so healthy he practically burst his skin growing."

Gunfer chattered on in the manner of humans suddenly admitted into conversation with their superiors, describing his boy's doings as a youth in exercises and games with the Drakwatch. Apparently he'd never once been caught in a game of Fugitive Hunt.

Gundar dropped and began a wild kicking dance, spinning like a child's toy. Then he jumped to his feet as though born on his own set of wings, landing lightly, black hair flashing—

The Dragonblade!

The youth might have been a statue cast in the likeness of the man who'd briefly ruled the dragons thanks to a foolish wretch of a Tyr named SiMevolant.

Humans and their infernal constant mating. It made bloodlines almost impossible to develop and decent breeding futile for all but the most diligent owner of human thralls.

"Yes, a very fine boy you have there, Gunfer," the Copper said, more to silence the annoying chatter without insulting a worthy warrior than because he wanted to converse. "He bears watching."

He dismissed the unhappy thought, saving it for another day. With that he raised his head high and watched the goat-track banner of the Grand Alliance flutter above the captured city.

Chapter 2

Wistala's polished scale gleamed green in the fall sunshine of the Upper World.

The dragonelle always enjoyed the fall season, and not just because of the plentiful summer-fattened game birds that could be knocked senseless or killed with one quick wingstroke. The pine trees smelled just a little bit more crisp, wood and charcoal smoke a little more welcome, and even as something as prosaic as a pile of horse venting could be called gratifying if you watched the steam's elegant little curtains waft as it dispersed into the breeze.

Of course the former circus-elf Ragwrist would joke that she was scaring the manure out of the famous white horses when she alighted in the paddocks sur-rounding her adopted father's estate house at Mossbell. Ragwrist's brother, Rainfall, had dragged her unconscious from the great river bordering his estate and succored her, educated her, and ultimately died next to her defending the land and order he loved. Taking his place, Ragwrist had settled down—at least as much as such a lively elf could settle down. He married a trick-rider from his circus and assumed the position of estate-head and landlord to a thriving little town growing up around a highway-rest inn with a green dragon hanging above its door, but he still walked the roads in a bright, colorful coat as though still advertising the spectacles of his circus.

Only one thing lacked to complete her happiness in the fall sunshine. There should be birdsong in the sheltered vales around Galahall, but the hammering and calls of dwarvish workers had chased them away.

The dwarf foreman, hearing some shouts from the roof, trotted over to her, whipped off his cloth sweat hat, and made a sweeping bow.

"Your Protectorship, there's another difficulty . . . "

Dwarfs were great ones for finding difficulty. The difficulty could usually be resolved at additional expense. This one had to do with the need for steel-reinforcing cable. There would be a delay of some weeks in completing the project, though they could finish other matters while they waited for cable.

Wistala felt her firebladder pulse with vexation.

Easy there, Wistala, she could almost hear her old guardian elf—and adoptive father—Rainfall say. *Civi-*

*lization is founded on mastering your emotions and guiding
your tongue.*

There's nothing less civilized than stomping a work-
man you hired into hot, soggy mush.

"I'll give you some funds to purchase it. If it's light
enough, I can fly it here myself. That would be a sav-
ings, yes?"

The dwarf bowed again. "Of time and monies. Your
Protectorship is judicious."

The foreman always complimented her when she
agreed to his solutions for difficulties. It lessened the
sting of suspicion that the dwarfs were padding the bill,
but didn't do much there for the vexation. At this rate,
she'd be beggared before she could assume the dignity
of her office from a proper resort.

Wistala, even by buying and eating blacksmith
scraps and rusted tools to feed her scales, still had little
coin left over for her own expenses—particularly since
she insisted on purchasing her own cattle and sheep
for consumption. Other Protectors demanded feed and
metal as their just due, but Wistala asked only for a
small yearly contribution from each town and village
she "protected" (mostly, she admitted to herself, just
by being in the thanedom), leaving it to the local thanes
and heads of households and mining interests and
craftsmen to work out among themselves. But they
tended to pay her in chickens or knitwork, neither of
which did much to fill her gold-gizzard.

The dwarfs were putting up a roof over the old ruins

of the thane's manor house, once called Galahall but soon to be renamed Northflight Resort, the local seat of the Thanedom's draconic Protector. Long ago, as an unfledged drakka, she'd infiltrated the place to retrieve her elvish guardian Rainfall's granddaughter, who had come under the spell of an ambitious young Thane. The Thane died in the vicious human-dwarf race-wars which had seen the Wheel of Fire, a clan of violent dwarfs who'd murdered her mother and sister, humbled. Since then, it had fallen into disrepair—Ragwrist, while technically the local thane though he considered the office well-managed by attending celebrations to offer toasts at births, marriages, and deaths, didn't care for tall, gloomy halls. To add insult to negligence, Galahall had been sacked by marauding Ironriders a few years ago in the war that ended with the Grand Alliance.

Wistala had grown sick of sleeping in a barnlike structure, half cave and half thatched roof, near Mossbell. Though warm, it made her feel a bit like a cooped chicken, and her fellow Protectors of Hypatia, when visiting, almost dropped their *griff* in amazement at the rusticity of her dwellings. They'd all long since at least started on stone palaces surrounded by gardens of water and stone. They'd laughed at her and said their thralls lived better than the sister of their Tyr.

She had plans to make Galahall her official residence, or resort, as Protector of the Northern Thanedoms of Hypatia. All the walls would be linked by a single roof, lined with her own dropped dragonscale and supported by iron melted and recast from captured Ironrider weaponry. She had great plans for its height. Such a roof didn't exist in the north, not in any temple or old Hypatian hall. Perhaps one of the great Golden Domes of old Ghioz, now reduced to dozens of quarreling baronies under an overgreedy dragon Protector named NiVom, could match it in size. Or the vast hall of the Hypatian Directory, but that was a wonder of the world.

Then of course there was the Lavadome, a crystal bubble an entire horizon wide buried deep in a volcano, but that was more than wonder. The Lavadome couldn't even be called architecture; it was a mysterious miracle of a forgotten age, claimed long ago by the dragons who went into hiding from their enemies in the Upper World.

Her brother had changed all that. Tyr RuGaard, Lord of Worlds, First Protector of the Grand Alliance, slayer of the Dragonblade—

If she recited her Copper brother's ceremonial titles she'd be remembering and counting all day. No, the dwarfs needed help steadying their dragonscale-laden machine—crane, it was called a crane—as it lifted its burden to the workdwarfs on the roof.

A green dart fell out of the sky. Suddenly its wings opened and it landed with a gust of wind that silenced the workers and sent ropes rattling against wooden bracing scaffolds.

Yefkoa, the swiftest dragonelle in the Firemaids, landed.

Wistala liked Yefkoa. The dragonelle had the energy

and interest in long journeys and had good directional sense. She rarely got lost, even when flying over unfamiliar lands. She also had an unusually passionate loyalty to Tyr RuGaard and would threaten any who disparaged his odd looks and awkward ways.

"Fill a trough for this dragonelle," she ordered one of the dwarfs. "What brings you in such a hurry, Yefkoa?"

"The Queen requests your presence at once," she panted.

"What, another war?" Since forming the Grand Alliance a generation ago, the Hypatians had acted highhanded toward their neighbors. They enjoyed the power of dragons at their back. Oddly enough, the Tyr encouraged their campaigns and excursions as though he thought to gain by all this enemy-making.

"I don't believe so, but it is a matter of some urgency. She bade me to fly quickly, though she gave no commands about you making haste. She simply said 'as soon as Wistala can manage the trip.'"

Nilrasha, Queen of Worlds, with other titles thanks to her being Tyr RuGaard's mate, must be obeyed. The Dragon Empire had an unspoken "or else" attached to such commands—most of the consequences involved loss of position.

Luckily, the northern thanedoms needed little protecting at the moment. Winter had already settled into the mountains, so Ironrider raiders would find all the seasonal passes closed, and the northern barbarians would already be filling their barns and cellars to wait out the snow and ice heaped about their mead-halls and hovels. "I shall attend her. But there must be a delay of a few days, thanks to minor difficulties in building my resort. The dwarfs need me in the air to lift and set the capstones."

It might be in my advantage to be away for a while, Wistala thought. *The dwarfs can't spend my last coin if I'm not around to buy them out of any more difficulties.*

The air was full of eagles.

It was good eagle country, here in the tangled foot-hills of the mountains with the ocean in sight and a dozen river-fed, cliff-shadowed lakes beneath. The inaccessible heights guarded future generations of eggs, and the ample updrafts made flying almost effortless for feather wings.

The vultures, bigger than the eagles but keeping a polite distance—of all the creatures she'd encountered in her travels they were the most sensitive and genteel of creatures. No raucous fighting, no territorial displays, and a philosophical diffidence as they waited to do their duty in disposing of bits and pieces, lest the flies grew so thick on offal they'd carpet the world.

Wistala marked an occupied nest above the Queen's lookout, and dropped to give it a wide berth. Though an eagle couldn't do much more to a dragon than put an eye out, a desperate attack in defense of eggs wasn't unknown.

AuRon told her once that his friend Naf—now long since King Naf of Dairuss—had hidden in this tangled border country while hiding with his rebels from the Red Queen of the Ghioz. It was a good land for someone who wanted to hide. *Vesk* after *vesk* of steep-sided river valleys, thickly wooded and vined, were inspiring from the air, but even a long-necked dragon would easily become disoriented on the ground.

She made a gentle call, both to alert the eagles so they wouldn't be startled by her presence and to announce her arrival.

She glided into the Queen's cave. It had a good view of the west and was warmed by the setting sun. She marked a few reinforcing pillars—someone had gone to the trouble to enlarge the cave. She'd visited a few times before, years ago when the flightless Queen had first been installed in her high resort. Since then, it had been much improved.

A few blighters, long-armed, hairy collections of appetites known for their strong backs and quick quarrels, greeted her with offerings of water, sweet wine, and toasted meat on wooden skewers. They wore colorful ponchos closed with brooches of green dragonscale. She accepted a little of each offering as an unusually tall blighter, with a careful request for permission in passable Drakine, massaged her wing tendons, first on one side, then the other.

The Queen had a homey cave. It had better air flowing through than the cave of her birth and the faint sounds rising from the thick forest below soothed when the air was still.

An aged *griffaran*, almost featherless and droopy,

stood sentinel on a hidden perch. A platter that smelled of fish stood near him on its own treelike stand. She wondered if he was some veteran of a dozen battles, now in a pleasantly airy sinecure as honor guard to the Queen. His beak and talon still appeared razor sharp, so perhaps it wasn't just for show.

Later it occurred to Wistala that the Queen might have encouraged eagles to build their tangled nests and settle about her quarters like a kindlewood crown. A dragon couldn't have too many sets of wary eyes to give the alarm when living aboveground.

There would be many an eagle jealous of that view, Wistala thought. Her cave looked out over sharp, rocky pillars with little soil, but what had collected in the nooks and crevices sprouted wind-twisted trees. Low clouds made the lush valley floors, echoing with the sound of rivers and waterfalls, hazy or invisible. Off to the west, a thin strip of the inland ocean could just be seen. Wistala, judging the sun's descent, decided that no matter what the Queen's concerns she wouldn't miss the view of the sunset.

She heard breathing from deeper inside the cave.

"My Queen, you called for me?"

"Ages ago, it seems. Thank you for coming. I long for company."

Wistala ambled into the Queen's presence and they clacked *griff* in greeting. Neither bothered with bows, they were relatives by mating fight. Nilrasha had lost her taste for courtly gestures since the war injury that left her with stumps for wings.

Queen Nilrasha was still beautiful, but it was the beauty of a ruin, like the old, fern-sided, weather-shaped stones of Tumbledown where she'd hunted for metals as an unfledged drakka. Her scales were still well-shaped, and she was still strong-limbed—probably stronger-limbed than most dragons, having to rely on them for climbing all the way up to her resort. She had a well-shaped head, which reminded her a little of Au-Ron's mate Natasatch about the nostrils and eyes, though the Queen's fringe, the pride of any dragonelle or dragon-dame, was clipped and stiffened and shaped into pleasing waves running down her back. Natasatch had a natural crest, much like Wistala's—a little ragged and bent from wear and fighting.

Only a little paint highlighted some of the scale around her eyes, nostrils, jawline, and *griff*. White polished teeth added to her other carefully groomed attractions. Wistala was relieved that the Queen didn't color her scale any of the garish pinks and purples that seemed to be in vogue in the Lavadome. She'd been told that many a firemaiden recruit needed a thorough scrubbing with a wire-tipped brush to get the paint off her scales.

Her cave was simple, adorned only with a few trophies of the Battle of Hypat, where she'd lost her wings in a dreadful crash.

She offered Wistala wine, or honey-sweetened blood, or hot fat. Wistala chose the fat, as she'd flown hard and fought winds. The Wind Spirit was sending air from the south and the north to do battle over Hypatia and the Inland Ocean.

Nilrasha called a female blighter and issued orders.

"Did you send for me all this way just for company?" Wistala asked. Nilrasha had become a much more serious dragon since losing her wings; she'd matured into a Queen to be respected and regarded, if remote.

"Wistala—I'm afraid."

Nilrasha, afraid? Wistala, from her time in the Firemaids, had heard the stories of the Queen's legendary ferocity in battle. She'd been the sole survivor of a futile attack on a well-fortified Ghioz city in Bant, struck hard in the uprising against the Dragonblade's hagriders, and sacrificed her wings in battle against the Ironriders.

She couldn't say she knew Nilrasha well enough to know whether she was being entirely honest. According to some of the Firemaids, Nilrasha was an expert at playing politics, hiding the jump and the tear behind an apparent interest in only your betterment. But Rainfall had taught her to start politely, and return courtesy with courtesy doubled.

"I am sorry to hear that. Is there anything I can do to allay your fears?"

Nilrasha loosed a quiet, friendly *prrum*. Wistala had an awful *griff-tchk* in which she wondered if she hadn't asked precisely what Nilrasha wanted her to ask.

"There is, sister. I need you to take my place."

Wistala thought she had heard wrong. First, she hadn't been called sister by anyone since she was a hatchling. Second: "Take—your place?"

"By my mate's side, in the Lavadome. He's set me up in these lovely quarters, it's like still being able to fly, in a way, not that I did much flying as Queen even in a place like the Lavadome. But I'm no longer able to perform even half my duties as Queen. There's something about a broken-winged dragon that inspires contempt in enemies and useless pity in friends."

Nilrasha waggled her wing stumps. It was a disarming gesture, so dreadfully unsettling it was humorous.

"Act as his mate?" Wistala managed, feeling her scales tingle as they resettled.

"Don't look so shocked, sister, there is a precedent for it. Back in the days of Silverhigh, of course." Silverhigh was a half-legendary dragon civilization, in an age long, long ago when dragonkind ruled the Earth and flew proudly in the sunshine. Before the assassins came.

Bother precedents and Silverhigh. Her brother? She didn't hate him outright. In her opinion, he'd turned into a rather noble dragon even if he looked, walked, and flew a little offbeat. Wistala had given him his bad eye in her fury over his role in the discovery and murder of their parents.

Nilrasha waggled her stumps again, pointing one at Wistala. "I don't mean you'd *be* his mate. It's true, we've had no luck with hatchlings, probably because we've both been so smashed about in our youth, but I don't mean a sort of substitute egg layer. Only that you'd act in my place in matters of rank and title."

"Why me?" Wistala asked. Surely there were more famous dragonelles—Ibidio, for instance. She was the well-respected daughter of Tyr FeHazathant, the greatest and most legendary of the Tyrs. Since Tighlia's death, Ibidio had always set the standard of how a great female dragon should act. If anyone deserved to display a proud side of green at court functions it was she. "Surely someone like Ibidio is more used to life in the Lavadome on Imperial Rock."

Nilrasha's wings froze and her *griff* flashed open and shut again with a *snick* that echoed off the cavern walls.

The Queen cleared her throat. "First, you're his sister. When all is said and done, I trust blood. Second, you're an outsider. You don't belong to any particular clan, so I suspect everyone would find you assuming the position agreeable. If we tried to put an Ankelene in, the Skotl and Wyrr would object, if Skotl—I'm sure you have made the mind-picture. These jealousies of clan and class are more dangerous to us than any hominid. But I'm showing my radical scale again; I must get back to cases. Third, you have tremendous experience in the Upper World—rank and friends in the Hypatian Protectorate—and no matter how knowledgeable some of us are in various wars and politics in the Lavadome or the Upholds, it's just a little hidden corner of the world. My mate could use the advice of someone as traveled as you. Fourth, you're one of the most impressive physical specimens of a dragonelle I've ever seen. It's clear you didn't grow up on scrawny bullocks and *kern*. If it came to outright physical intimidation, you'd make any of those pretentious, overgrown asps in the Imperial Line back off."

Lavadome politics were still a vague business to her, but she did know the three "lines" of dragons mistrusted one another, a holdover from terrible civil wars generations ago. "I always thought myself rather thick and lumpy. Most of you are so sleek and graceful."

"You'll find there comes a time when you simply must draw yourself up and bellow with that collection of iron-brained self-importance of the Imperial Rock, Wistala. Even if you can't break heads, you can give their ears a good pounding. You're the dragonelle to do it, I believe."

"I've no ambition," Wistala said, wishing she'd stayed to see her roof finished. "I'm happy living among my friends in the northern provinces. It's a fractious part of Hypatia, my Queen. Barbarians to the north with a few mercenary dragonriders left over from the Wizard's days, grumpy, begrudged dwarfs in the mountains, infiltrations by clans of Ironriders in the woods and dales committing banditry, and the human thanes who are ostensibly our allies don't care for the Hypatian Directory being high-handed thanks to our Tyr's backing. You see 'dragons out now' scrawled on mile markers in some of the other provinces, especially where their 'Protectors' demand much in the way of food and coin. Not that I'm not immensely honored—"

Nilrasha clacked her teeth to cut her off. "Fifth, you

analyze rather than emote. Half the dragons I know would be cursing the dwarfs and barbarians and already have a war going. You talk like an Ankelene sage but display like a Skotl and persevere like a Wyrr. I hope you'll take no insult at the comparisons."

"I'm flattered you think so much of me."

"When you held the Red Mountain pass against Ironriders and Roc-riders alike I knew you were a dragon who could set her backbone and stick."

Blood in the snow. Wistala didn't care for those memories. Battles terrified her beyond words and she still dreamt of young Takea, dying in that dreadful pass.

"What about my duties as a Protector?" Wistala asked. Mossbell was in good hands, but who knows what kind of greedy fool might replace her.

"I'll find a substitute. Or I'll take it on myself, and just send and receive a few messages a year so your more ambitious fellow protectors don't get ideas. Now let's not look so disheartened; it won't be forever. Besides, I have another need." She lowered her voice, but Wistala couldn't imagine who might overhear, save blighter servants she presumably trusted. "What I'm about to tell you is a great secret. By your oath as a Firemaid, do you promise to keep it?"

"I shall."

"Your brother will not be Tyr much longer. Once Ru-Gaard has a successor in place, he'd like to lay down his duties. I know the Ankelenes call him power-mad and other worse names, but nothing is farther from the truth. He's carrying out the honors and duties given him, honors and duties he didn't seek, whatever the whisperers might say."

She looked at her battle trophies. "Too many Tyrs have died atop the Imperial Rock. Right now the one thing we don't have a tradition for is the peaceful transfer of power and responsibility. Can you believe, these Hypatians are more organized about such things than dragons! Short-lived, scatterbrained little mammals arranging their affairs better than, well, their betters. He'd like to learn that one practice from the humans and change that tradition to a happier one—a solemn ceremony where he turns over the responsibilities of rank to another with sense and energy."

Nilrasha shifted her weight with a lunge and Wistala heard the *snap-crack* of her tail strike the floor.

"I told you not to listen," she roared at her hindquarters, where a blighter hopped on one foot and long arm, cradling the other foot in her hand. Wistala smelled blood. "Oh, I am sorry, Obday, I didn't mean to strike you, just startle. Go get it braced and bandaged and have some soup."

The servant hobbled off toward a curtained partition and disappeared.

"I still don't understand why you're afraid," Wistala asked.

"There's a plot against my mate's life. I feel it in my bones."

"A plot? As in . . . as in *murder*?"

If the suggestion bothered Nilrasha, she showed no sign of it. "Come, let us watch the sunset."

Wistala followed her out to the entrance. The sun blazed orange red as it sank, making Wistala think of DharSii, the odd tiger-striped dragon she'd met thrice, each time under unfortunate circumstances.

"I'm not one of these brilliant dragons, Wistala," Nilrasha said. "Everyone is always a move ahead of me in their little games. I'm not that great a fighter, either—if I were, I'd still have wings rather than stumps."

She waggled them again, then continued. "What I do have, though, is luck. Luck and an instinct for when to move. I've lived quietly here for years, doing the best I can to be an absent Queen through messengers and the good offices of court dragons like NoSohoth and He-Bellereth. Word has come to me through a variety of sources that something is reaching *sii* and *saa* for my mate's throat. For all that he's suspicious of hominids, he's entirely too trusting of dragons, especially those close to him.

"I'm going to tell you something, Wistala, about one time when I had the instinct to be in the right place at the right time and I didn't act."

Nilrasha watched the sun turn red. "Your brother had a mate before me, a very frail dragonelle, one of FeHazathant's line, daughter of Ibidio and AgGriffopse, one of the best dragons who ever flew in the Lavadome. My mate was an upholder at the time, in an important but remote province called Anaea. I was on hand the night she ate an enormous meal and choked on a bone.

"Some people say I choked her. Well, I might as well have. I don't know if you've had this lesson in the Firemaids, Wistala, but in my day we learned how to help a choking dragon. You pierce the weak spot in the windpipe just above the breastbone with a reed, a pair of arrows, anything you can find. It opens the lungs to the air and you can still breathe, after a fashion.

"I had the presence of mind to grab a horn off the wall, the brass tubing would have served admirably to feed her air once I punched it through her throat, but then I froze, unable to act. I think part of me, the part that wanted to be mated to your courageous brother, wished she would die. I stood there, watching her choke, seeing the pleading fear in her eyes, and I knew what I had to do. But I stood there, rooted. Then she collapsed and quit breathing, and too late I tried to intervene. I dropped the horn and went to her side. I thrust my *sii* down her throat and tried to take out the bone in a panic, and your brother finally appeared in answer to a human thrall's signal.

"I've always regretted those moments when I stood there, doing nothing. As usual, I was lucky enough to be at the right place and the right time, and as usual, the world came down on top of me, just like in that attack in Bant."

Wistala respected Nilrasha, but had never felt warm toward her. For the first time, she found herself in sympathy with her queen.

"I tried to save my wounded father," Wistala said. "He had—terrible injuries. From war machines, weighted dragon harpoons. I brought him water and food. Later I looked for coin and metals to help his scales heal. I found some in an old ruin, but I ate most of them on the way home. I couldn't help myself. Even worse, men followed my trail, and the hunters found him. I led them right to his refuge."

Nilrasha rubbed *griff* with her. "Thank you for that confession. But at least you tried from the first to save your father's life. Poor little Halaflora, who'd never said a cross word to even a waste-barrow thrall, died while I stood there like a rooted elf."

"Even when you do try, sometimes fate is too much for you," Wistala said.

The sun was half-gone now, and mostly obscured by horizon-hugging clouds. The sky above it had turned purple. Queen Nilrasha emptied her lungs. "So, what is your answer."

Could there be a plot against her brother? Would it be worse if it failed, or if it succeeded? In the Firemaids she'd heard terrible stories about the dragon civil wars, where the clans even made unhatched eggs the target of their vengeance. "I can try. But in trying, I may bring disaster."

"You must have faith in my mate. Don't listen to the whisperers—me excepted, of course. He just needs time to see Hypatia grow used to living and working with dragons."

"If there's a plot against Tyr RuGaard . . . how would I learn of it?"

"Some dragons have a natural gift for sniffing out secrets and finding weaknesses. It's quiet up here. I have visitors. Most of them are important Hypatians, or Hypatians who want to be important. They come here to seek my help, an intervention from the Tyr. They're always awestruck, at first, and tell me about the only other time they met a dragon. I've heard an elf named Ragwrist used to have one traveling with his circus; it seems she told fortunes and somehow worked her way into the Wheel of Fire. She humbled a dwarf-king's fortress that entire armies hadn't managed to breach."

"I've heard that story too," Wistala said. "I think storytellers look for ways to improve on the truth."

Nilrasha cocked her head and flexed her stumps again, as though brushing off imaginary birds perched on her fringe.

"A dragon who can bring down a dwarvish fortress so mighty that no army could take it might find herself in another conspiracy, wouldn't you agree, sister?" Nilrasha looked at her sharply.

Was Nilrasha testing her to see if she was already involved?

"We'll talk more in the morning. Would you like my thralls to clean your scale before you retire?"

Wistala enjoyed their services that evening. She wanted to think, and strangely enough, having the Queen's servants cleaning and polishing claws, teeth, and scale gave her strange powers of concentration in their busywork. When they were done she fell into a deep, post-flight sleep and dreamed of moss-covered ruins filled with stalking cats and furtive rats.

They breakfasted on freshwater fish hauled up to the Queen's eyrie in a woven basket on a line.

"You'll not mind if we climb down so I can show you something? After, there's good hunting in those woods, if your taste runs to wild goats or small deer."

Wistala agreed. The Queen had the good manners to ask if she'd changed her mind about serving as Queen-Consort.

Wistala had assured her that she had not, but had more doubts than ever about how well she'd fit the role. "I'm no social dragon. I learned my manners from an elf."

"That's the great thing about being Queen. Blunder away. Your manners are never laughed at, at least to your face. Perhaps you'll introduce a few new traditions," Nilrasha said, giving an unsettling laugh.

Wistala's family hadn't been laughing dragons, though she'd learned humor in Rainfall's gentle school.

They began their descent and Wistala found it exhausting, despite the chisled-out holds for *sii*, tail, and *saa*. She hadn't had to cling vertically in years.

"I see now how you stay so fit," Wistala said. "Hanging on for your hearts' dear life is good exercise."

Nilrasha held on with her tail as she negotiated a difficult overhang. "Better than flying in many ways— the constant strain of unusual angles brings a muscular warmth and a healthy fatigue that much faster."

They circled the pillarlike mountain of stone in the long climb down. Not even a goat would call it a path, but it was a series of *sii*-holds.

"Do visitors come up in that same basket that brought the fish?" Wistala asked, watching a wary blight cling tightly to the knot-and-handle as the basket descended.

"If they're invited, yes."

"What if they're not invited."

"They find their own way up. And a much faster way down. So far, my luck has held. As you are about to see, sister."

Nilrasha took her to a sort of dimple in an outcropping from the mountain, out of the wind and big enough for a mother dragon to use as an egg shelf.

"I used to use this to rest during my climbs," Nilrasha said. "You're breathing hard. Perhaps we can catch our wind among some more of my trophies."

The shelf didn't hold eggs, or captured banners and broken swords and helmets. The shallow rocky well held bones, some with bits of desiccated flesh still on. Skulls of at least two kinds of hominids, broken blades, pieces of rope and chain and broken dragonscale, even bits of demen back-carapace lay in a jumble. It smelled of rats, though how rats could live halfway up a mountainside Wistala had to wonder.

They smelled of sun-bleached death, a crisp dry odor like shed snakeskins. Wistala saw that the pieces had been arranged as though they were at a human dinner party, with shields and sagging packs serving as furniture. The display showed a grim sort of humor, skulls sat on shield-platters staring back at their own bodies and weapons were substituted for missing limbs. "Who are they? Were they, I mean."

"They were assassins," Nilrasha said. "There have been several attempts on the Tyr's life. But many more on my own. Certain members of the Imperial Line think that if I were out of the way, RuGaard will mate again. What some dragons will do to become Queen. Also, there's old Ibidio's faction, who think I outright murdered poor Halaflora. I've saved a souvenir or two of each assassin."

Wistala thought the collection a macabre one. Some of the Firemaids kept a trophy of a broken sword or shield or an old helm to commemorate a battle, but pieces of the enemies' bodies?

At least there were no dragon heads. None that Queen Nilrasha wanted to put into the tableau, anyway.

"You spoke of exercise. Climbing down here and looking at these remnants are my exercise. The mental exercise is as important as the physical. I'm reminded that we have enemies who will stop at nothing. You would do well to keep that in mind as well, sister."

As if reading her thoughts, the Queen continued: "I could have put dragon bones in this collection as well. We had a mad young renegade try to knock my mate out of the sky during the war with the demen. While I admit it's a strange collection, I've no desire to outrage my fellow dragons. Just assassins on their way up. I like to think I'm doing a service. Perhaps some took the warning to heart, and turned back rather than climbing all the way to their deaths."

She stared Wistala straight in the eyes. "You'll need to keep your wits about you, Wistala, if you go into the Lavadome with a plot in your heart. Don't do that. Be like water, or the wind. Just follow the path of least resistance to the bottom of it."

"If I do learn anything, what do I do?"

The Queen righted a wind-toppled corpse with her tail and tamped it firmly into place. Wistala heard old bones break. "That depends on the names of the dragons involved. It may be too widespread to uncover. Too powerful to resist. Your only chance for survival may depend on you joining. Not as play, you understand—to really join it. I'll try and understand. Save my mate if you can."

"Yes, my Queen."

"Now, on to more immediate concerns. There's one other worry on my mind. An unnecessary war is about to start. Dairuss, once a province of Ghioz, has kicked out its Protector, a self-important dragon named SoRolatan. He spends all his time chasing dragonelles a third his age or eating. Fat lout. You'd think the jade-chasing would keep him trim. A few of the sly young wings lead him on, as he's quite wealthy, though if you ask me, they're better off without him. But the Dairussan king sent him home. He's a fellow named Naf, older, one of our principal allies in the fight against Ghioz. He claims he won't have any dragon back.

There's no provision for members of the Grand Alliance to leave, so you'll need to smooth things over somehow before it comes to fire. Now, let's finish this climb and hunt. I hear you're quite the famous hunter, sister."

A conspiracy to discover and a civil war to prevent. Here she thought being Queen meant licking new hatchlings and presiding over feasts.

Chapter 3

The sun hadn't visited the Isle of Ice in scores of days, it seemed.

Of course winter always came early this far north. Once it became truly cold, the inhabitants could look forward to long stretches of clear daylight, for the sun only set for a few hours over the winter solstice.

AuRon the Gray had settled on this island to be cut off from the world and its mad hatreds. Man against dragon, dragon against dwarf, elf against man and dragon . . . it was a long and bloody list of enmities. Just in his brief lifetime of a few decades he'd seen new ones form, hot and fast, and others burn down into charred lumps like dry wood. But even so, as much as he enjoyed the quiet of this remote, hard-to-reach island, come the winter storms the feeling of being cut off intensified, for you could hardly see your own tail when the snow was blowing.

"My love," Natasatch said to AuRon. She was his mate and mother to his four now-fledged offspring and sometimes she chided and nudged him as though he still had bits of egg clinging to his skin. "You must attend the ceremony."

AuRon didn't like the pomp and pageantry of his Copper brother's cursed Dragon Empire. He'd seen it born in bloodshed, even if he grudgingly granted its success in allowing dragons to live openly aboveground in safety. Trumpets and banners and dragon roars, with those blowing and roaring the loudest the ones farthest from the fighting.

"It wouldn't hurt for you to mix a bit more with the Lavadome dragons. Even your brother sent us a bullock with his compliments. A fine fat beast it was and that messenger had to carry it all the way out of the south. This old enmity deserves to be laid to rest. The Tyr's put it behind him."

Had he? AuRon wondered. Or was it some elaborate treachery?

Of course, if his brother really wanted to do away with him, he had the power. He could put forty or more fighting dragons in the air over the Isle of Ice if he wanted. He might escape two, five even, but forty?

No. Still, just because his brother had the power to end their old feud and chose not to use it, it didn't mean he had to like him, or his empire or Grand Alliance or whatever he was calling it lately.

"It will be a celebration of magnificence. It's not every day a new Queen is announced. Well, Queen-Consort, they call it. And your sister no less! Plenty of coin to eat. The Hypatians own the seas again, south of the neck. It's a chance to mix. Besides, the last two winters have been dreadful here. I'm not sure I feel up to facing another, the island could do with a couple less appetites to feed. Your wolves may like the howling wind and blowing snow driving bighorns into the valleys, but I don't."

Natasatch had spent too many years chained in a dark cave. She loved going hither and yon on social calls and sometimes was away for weeks when she visited Queen Nilrasha in her refuge to hear the news.

He couldn't deny his mate the pleasure of company, or seeing their newly fledged son promoted into the Aerial Host. Besides, there'd be little enough to eat besides fish on the Isle of Ice if it was another hard winter, and the blighters complained if he went after their seals and such. Maybe that was the reason for his foul mood lately, not enough variety in the diet. He was still growing, after all.

Youth. He was still a young dragon, even if the knowledge that there was now a generation behind him made him feel old at times. Some dragons went on and on, in and out through whole nations of men.

Perhaps Natasatch was right. This mania of his to be isolated, remote, out of the affairs of the hominids— lurking in a cave listening to groaning glaciers between flights to warn off deepwater fishing boats or treasure hunters chasing legends of an entirely imaginary "wizard's trove" on the Isle of Ice wasn't much of a life. Besides, he owed it to his mate that she might see some of the world. He'd traveled all those years she'd been chained in a cave.

Don't be a blockhead, gray dragon. The outside world isn't that bad.

"It will be a long flight," he said, giving her both a warning and a chance to bow out gracefully.

She fluffed her wings with a leathery crackle. "I don't mind at all."

"Oh, very well. Let's enjoy ourselves. But, Natasatch, try to keep out of the business of my brother's alliance. I don't want us joining any factions."

"Factions? Us? No, my love, you're quite right that we should keep out of politics. I just want us to be sociable with our relatives to the south. It never hurts to have friends for when we desire a change of scenery, and I do so want to be able to congratulate AuSurath in person."

"To tell the truth, I'm curious to see how he looks, now that he has wings. I always thought he rather resembled my father."

Natasatch looked downcast for a moment. She hadn't known her parents at all before being snatched away to the Isle of Ice. "Very well. Shall we bring Istach?"

"She has young wings," AuRon said. "The exercise would do her good."

"My lord is wise," Natasatch said. Her tone was

light, and the wording was the one she used when she teased him for dispensing what she called "the wisdom of the obvious."

He snorted. "You're right, my love. You mated a dragon with delusions of sagacity."

Istach, their striped daughter, was a bit of an odd-hatchling out. Always had been. Quiet and thoughtful, she stuck close by her home cave, learning the tongues of blighters and wolves and sea mammals. She brought home game almost every day. It was unusual for a dragon her age to dote on her parents so, but again, she was an odd-hatchling.

Her sister Varatheela was a Firemaiden and took after her mother in her desire to enjoy the social struggles with other dragons. He doubted he'd see her; from what he understood, the Firemaids and younger Firemaidens spent most of their time guarding the beating heart of the Dragon Empire, the Lavadome, running or flying messages, or learning about the lands under their Tyr's subtle control.

At least that's how Wistala explained it to him when he asked her advice about Varatheela joining. But Varatheela was a full-fledged dragon now, and able to shape her own destiny.

It was a longish flight to Hypatia. AuRon, being scaleless, could make it in three hard days, but Natasatch and Istach were weighed down by scale and inexperience in distance flying.

To give themselves energy for the flight they feasted

three days on a dead whale AuRon found beached on one of the tiny islands surrounding theirs. The gulls hadn't torn it up too badly. There was still plenty of juicy fat and it was too cold for flies. Then they spent a day in short conditioning flights, cleared their digestive systems, and accustomed themselves to the air. They flapped off to the south the next day, as the weather promised fair.

Though he'd steeled himself against the departure, AuRon couldn't help but leave his island with regret, the pain all the sharper for Natasatch's eagerness to leave.

To think, when his hatchlings were first above-ground, his worry was overpopulation on the Isle of Ice and running out of sheep or goats in consequence. Now most of the dragons were gone, eager for the gold and glory of his brother's glittering new empire. Save old Ouistrela. Too cantankerous for dragon society, always hungry, she rained contempt on the young dragonelles who flew north with messages. The Firemaid who brought the message from the Tyr, letting him know about the victory against the men on the western side of the Inland Ocean and his son's promotion into the Aerial Host, had had her tail shortened by a mouthful for taking a sheep without permission to refresh herself.

He had paid Ouistrela a visit to bid her good-bye and heard the story about how she'd seen off the "trained dog of a dragonelle" with noise and teeth, the one resource of the Isle of Ice's old Ouistrela made free with. He'd brought her some of his pitifully small hoard in return for keeping an eye on the cave and not causing his wolves too much grief.

"Some price for my services. If you're gone longer than a year, I'll go looking for the rest," she said.

The trio traveled with the wind; with winter coming it was blowing hard out of the north, their flight alternately serious and playful. Istach had the energy of a newly fledged dragon and enjoyed swooping around her parents and experimenting with surfing the air currents created by their hard-beating wings in their wake. AuRon, unhindered by scale, could outfly any dragon he'd ever met without sucking wind much deeper than he did on the ground, and continually asked his mate and daughter if they wanted to float and rest. Natasatch responded, as a proud dragon-dame should, by flapping harder and forcing him to catch up.

Istach simply took over the lead position, so her parents might suffer a little less drag by riding in her wake.

From the air, AuRon always thought Hypat, capital city of the Hypatian Empire, looked like a white vase dropped on a coral-strewn shore and shattered. From a beautiful core bits of it were scattered in all directions; even the toothlike sails in the great sand-choked estuary of the Falnges River might be mistaken for broken pieces of a greater structure.

Whoever had first laid out the city had thought the

design through, with a star of broad avenues running out toward the old city walls and riverfront. The heart of the city held several magnificent buildings and pillars.

In human fashion, something well begun was finished badly. The wide avenues were choked with barrows and carts and wooden shacks and some of the graceful buildings had fallen into disrepair—though AuRon noticed sets of scaffolding and canvas marking where restorations had begun. The city's lovely gardens, run wild and crawling with livestock on his last visit, were still in disorder, but the worst of the overgrowth had been cleared and there were no longer pools of distressingly fouled water. Outside the old walls a jumble had built up, beautiful homes and buildings looking out on the sea, and a rat's nest of tightly packed dwellings growing around the docks and wharfs like barnacles.

Hypat was thriving again, if in a messy and disordered fashion.

A fast-flying dragonelle rose to greet them. Istach swooped down to interpose herself between the stranger and her parents.

"Welcome, AuRon of the Isle of Ice, on behalf of the Tyr of Worlds Upper and Lower and Keeper of the Grand Alliance. Welcome, AuRon's family."

The lack of reflective scale did make him recognizable, even from a distance. He'd been quietly called a "plucked *griffaran*" by some wit in the throne room of his brother's rocky home in the Lavadome, according to his hatchlings. He bore the moniker without challenge. He'd learned long ago that words couldn't pierce your skin.

Natasatch panted out a response and asked about a place to stop and take refreshment. The dragonelle offered to guide them in.

AuRon only half-paid attention as they descended toward the outskirts of Hypat, capital city of the Hypatian realm.

Tyr of Worlds. His brother did enjoy his titles.

"I'm bid to tell you your sister Wistala, soon to be formally named Queen-Consort, invites you to reside with her at the circus campground," the dragonelle said. "I will guide you to a safe landing," the dragonelle continued. Natasatch beat her wings vigorously and lazily performed a few acrobatics, showing she was a match for any young thing who'd only been in the air a year.

It was easy to determine where his brother was residing. Bright-colored creatures, half feather and half skin, sunned and preened over a sort of open clamshell of masonry, wood, and canvas near the great round building where the Hypatian Directory met. Near both, the layout of an impressive palace was growing in what AuRon remembered as a pile of rubble and wreckage along the inner walls left over from the invasion of the Red Queen's Ironrider horsemen.

Such magnificent works. AuRon wondered if it was all to succor a twisted little dragon's vanity.

Other dragons were enjoying themselves in the

rough waters off a rocky point that flanked the city from the seaside, swimming, fishing, or taking the sun on their own private perches. A few humans watched, and little boys dashed across sand and surf to collect dropped dragonscale. Older servants brought the playful dragons platters of food and roast meats suspended from poles borne by two stout servers.

Empire had its privileges, he supposed.

"Brother, welcome," Wistala said as they alighted outside a brightly painted wall. Images of animals and performers decorated the walls of the circus. It was much as AuRon had remembered it from when he stayed briefly before, but now a flag fluttered above, green and white with a dragon's profile on it. Below the flags, angled masts, a cross between ship's timbers and lifting cranes, held up canvas to shade the seats. "Natasatch, you are most welcome. I'm glad you could come. And young Istach. Your sister is doing well as a Firemaid, though I don't expect she'll take the Second Oath. She's beginning to display a bit in front of the young dragons, so we will lose her to mating one day, I suspect. Your young dragons are both fine examples of dragonkind."

"Thank you for news of the offspring," Natasatch said. "We're so cut off in the north."

A crowd gathered but kept a respectful distance. Wistala sidestepped and gestured with her neck and tail. "Perhaps we should retreat within the gates. There'll be beggars here any moment, asking for loose scale."

They proceeded into the circus arena. Piles of sawdust and matting showed that several dragons were staying for the duration of the celebration.

"Sister," AuRon said. "I am told you are taking an important new role soon."

"Formally, yes. Informally, I'm already helping the Tyr."

"Rounding up slaves for the Lavadome?"

"Nothing so distressing, AuRon. My duties are mostly to represent the Tyr at minor functions when he's busy elsewhere. But sometimes problems are brought to me when it is thought that NoSohoth or our brother will refuse aid. I wish I had a mouthful of gold to offer, but it flows out as quickly as it flows in. I have some copper scraps, however."

His mate and Istach gratefully swallowed a few battered remains of cooking pots. With so many dragons about, AuRon wondered what even these odds and ends had cost his sister.

Natasatch asked Wistala about arrangements for the celebration, who would be there with whom, whether there were any important humans she should greet or defer to, what kinds of dishes might be served—"all the flying put me in good appetite, and I've long been hungry for society."

Her life wasn't yours. Try to understand.

Did he expect his mate to always trail along in his wake, dutifully waiting for the next clutch of eggs? No, if she was as hungry for company as she was for precious metals, he could put up with a few cheers for his brother. He might even have done something to deserve them.

Wistala assigned them a thrall to help them with her traveling household, and made her excuses. Already she reminded AuRon of one of these smooth-talking dragons of her brother's court. What had his sister grown up to be? Not another preening decoration, he hoped.

At least Natasatch wasn't vain. The dragons of his brother's empire accumulated small armies of human retainers and servants. Every scale polished, filed, and aligned, claws smoothed and sharpened, teeth picked as clean as a corpse in the desert he'd crossed in his unfledged youth with the girl Hieba.

He consented to a bristle-brush scrubbing of his skin, more to keep his mate company while they worked to clean beneath her scale. She chattered happily to him the whole while, and he suddenly felt better about the trip south. Maybe he'd encourage her to visit Hypat more often. Wistala seemed to like her and might appreciate a companion on her rounds, doing whatever a Queen of Two Worlds did.

She'd refused several friendly loans of "body thralls"—slaves, really—to help her prepare for the victory banquet by filing and shaping her scale. "A healthy dragonelle is perfectly capable of attending to her own scale, and I wouldn't care to go into a fight with those oversharp talons you underground dragons seem to favor."

Fashionable dragons are such a bore, she thought to him. He'd never been more proud of her.

* * *

They had good weather for the feast, with just enough wind to disperse the dragon smell so that the humans could enjoy themselves. The only part of the banquet AuRon enjoyed was the fact that Natasatch gloried in the polite exchanges and friendly conversations. It did his hearts good to see his mate so happy.

It was held before the Directory, a vast building where the Hypatians met and schemed and governed, a place of alliances and betrayals, of promises public and secret agendas, or so Wistala's quick history of it explained when AuRon and Natasach were shown inside. There were circular ranks of benches fitted for humans running around the walls looking down on enormous statues of the beasts of the world: oxen and dolphins and lions and such, along with a dragon who had the wrong number of toes and his crest-horns growing in the wrong direction.

Wistala had a high opinion of the traditions of the place, something to do with some old elf friend of hers who'd been a "Knight of the Directory." To AuRon the place only echoed with noisy vanity.

AuRon noted an empty place next to his brother—where his Queen Nilrasha would be had she not been restricted from travel by injuries. Perhaps for the first time since their hatching he felt a pang of sympathy for the Copper. Tyr RuGaard was grave and ate little, though he offered elaborate praise and politenesses to his guests. On his other side Wistala reclined, supplying him with names when he forgot the identity of this, that, or the other so-and-so.

"My tongue does you an injustice," his brother said, after mispronouncing the name of a human thane from the north.

The human, awestruck and uncomfortable in the presence of a throng of dragons, assured "my Tyr" that he was utterly unable to pronounce half the names of the dragons in attendance.

When it came time for the banquet, the dragons ate on the great pillar-bordered street leading up to the immense Hypatian Directory. Even that vast building couldn't fit this many dragons, at least in such a way that they might be fed. Using a road allowed oxcarts to carry food to the dragons, stretched out on their bellies in a vast rectangle—the oxen were blindfolded and had Ghiozian camphor rubbed in their noses to cover up the dragon smell to forestall panic.

Dragons, humans, and a smattering of elves and dwarfs and even a blighter or two with hair neatly bound and ribboned dined in two long lines flanking the road. The dragons lay on their bellies to eat and many of the humans and elves did likewise, reaching for tidbits from bearers carrying plates in endless procession.

AuRon and Natasatch, with Istach trailing behind, were both last and first. They were the last dragons to be introduced—as "distinguished visitors from the north and relatives of our great Tyr"—ahead of various humans and elves and dwarfs representing their kind.

In the interval between the feast and the ceremonies Wistala talked with a dozen rather wizened, bent-over humans, whom she introduced as "librarians"—keepers of knowledge and secrets.

"Oh, would you look at that little bit of tail?" Natasatch said, spying the mate of one of Hypat's "Protectors." "Dyed all in red. She looks like she's trying to pass as male."

AuRon glanced over at the dragon, who'd chosen a bright shade of red favored by the Red Queen, who'd ruled Ghioz until she settled on war against the Dragons of the Lavadome. He'd had more than a claw in the killing of the strange creature who claimed to be too busy to ever die. He half-hoped one of her supply of bodies still lurked at the edges of his brother's realm, ready to wake him out of his dangerous dreams of an ever-expanding rule.

"Oh, and look at that painted advertiser," Natasatch said, referring to a graceful young dragonelle, some sprig of dragon nobility with fledging scars still dripping and wing skin hardly dry, who'd painted the fanlike *griff* that protect a dragon's neck-hearts with gold and added jeweled designs to her claws. "Practically simpering in hopes of a mating flight," she thought to him. "Some young dragon will get a mate and a hoard in one quick flight. Weighed down like that, she could get caught and breached by an eager eagle."

His mate displayed a rather perverse sense of humor at times. She explained it as the product of long years sequestered on an dismal egg shelf with nothing to do but dream erotic dreams.

"Mother!" Istach said, scandalized.

"Isn't that Varatheela with her?" AuRon asked aloud.

"No, surely she would have greeted us," Natasatch said.

"It is Varatheela," Istach said. "She's with some fire-maids, if I read the designs on their wings correctly, that is."

Well, dragonelles had to grow up sooner or later, AuRon decided. Still, it felt odd to be at a feast without even a word from your own offspring.

The hominid guests, AuRon noted, ate on their stomachs in the fashion of dragons, perched on cushioned benches. The oddly proportioned human frame looked only a little more dignified in that manner, though some of them stuck their hindquarters rather high in the air like a cat seeking a mate.

A silver-with-black-tipped dragon settled everyone down and introduced Wistala as the new Queen-Consort to roars of approval. The dragon went on for quite some time, lauding her ability with languages, her rank in the Hypatian hierarchy—AuRon wondered how she managed that—and her prowess in battle. The stuffed dragons, with ample coin in their gold-gizzards and juicy joints in their bellies, roared their approval in a manner that sent pigeons in flight all over the city like little feathery fireworks.

"I cannot replace Nilrasha," Wistala said. "But I can try to follow her example of diligence and devotion to the dragons in her care. I will also do my best for the hominid half of the Alliance. Let our Hypatian allies know that they now have a voice even atop Imperial Rock in the Lavadome."

The humans sprang to their feet and cheered and waved their arms at that.

The Copper's good eye narrowed upon hearing those words. AuRon suspected that he hadn't been told of that part of the speech beforehand. But words once spoken were as lost as yesterday, as NooMoahk the Black used to say.

He felt proud for his sister, even if he thought her a bit too trusting of their copper sibling.

They heard a song about the battle with the Pirate Lords in Swayport, and a scarred dragon named He-Bellereth introduced the newest member of the Aerial Host: AuSurath the Red. His rider would be Gundar, son of Gunfer. They both proceeded between the lines of dragons, AuSurath walking slowly so his rider could keep up.

They ascended to the stairs of the Directory, where the Copper now sat with Wistala and the Hypatian directors.

"All mark and hail AuSurath, newest member of the Aerial Host. All mark and hail Gundar, his rider and attendant."

Gundar drank a ceremonial drop of blood placed in wine from a golden chalice. Then AuSurath bit off the end of one of his rider's fingers of his off hand. AuRon wondered how that tradition ever was started.

A tremendous volume of wind from one very fat Protector from the cattle-rich south spoiled the solemnity somewhat, but everyone pretended not to notice.

"I'm so proud of our offspring," Natasatch said.

AuRon watched the new dragon and rider pair look at their off-kilter Tyr with naked adoration and felt his summer go sour.

AuMoahk visited them late that night, dropping exhausted from the sky. He was serving the Grand Alliance as a messenger, and while he was given leave to attend the ceremony involving his aunt and brother, winds had delayed wings not long used to flying.

Even Varatheela snuck into the circus arena to pay a call on her parents, coming in the dead of night and smelling of wine and fragrant oils. She made her apologies, and talked nonstop of social matters with the Firemaids, who had been assigned to which part of the Alliance, what entrances to the Lower World were being explored, which members of the Aerial Host were to take mates this year.

Her nonstop chatter of matters he didn't care about, with his mate hanging on every detail, bothered AuRon more than he could put into words. It seemed he was losing his family to the glories of his brother's empire.

He decided to take the night air outside the circus. He heard wings above and glanced up, but whatever had been there vanished behind one of the canvas shades. Curious-sounding wings. Small but almost dragonlike—no feathered creature would have made such a leathery flap. He wondered if the Copper had dispatched one of those *griffaran* of his—no, they were feathered, too.

What was it?

He opened his wings to go investigate when Wistala tipped her head over the circus wall.

"AuRon," Wistala said. "May we talk? I have a duty for you to perform, if you're willing."

"With all these polished dragons coming and going?" AuRon asked. "They're much more impressive. I'm sure one of them will serve."

He hopped over the wall and joined her, landing as silently as a cat—were there a cat that weighed as much as a strong pair of horses, that is. *Let's see a scaled dragon do that!* Why he decided on an athletic display he couldn't say, just his general feeling of dissatisfaction with events of late made his muscles twitch.

She ignored him. "It's rather a delicate situation. Your friend, King Naf of the Dairuss. He's proving a problem for the Grand Alliance. He's kicked out his Protector."

"Good old Naf," AuRon said. "I'm glad he hasn't changed."

His sister dug her *sii* claws into the dirt of the arena and tore some up. "Dairuss is in an odd predicament, as far as the Empire and these Hypatians are concerned. It was a province of Ghioz, and before that a part of the Hypatian Empire. The Tyr put SoRolotan there—do you know him? Well, never mind. The Tyr put a dragon he didn't care for much as Protector there, as it was an unimportant province, more to get him out of the way, I suppose. Something about the Tyr preventing him from taking a mate he wanted. In any case, it ended badly. I understand SoRolotan barely escaped with his life. Are the people of Dairuss unusually contentious?"

"I'm no expert on human history," AuRon said. His stomach was growling. He hadn't eaten much at the celebratory feast and the smell of all the draft animals brought fierce hunger pangs.

"The old Ghioz empire has been broken up. Each province has a dragon to help the humans there, save for Dairuss. We're afraid they'll declare independence from the Grand Alliance. The Hypatians would never allow that."

"You mean a war."

"Not if I have my way," Wistala said. "I'm sure you don't want to see your friend killed or humbled."

"Of course not. I have few enough friends left."

"Would you like to hear my solution?"

AuRon sighed. "Probably not. I'm sure I can guess what it is."

"You'd have a title. 'Protector' is one of the most respected of positions, second only to the Tyr himself in responsibility."

"Title? I don't care much for titles."

"Dairuss must be a more congenial climate than your island."

"You haven't spoken about this to Natasatch, have you?"

"I dropped a hint. She swore not to mention it unless you brought it up."

"You do know how to sink your claws into your prey, don't you, sister."

"AuRon, can't you see what I'm trying to build here? Your help would be invaluable. I'm trying to make a world where dragons have faith in humans, and humans in dragons. A Hypatian family out riding the Great North Road no longer gallops to the trees at the sight of a dragon overhead. Dogs aren't sent into caves to sniff out dragons anymore. What happened to Mother and Father will never happen again, if I have anything to say about it."

AuRon thought he heard that quiet flapping again, somewhere among the wooden spars. Were they being spied upon? "You forgot to add, thanks to our brother: He's the one who put this Grand Alliance on the map, so to speak."

"And I admire him for it," Wistala said.

"I find it hard to forget—the cave."

Wistala looked up. Maybe she'd heard that small flapping noise too. "I'm not excusing that hatchling. Every time I look into his face, I see my anger in that lazy, scarred eye of his. He did a great wrong to us."

She tried to read AuRon and failed. Her scaleless brother had a way of drawing in on himself, disappearing against the background as his skin changed color. Most dragons were easy to read: rage, hunger, lust, triumph, they huffed and stamped whatever they felt. AuRon and DharSii were the only two she'd ever known who could hide their emotions completely. Even the courtly dragons of the Lavadome gave a little away. She continued: "He's done right by his dragons now. Our family was just five dragons—six if you count him, which no one on our egg shelf ever did. But to the dragons he leads, a hundred times that number and more . . . he's brought them out of hiding and back into the sun, in safety."

"My dragons were safe on our island, too," AuRon said, feeling a bit like a petulant hatchling immediately after, yammering that his appetite was just as big.

"I'm sorry, Wistala," he continued. "This doesn't really matter, at least to anyone but us. Naf and Hieba—King Naf and Queen Hieba, that is—are my friends. Are they really in danger?"

"The last to defy the Grand Alliance was the old colony at Swayport. Now the new old colony, much impoverished. I once pretended to predict the future but I can't anymore, brother. But if they continue to resist, it may involve the Aerial Host again, if the Hypatians come up with a pretext to settle old scores. I understand a number of Hypatians who didn't much care for the Grand Alliance fled. Dairuss is a place of refugees. During the Dragon Wars many elves and men fled from their troubles on the Hypatian coast to their lands across the mountains. Some old Ghioz aristocrats are still important men there, there are even Ironriders who surrendered to them rather than face the wrath of the Hypatians and the dragons of the Grand Alliance. It wouldn't be difficult for our brother and the Hypatians to justify a war."

"And how am I to prevent that?"

"By getting Naf to rejoin the Grand Alliance. I spoke to him personally about the issue. He swears he'll have no dragon on his lands as Protector—no dragon except you."

AuRon returned to his family deep in thought. Their offspring, exhausted by the excitement of the day, slept in the style of hatchlings, near the belly of their mother.

Only AuSurath was missing. He was probably off somewhere, watching his rider numb his wounded hand in ice.

They made a pretty picture.

AuRon could not help but feel some pride at the achievements of his hatchlings. This awful empire of his brother's inspired them in a way he found disturbing. He'd done his best to educate them, to warn them of the example of Silverhigh . . .

He couldn't blame them for not wanting to stay among the fogs and reefs of his island. Conversations with wolves couldn't match the splendor of these elegant dragons.

"That was another time, Father," AuMoahk said, earlier that evening. His son's rebuke still echoed in his thoughts. "Besides, we don't make enemies of hominids, we make friends."

"I'm sure that was how it was in the early days of Silverhigh, too."

Perhaps fate had just decided to repeat itself. AuRon had read enough histories in NooMoahk's library to know that sometimes events repeated themselves even when all the parties concerned knew full well the details of past tragedies.

Natasach opened an eye.

Did you enjoy your walk? she thought to him.

"I met Wistala. It seems she has a problem she believes I can help her solve. It involves my friend, King Naf in Dairuss. She asks me to fly there and engage in a little diplomacy on her behalf."

He decided not to tell her about the possibility of a Protectorship.

Natasatch's scale lifted in excitment. "So what did you say?"

"I said nothing. I wanted to get your opinion first. You see, it would probably mean several years away from our island, and I know how much you enjoy the winters there."

"Oh, AuRon, don't tease. What will you do, my love?"

"Do my best to resolve the issue, I suppose. I can't leave Naf at the mercy of these unscrupulous, greedy dragons. Will you accompany me there?"

"Silly. Nothing would please me better. I'm happy to see more of the world, especially with you."

Chapter 4

airuss and the City of the Golden Dome had grown since last AuRon had seen it. It rivaled even Hypat in size, though probably not in population; there were still many fields where sheep grazed within the city proper.

AuRon took the precaution of first visiting the guardpost in the high pass of the Red Mountains, once Naf's station, and sending word by Dairuss messenger that AuRon the Gray had returned with mate and offspring to visit and consult with King Naf.

The men of the guard watched from their tower slits. Mysterious clanks and clatters echoed from within—were they pushing furniture to barricade the door, setting out fire buckets, or preparing war machines to fire harpoons?

He assuaged his anxiety by telling Istach stories of how he and Naf met, back when he was just a lowly sword-for-hire guarding dwarven gold. How he raised Hieba up from a little girl stolen from a ravaged trade caravan to Queen, and how Naf's people had been the first to fight back against the Ghioz empire.

So when word returned, flashed by a great mirror atop the Golden Dome, that AuRon was to land in the Dome's gardens, AuRon half sighed in relief.

They alighted in a meadow filled with white-painted decorative stones. From the air, or the top of the dome, they made patters that AuRon recognized as human astrological signs.

"Hello, AuRon. I'm glad to meet your family at last," Naf said from behind.

AuRon had been watching the elaborate, fountain-flanked steps leading up to the onion-shaped, gold-painted dome. Instead, he'd come out of a ordinary stone dwelling, not much more than a cottage, really.

"You aren't in the old palace residence?" AuRon asked.

"Ach, no. Everything is such a walk in that place. I like my pipe, my water, and my hearth all within reach of a good solid chair, and these days a long hike to bed is not my favorite way to end a day."

"AuRon! You haven't changed a bit," Hieba said. She was still beautiful, only careworn.

AuRon introduced Natasatch and Istach.

Naf's forehead bore a fringe of white—a sign of aging in a human. What had been gray before was now white, making the remaining darker hair toward the back look all deeper in color, as though it were steadying itself for the final desperate battle from the white encroachment at the temples and forelock. Hieba's eyes had lost much of their sparkle. They'd seemed to have fallen back into dark sockets, but were steady and alert and the teeth she showed in her mouth were still in order, even if they'd gone a bit yellowish brown.

"It's from all the bitterbean I've been drinking," she said, when AuRon asked about it, since he couldn't discuss the condition of her scale and had no idea what human standards applied to the night-black hair bound in elaborate cording of three colors. "The taste is so familiar, I must have had it as a child, before you found me."

"Some of the Ghioz trade routes are still intact," Naf said. "They're not bad fellows, once you yank the whips out of their hands and don't curse their dead Queen—to their faces, anyway."

Naf wore the coats of state of his people. The Dairuss kings of old, evidently, did not go for flashy apparel, perhaps befitting a simple people who grazed a dozen different animals depending on ground—Dairuss was everything from high-mountain passes to rolling, well-watered hills near the great river. While it had never been a land rich in gold or gems, they'd fallen from the heights they'd once, briefly, known when they'd overthrown the evil wizard Anklemere, who'd ruled an empire vaster than even the Hypatians had known in their glory.

"And Nissa," AuRon asked, dredging up the name from his memory.

"Nissa means 'morning dove' in my language. Our

nickname for her. Now she only answers to the Ghioz court name the Red Queen gave her, Desthenae."

"Married at eleven, to one of the Princes of the Sunstruck Sea," Hieba said. "Not our doing, some Ghioz title in charge of her sold her maidenhood and absconded when the Queen's rule collapsed. We're just grateful this Prince made her a wife, instead of a concubine, as the men in those parts are wont to do."

"Those white-turbaned fellows?" AuRon asked. He'd fought them once, to defend his blighter allies in the mountains of Old Uldam.

"It's a fractious land," Naf said. "For the most part they keep quarrels among themselves."

"I hardly know the world outside our island," Natasatch said, in her shaky Parl. Istach corrected her pronunciation.

"Hieba made an unofficial journey to see her," Naf said. "She's, well, even influenced her husband to prefer us to the old Ghioz states in matters of trade routes. Their caravans off-load here now, rather than in Ghioz."

"I'll be happy to fly you down there," Natasatch said. "I'm learning that I enjoy travel."

"Very kind of you—lady . . ." Naf said, searching for a title.

AuRon harrumphed. "We don't have any sort of rank you need to refer to. Though we have come to talk to you about this business with the Grand Alliance."

"It's a pleasant day," Naf said. "Perhaps it would be easier for us all to talk outside. I'll have some chairs brought."

*   *   *

Once they settled in, Hieba and Naf seated with a few of their court in attendance, AuRon and his family facing them, and some roast mutton long since gone down dragon gullets.

"I'm here to convince you to rejoin the Grand Alliance," AuRon said.

"That fat SoRolatan was almost as bad as the Ghioz," Hieba said. "He'd pluck cattle right out of a field or dip his neck right into a net full of fish. He threatened to burn down the dome if we didn't bring him more coin."

"Did he protect you from anything?" AuRon asked.

"Biting insects, I suppose," Naf said. "They avoided his reek."

"Your kingdom is in an odd predicament," AuRon said. "I understand it fell into the Grand Alliance rather than joining."

"I would have your counsel," Naf said. "Perhaps fresh dragon eyes can perceive that which is puzzlement and dilemma."

"Counsel? My eyes won't help you much in political murk," AuRon said.

"Then let's escape it. Come, AuRon, I'll fly, if you'll humble yourself to bear a human on your proud and unconquered back. Like Tindairuss and NooMoahk of old, eh?"

They brought out sewn-together sheepskins rigged with stirrups and horn. "It's a saddle for an elephant, if you must know. They're used down in the logging camps to the south."

AuRon's mouth watered at the memory of elephant. Chewy, but one could dine for days.

It took some time for Naf's saddlemaster, or whatever his title was, to adjust the straps so they fit snug on a dragon. Naf eventually put on a heavy cloak and climbed on.

"Keep your scarf about you," Hieba said, rechecking his stirrups. "It's cold, flying on dragon-back."

"Ah, AuRon," Naf laughed, "you're wider than the hunting horses a king rides for pleasure. It's like sitting atop a flat old plowhorse."

"Be sure not to tip him," Natasatch said. "That would be a terrible beginning to our diplomacy."

"He's tougher than he looks," AuRon said. "Ready? Don't be alarmed, I flap the most taking off."

With that, AuRon launched himself into the air. Naf kicked him hard in the throat as his heels sought purchase, hanging on for dear life.

"What direction first?" AuRon asked.

"North," Naf said.

AuRon swung toward the blue green of the Falngese river.

"Here, to the north, is where we first met. Wallander's an ally of ours, of sorts. The traveling towers don't cross the lands since the Ironriders waged war on the lands west, but there is still trade. The silk and dye chain of trading posts bring their pack trains here, and a good deal of the Sunstruck Sea trade finds its way here as well. Your dwarf friends rely on us as allies in case of trouble, and there's always trouble when the Ironriders are your neighbors.

As if to prove his point, AuRon saw galloping figures on the far side of the river.

"Yah-ha, what's this?" Naf said. "AuRon, by the riverbank, the long sandbar with the trees."

AuRon descended, willing to take a closer look.

Even the great Falngese sometimes ran shallow, and a barge had caught itself on a sandbar. Its crew had been trying to move it back into the main channel by means of a small boat, lines, and anchors.

The problem was the boat was stranded on the far side of the river, not yet to Wallander and in the open country of the plains.

Ironrider lands.

More and more Ironriders galloped up to the riverbank, like hyenas gathering at a lion's kill.

AuRon's battle blood wasn't up. Nothing particularly vexed him about the scuffle below, just humans robbing one another. For every fishing ship he'd seen coming to the rescue of another in distress, he'd seen two stealing each other's pot-markers, or cutting a rival's nets away. "Naf, I'm not some kind of warhorse. I'm not even a scaled dragon. One lucky bowman—"

"Drop flame on them. Anything to frighten them away!"

"That I can do. But you'll owe me a hearty meal, my friend."

If it was to be done, it might as well be done well. Where had he heard that? His brother? He must be getting mazy from too much change of altitude, if he was quoting his brother.

AuRon read the wind in the grass before deciding on a direction for the attack.

Mind made up, he swooped in low, making as much noise as he could. The horses reacted as horses usually did: They danced and shied and the arrows drawn went well off mark.

He loosed his flame in the shallow waters at the riverbank. Billowing clouds of steam erupted, and a small grass fire sizzled.

"The King! The King!" the crew shouted as AuRon passed overhead.

"I'll dislodge them. Hang on," AuRon said.

With a wary glance at the bank, where the Ironrider raiders had discovered that the prize wasn't worth a possible scorching and were scattering to parts east, he landed. Gripping the barge's stern with his *sii*, he found purchase in the sandy riverbottom and shoved, then swam, the boat back out into the main channel.

"You should get one of those monster herbivores the dwarfs use for this," AuRon grunted.

Naf waved to the cheering men. *Ah well*, AuRon thought, *the king always gets the credit. Or the blame.*

With that he took off again, and they followed the course of the Falngese river.

AuRon had overflowed it before, but he'd never

seen this much traffic on it, from little fishing boats to bigger, grain-filled barges.

"Hypatia is growing rich again," Naf explained. "They're buying, and when there are buyers there are sellers jostling each other to be first to their markets."

AuRon shrugged. He didn't care one way or another if the Hypatians grew rich or how much grain they bought. He did fear for what a rich and powerful neighbor might intend for Naf and his people. It could be like the Ghioz all over again—Naf's poor country was at an important gap in the mountains.

"This is the east. We claim this length of the Falngese river, but by long tradition it's a free-flow. I can claim no part of the commerce that doesn't come into or leave my shores. The Ghioz abide by the tradition as well—for now. Beyond the river are the forests of the old provinces, now claimed by both us and the Ghioz (who, under this Grand Alliance, aren't all that different from the old), and beyond that are the mountains where you and Hieba lived with the blighters. The mountains are thick with blighters and their herds and they are settling here, there and here again before you know it. Do they grow on rocks?"

"I read a study in NooMoahk's old library," AuRon said. "In times of war and stress blighters will produce more male children. In times of peace, more females are born. Back when I lived there, I advised them to stay out of wars and battles; it seems they still do. Wiving years and knifing years, the Fireblades used to call such intervals."

"I fear they will see some knifing years. There are

the usual disputes about grazing lands and stolen livestock between my roving foresters' camps and the
blighter settlers and the Ghioz."

"Or your settlers and the roving blighters, as a
blighter-chief might have it. But don't worry too much
about border disputes here; I may be able to help you
with this. There may be some old fireblades who remember me."

Naf needed a rest out of the saddle and they broke
their journey at a village. After a moment of terror and
slammed shutters as AuRon passed over, once he
landed and Naf called out for his people to come help
their weary old king dismount, they forgot their fear
and children seemed to be peering at him out of every
doorway and windowsill. Naf bought some bread for
himself and two fat hams for his mount, and they
stretched out for some of the afternoon before mount-
ing again.

"To think, to be able to travel from one end of my
kingdom to the other in a day," Naf said. "Dairuss is
not big by any means, but even riding hard with fresh
horses at every station it takes a messenger more than
a day to go from north to south."

AuRon was used to the saddle by now—though he
resolved none but Naf could ride him—and they took
off again.

"And the south. Our source of sustenance and of trouble. We love the Ghioz for their plentiful food, barges full
of grain and feed they send from their southlands, but it
has always come at a price of arrogance, or domination.

They outnumber us and frequently outwit us; more than one Dairussan has borrowed from their ample coffers to find that it must be paid back through Ghioz tax collectors and market law. They think of us as upright blighters in need of direction and management."

"You should be honored to be thought of as blighter by such as they. I would rather freeze in that pass with you than pass a holiday with the Ghioz, from what I've seen of them. Always trying to get others to do their dirty work."

"They're slavers, one way or another. Now they've got that great white dragon and his mate as their dragon lords, when others aren't coming and going to keep an eye on those two. I'm—ho, what's this, Au-Ron? Name a specter and he appears."

Naf pointed to what AuRon's sharp eyes had already picked out—a green dragon flying up from the south.

"I don't recognize her," AuRon said.

"Is there danger?"

AuRon judged the green, trying to close distance. She didn't move through the air with the slow, steady beats of an experienced flier, he suspected she spent most of her time on the ground.

"I should think not. She flies like a dragon born for swimming."

"She's coming straight for us."

"Let your fears go like a loose scale. I can outfly anything with scale," AuRon said, getting height advantage, just in case. "Though I don't want to take you too high. Your nose will bleed or you'll freeze."

The lumbering dragonelle waggled in the air as she approached, showing her belly. AuRon guessed she wanted to talk, the gesture struck him as funny or playful, though he didn't know what the signals might mean to these dragons of the Lavadome.

He circled her, she circled him.

"I believe that's one of the Ghioz Protectors," Naf said. "She visited our dragon."

AuRon came up alongside her. "Happy to meet a new dragon," she called. "Might we alight and talk? My name is Imfamnia, my mate is the Protector of Ghioz."

And so it was that AuRon met the former Queen of the Lavadome, Imfamnia, called the Jade Queen, and now an exile.

They alighted on a rocky hilltop, sending hares fleeing for their lives.

"I am AuRon. I'm carrying my friend, King Naf of the Dairuss."

The dragon-dame tipped her head to the King. "Very pleased," she said, in stilted Parl.

She had too much paint on her by half for AuRon. A health-tonic-selling dwarf's trade wagon looked subdued compared to the purples and reds and golds about her eyes, *griff*, nostrils, and ear-buds.

"NiVom is feeling unwell this morning, otherwise he would have been up in this delightful air," she panted, sucking in a good deal of it.

"The white?" AuRon asked. "I met him in the war against the Red Queen. Where he changed sides."

"To the nation of his birth, who'd cast him out before your brother took power. He never wanted to make war on them, and reverted to where his true loyalty lay at the first opportunity."

Naf hopped off the saddle chair and stretched his back.

"It's getting late, AuRon," Naf said. "We'll want to find a place to overnight."

Imfamnia cocked her head, puzzled. "Perhaps I misunderstood, but did that man just order you to rest for the night?"

"He hasn't flown before, and I've no wish to tax him."

"Curious. Well, pleased to meet you, AuRon. I hope we shall be good friends. I know we will. There's a terrible shortage of new anecdotes at our feasts these days, in Ghioz we're cut off from most of Lavadome society. I don't know if you're aware, but I'm not exactly welcome there."

"You didn't fly all this way to tell me this."

She tucked her shaking wings in to her sides a little tighter. "We heard a rumor that you were to be our new neighbor."

"Neighbor?"

"Fellow dragon lord. Protector of Dairuss."

AuRon shifted his gaze to Naf. "That would be up to him."

"Up to—a human?"

"King Naf is lord in Dairuss. I wouldn't presume to tell him how to arrange his affairs."

The dragon-dame bent her neck without moving

her head. Some might interpret it as a bow, others as a twitch. "I'm pleased," she said, in that halting Parl. She shifted back to Drakine: "You know, AuRon, if he's fatigued, a little dragon blood would help revive him. Does wonders for older human males. Might even help with the brittle hair."

"Dragon blood?" AuRon asked.

"It's all the rage with certain allies of ours. Sometimes, at banquets, NiVom and I are quite drained."

AuRon looked over her perfectly formed lines. "You don't look like you've ever shed a drop of blood in your life."

Imfamnia chuckled. AuRon still wasn't sure he liked laughing dragons. Silliness wasn't befitting of dragonkind.

"I've never claimed to be a fighting dragon. There are more pleasant things to do with one's life. You're mated, aren't you? Too bad. With so little scale you must be quite an experience."

AuRon stilled his *griff*. Mating, perhaps the single most important decision a dragon could ever make, reduced to an *experience*. Less and less he was liking this dragon-dame.

"I'm sure I don't have your experience to judge," he said.

"I'm sure you don't. But that's easily remedied." She brushed him along the side with her wing.

He'd never encountered anything quite like her. She appealed in a way that was hard to define, a less dragonlike attitude could hardly be imagined. She behaved more like a blighter who'd had too much rice wine, or an elvish jester.

"You didn't fly after us to joke."

"No. Flying is wearisome. My mate and I thought we would invite you to our residence. Surely with two lands sharing a long border and a longer history, we have matters to discuss, so that the thralls don't become restive and take matters into their own bloody little hands. Cooler dragon heads should be called in to resolve things, don't you agree?"

"How did you learn I was to be sent to Dairuss?"

"You're new to the Grand Alliance. News travels faster than wings. Especially in matters of mating, dueling, or politics."

"Again, matters I know little of and care of less. I'm already mated, I've had my share of duels and won't seek another, and as for politics, I don't know enough to have an opinion."

Imfamnia made a noise that was half laugh, half *prrum*. "An admirable disinterest. To tell you the truth, sometimes I have difficulty distinguishing them myself. What is your mate's name again?"

"Natasatch."

"Please send her my regards. Should your King Naf there decide to accept you as Protector, I hope we'll see you in our resort soon. The change of company would be most welcome.

"Hail and farewell, King Naf," she added, switching back to Parl. "I hope the next time I visit your city, no one shoots arrows at me.

"Enjoy the rest of your tour, AuRon. It shouldn't take long, unless you enjoy counting sheep."

With that, she trotted away and launched herself into the sky.

They rested in one of the towns near the Ghioz border, in a broken-down old castle overlooking a village nestled along the Ghioz road through the hills.

Naf told him a story about the defense of the castle against the Ghioz, long before he was born. Dairuss had lost, of course, but they resisted gallantly while they could.

He wondered what difference it made in the long run. Sometimes you just had to give up trying to fly if the winds were too strong. He hoped Naf wasn't nerving himself for another gallant but futile resistance to the Hypatians and his brother's empire.

Naf wandered into town cloaked. He liked to go among his people disguised, it seemed, and returned with two plucked turkeys and some bread and wine. After eating, AuRon curled up in the foundation of a collapsed tower and slept.

The beautiful and slightly silly Imfamnia invaded his dreams.

They were up with the larks the next morning. Naf settled himself rather stiffly into the saddle chair. "Old bones don't take quickly to new tricks."

They flew back northward on the Dairuss side of the Red Mountains.

"And at last, the west. Hypatia. We bled plenty for

them when they were bowing and scraping to the Wizard Anklemere and we were the only men west of the great desert who wouldn't submit. We won our freedom then—only to lose it shortly after to the Ghioz. It appears my land is fated to remain free for only brief periods in between conquerors. Now, with the Tyr's dragons at their backs, they're haughty and demanding."

"Are you worried about the dragons?" AuRon asked.

"Oh, they send smooth talkers over, to tell us all the advantages of joining your Tyr's 'Grand Alliance.' Safety"—he spat. "Security"—he spat again. "Order *psht*! Those words go like chains about the wrist. Only they're worse; you can't see the manacles until they've bound you hand and foot like a pig to slaughter."

If Naf went on much longer about his brother's Dragon Empire his shepherds below might think it raining.

"I know what will happen," Naf said. "The Hypatians will create some pretext to reclaim us, and we won't dare resist with dozens of dragons ready to sweep over our poor lands."

AuRon knew what it was like to be the weakest of a team of rivals. He'd always thought that the more the hominids fought each other, the better off dragons were—fewer two-legged warriors to go after his kind.

Hard to think of a good-hearted fellow like Naf being ground up in a war, though.

"It's a good land, AuRon. The elven refugees have

settled and set up craft houses and theaters and schools and hospitals. We have dwarfs coming to and fro from the Diadem, setting up mines and wells and trading posts. You ever tried dwarf-drink, AuRon? Most refreshing, like beer that doesn't give you a headache, just the burps. We even have some Ghioz who don't care for their new Dragon Lords setting up households, and say what you want about the Ghioz, they know how to organize and smooth and build. They're doing very well as stonemasons and bricklayers. We could be as great a people as we ever were."

He didn't like the idea of flinging himself into the rivalries and politics of the Lavadome, but if it would help Naf . . . He gulped and took the plunge: "I promise you, my friend, if you'll join the Grand Alliance, with me as your Protector, I'll do my best to truly protect your lands. My sister, who's now serving as Queen-Consort to the Tyr, she wants the Alliance to benefit both."

"I've met her," Naf said. "She speaks superbly. But she's just one voice. For every dragon like her, there's at least one SoRolatan."

They traveled over central Dairuss on their way back to the City of the Golden Dome, and Naf had him stop in some marshy country.

"This is a famous holdout of robbers and partisans fighting against our conquerers. Many a king has removed his throne to these swamps."

AuRon had perfected his swamp-feeding technique

in the jungles south of NooMoahk's old cave. (Ah, if he'd only known about the trouble that crystal could cause—he would never have willed it to the blighters when he quit that old library-cavern.) You simply plunge your jaws into the swamp vegetation, suck up a mouthful of roots, stems, leaves, and petals, then hoist your head high in the air and drain the water down your throat. Any number of fish, frogs, crustaceans, worms, bugs, and leeches would then cascade down your throat. Then you'd simply spit out the green stuff. Not the most tasty meal—stagnant water always made one's belches reminiscent of sewage—but it filled one with water that could be quickly processed and the food digested quickly without a jumble of bones and joints clogging the gut.

"A man could get gut-sick on such water," Naf said.

"I've seen hominid innards. It's a wonder your food makes it through at all. All those bends and turns."

"The scientists say you need more guts for grains and roots. Thanks to all that, we can make it through a hard winter without starving on stored food. They keep for months."

"So can we. We just get out of the wind, curl up, and sleep and wait for the smell of thaw."

"No fun in that," Naf said. "Winter's a time of beer tapping and storytelling." He turned sour. "Or it used to be."

AuRon spat out another mouthful of swamp growth, pretty sure he'd swallowed a couple of turtles this time, something was rattling as it went down his throat. "I thought human kings had the best beer and professional storytellers to keep them entertained."

"Yes, but I'm always drawn away from my own parties, so the tales and songs are played for others' benefit. I wish I were just riding with my old Red Guards again, at times. Yes, I was in the Red Queen's array and war livery, but duty for a soldier is easy and cares can be thrown off at night as you put off your day clothes. Duty as a king—finding it is like reading stars in a fog."

"Can't you leave or stop?" AuRon knew what word he was seeking, he'd read it in some dwarfish text or other, but fumbled for the Parl equivalent.

"Abdicate," Naf said. "It crossed my mind. Hieba and I have discussed it, we considered renouncing the throne to search for Nissa—Lady Desthenae, to use her Ghioz court name. But even if I named my successor, there's no telling who might be on the throne in a year's time. We've just gained our independence. Dairuss has no traditions to speak of. Whatever I do will become tradition. It'll be a poor start for my people if their king renounces his throne to go seek a married-off daughter."

"They must think well of you," AuRon said. "It's not everyone who can work up the nerve to face down a dragon."

"SoRolatan didn't put up much of a fight. He was raiding a marketplace and some old women started pelting him with garbage. When he flew back to the Golden Dome, sputtering outrage, I met him there with some spearmen. He roared a warning but fled as fast as his wings could travel."

"Your people chose well, picking you as king."

"They had few enough choices. All I had going for me was the knowledge that I fought the Ghioz when no one north of Bant dared defy them, and retrieved our old throne from the heart of the Red Queen's Empire."

AuRon remembered him sitting in it, bloody and battered.

Naf looked at the sky, chuckled. "You should hear the tales that pass for the official history of my battles. Back in Dairuss, they whispered that I was striking left and right, winning smashing victories and leaving a series of Ghioz generals embarrassed. Culminating, of course, with our great raid on the throne-city you helped us win. Oh, AuRon, I have been closeted with two very disappointed historians, correcting their texts so they know my gallant band spent most of their time in desperate flight from superior numbers."

"Most of my victories are little but escapes as well," AuRon said, thinking of his encounters with the Dragonblade. Strange to think his brother, of all dragonkind, had been the one to kill that remarkable human.

"So, what will it be, Naf? Another gallant fight, defeat, and you'll end your days in these swamps or some valley in the Red Mountains? I promise you, if you accept me as Protector, you'll hardly know we're here. My mate and I will find a comfortable cave, and bide our time there until you need us."

"I suppose mock independence is preferable to no independence. I just don't want a court full of Hypatians running my country for me."

"We'll keep them away."

"Then let's call it a bargain," Naf said, grinning. "That Imfamnia, I thought she said something about dragon blood?"

"You speak Drakine?"

"I picked up a little from SoRolatan," Naf said.

"It's the first I've heard of it, but if you want to taste my blood, you're more than welcome. Try some out of my tail, there are fewer nerve endings there."

Naf carefully cleaned his knife and gave AuRon a small nick, then drank from his waterskin cup.

"Most invigorating," Naf said.

"Try not to get used to it," AuRon said. "I don't care what my brother does, but I don't want to bleed every time you hold a feast."

He returned to his family with the small nick already healed. They awaited him at the king's stables. Istach was sleeping atop a barn, watching the stars. She was an odd one.

"You look tired, my love," Natasatch said, comfortably curled up in an old cow basement.

"I flew a great deal with Naf in the last few days. We covered his whole kingdom."

"How goes the diplomacy?"

"I have to tell you something, highlight of my song.

My brother—well, Wistala, mostly, has put me forward as dragon lord—Protector, or whatever they call it—of Naf's Kingdom. Naf has agreed that we might serve."

Natasatch's eyes brightened as though filled with dragon-flame. "A Protector!"

"You would like me to take the role?"

She let out a loud *prrum*. "They're all respected. Most are considered powerful. I've heard some become very rich."

"My brother was one before he became Tyr, I understand. We won't grow rich here, though. Dairuss is a poor land, it just happens to be situated at a crossroads between south, east, and west."

"But you don't like the idea, it seems."

"Getting mixed up in this way with hominids. It's dangerous," AuRon said.

"But Naf wouldn't hurt us. Did you not tell me he is your oldest hominid friend?"

"That's exactly why I don't desire this position."

Natasatch asked, "To be of use to a friend?"

"This 'Grand Alliance' my brother imagines, and Wistala is refining, could be the death of that friendship. I'd help Naf if it meant tearing my wings to pieces flying for him and losing teeth in his enemies' necks. But he'll only live so long. Who knows what manner of king might replace him, or what the Grand Alliance will one day demand of Dairuss. I fear that dragons who set themselves up to rule an empire on the backs of the hominids will only find they've left their undersides vulnerable."

Chapter 5

T he throne room atop the Imperial Rock in the Lavadome was buzzing. Oftentimes, it seemed that
the Tyr was the last person to know what was going
on. NoSohoth had gathered a crowd of important
dragons—well, with so many living on the surface as
Protectors these days, what passed for important dragons in the attenuated Lavadome—so he assumed it
would be good news. Bad news always ended up being whispered in his ear.

"He's done it," Wistala said, marching up toward
the throne room with a smaller striped dragonelle just
behind. "There, my Tyr, no threats or battles required.
Instead of a defeated enemy, he brings an ally."

The Copper was still getting used to Wistala as his
Queen-Consort. When Nilrasha had first brought up

the idea of someone to stand in for her at the ceremonies and so on, that the Queen was expected to attend, he simply said that she should pick her replacement. He assumed it would be Ayafeeia—she was of very noble birth, being the granddaughter of Tyr Fe-Hazathant, and though she had no interest in politics could be counted on to show her face at a feast or a hatchling review.

Instead he ended up with his sister, Wistala.

She was a capable enough dragon and happy to forget the wrongs they'd done each other as hatchlings. Wistala had some obtuse ideas about how hominids should be treated. The Copper wanted the Hypatians as a privileged elite, who would keep the other hominids in line. Wistala seemed to think that the Hypatians should be dealt with as equals.

"The easier an ally comes, the easier he goes," the Copper said, quoting the Tyr—or rather FeHazathant. FeHazathant would always be "the Tyr" in his mind. The great old dragon who had adopted him when he'd virtually drifted into the Lavadome could only be emulated, never replaced. On the rare occasions when NoSohoth could be diverted from his blather about trade routes and thrall markets, the Copper liked to have him quote FeHazathant's sayings.

"How many dragons will he need?" the Copper asked.

"Just himself and his mate, and their daughter while she remains with them. Istach is her name. She flew here with the news that AuRon the Gray is the new Protector of Dairuss."

"The other went into the Firemaidens, did she not?"

"Varatheela. Yes, she's taken her second oath," Wistala said.

The Copper wasn't sure he liked Dairuss watched over only by dragons of his brother's family. It was an important province. It guarded the Iwensi Gap in the Red Mountains, the route by which Hypatia had been invaded any number of times, most recently by the Ironriders under the Red Queen. There was a dwarf trading settlement at the falls, hanging there in the river's neck like a stuck bone.

He'll have to see about getting a wall built. The Hypatians had started such a project several times in the past, with little to show for it but some scarring in the mountainsides where quarries were dug and a road running the purported path of the fortifications selected by Hypatian engineers. The gap was cold and windy, even in summer, and if there wasn't dust blowing off the plains there was cold rain or sleet piling up off the Inland Ocean. Anything but dwarfs and sheep quickly sickened and died in the cold and wet.

Well, there were dwarfs in the pass already. They might be persuaded to build the wall. Dwarfs couldn't be threatened or bullied into doing something, but they might be bought. He suspected the dwarfs of the Diadem, who never put on their boots without calculating profit and loss, would command a hefty price to see it through.

Why this sudden interest in the wall? He'd known about it for years. Did he seek to put a barrier between himself and his brother? If he hadn't once fought over an egg shelf with the fellow, he'd think him another inoffensive, unscaled gray. But grays could be tricky, with their ability to blend in and creep up on you without a sound.

Back to business. The young dragonelle behind Wistala stepped forward.

"Just as I told you," Wistala said in her ear.

"Tyr, I ask leave to make a report," the newcomer said, a little wide-eyed at being atop Imperial Rock, the heart of the Lavadome.

By Susiron, fixed forever in the sky! Jizara, how can this be? Winged and beautiful as I knew you always would be.

The Copper couldn't find words.

"Tyr?" almost-Jizara repeated.

"'My Tyr,' you mean," NoSohoth prompted.

"I don't know that he's my Tyr," almost-Jizara said.

"Why—" HeBellerath started. "You young—"

"Oh, bother the court protocol," the Copper said. "She's not a dragon of the Lavadome, and 'Tyr' is ample honor for me."

No, it wasn't Jizara. She has stripes; Jizara's scale was as uniform in color, save for a slight lightening along the belly, as any dragonelle. The young dragonelle just looked like her. Jizara as she might have been.

But still.

"What is your name again?"

"Istach, daughter of Natasatch."

"I don't suppose you can sing, Istach?"

The assembly murmured at that. Wasn't there a report to be heard? Had the Tyr taken leave of his senses?

Bother all that, the Copper thought. *I want to hear her sing*.

"Sing?" Istach said. "Just to pass the time when I'm preening scale."

"Let's hear you."

Her eyes widened, and the Copper wondered if she thought him a bit mad.

"Go on, you can never go far wrong doing as the Tyr requests," NoSohoth said.

"On our island we have some blighters. They sing a song when they're digging—I'm not even sure what the words mean, they speak to us in a bad mix of Drakine and Parl. But it's good for breaking open marrow bones, or piling cod for a roast.

> *"Fee-yo, fee-yah, mumabak, mumakhan—*
> *Uf, duf, tref, dza! Brekogal hu soupapan."*

"The last bit is counting and about supper at the end of the day. That's all I understood," Wistala said.

"Thank you, Queen-Consort."

The Copper tasted the air about her. No, she wasn't much like Jizara after all. But she intrigued him anyway. Imagine singing a simple blighter work song in the Tyr's court.

"So are you being courted?" he asked.

She dipped her head in embarrassment. "No, Tyr. I don't mix much."

"Joined the Firemaids?"

"No, Tyr."

"Not even tried?"

"Never," Istach said, growing bolder and learning to ignore the stares of the great dragons. "My sister joined, and is doing very well, I understand. You've recently promoted my brother AuSurath into the Aerial Host and my brother AuMoahk studies with the Ankelenes. I did not wish to see my parents left alone."

"Surely you want to do something useful," the Copper said.

Some of the court was exchanging looks. Well, he wanted to know about this young dragon, so he'd ask a few questions. They'd indulge their Tyr.

Istach flicked her tongue in thought. "Oh, I learned the language of the wolves on my home island, I keep the blighters from stealing our sheep, and once I pulled some storm-wrecked fishermen to shore and brought a boat to pick them up. I'm useful to my father's island."

She spoke heartfully. Another dragonelle might simper and flatter in the presence of so many young males of the Aerial Host. In any case, those who spoke to him almost always wanted a favor from the Tyr. The Copper wasn't used to such an open manner. Most dragons of his Empire either wanted his judgment and decree in their favor, advancement for themselves, or mercy for some crime. A very stupid dragonelle might not realize all the power he represented, but he didn't think her cloud-brained. But why feign such nonchalance? No, she must be hiding some other agenda.

"I'm sure my brother AuRon is proud of you."

"I would still guard his throat were he not," she said.

"Such loyalty to her sire and dam at her age, newly fledged," HeBellereth said. "Entirely admirable."

"You interest me, Istach. I hope, now that your message is delivered, that you will stay and join the festivities."

"Festivities!" one of the more robust dragon-dames said. "Is there to be a feast?"

"We shall celebrate the latest proof of the strength of our Alliance. Let word go out that twenty-one days hence, there will be a feast to celebrate. Let them feast in the Lavadome, let them feast in the Uphold of Swayport on the western shores, let them feast in Ghioz. Of course, the Tyr's court and select members of the Aerial Host shall enjoy the finest feast of all."

"Where is this feast to be?" NoSohoth asked.

"Dairuss, of course," the Copper said. "I must congratulate my brother on his triumph. Istach, would you be kind enough to act as the Tyr's messenger, and tell your parents that we are coming to celebrate his new position?"

"Yes, Tyr," Istach said. NoSohoth stamped at her not using the more proper "my Tyr" but it did a little good to have the old goldeater get some exercise being aggravated.

"A feast," AuRon asked. "Here?"

"That is what they said. They shall be here in nineteen days. I flew hard, Father, to bring you the news. To tell the truth, I'm famished."

AuRon and Natasatch had taken possession of an old Ghioz mine in the Red Mountains above the City of the Golden Dome. Naf had worked out a signal with the mirror or a firework if he was needed, day or night. So far, he'd not called on his dragon Protector, but he had sent gifts in the form of herds of sheep and goats and a few blighter herdsmen. They were cattle thieves captured in the borderlands and pardoned to serve the dragons. AuRon didn't think much of them, but Natasatch was training them with a will, eager to start having her own servants to attend them.

"It would help if we knew what a feast entailed," Natasatch said, dryly.

AuRon had been around the Lavadome dragons enough to at least know what a feast entailed. "Oh, roast cattle, pork, mutton, fish and fowl, if any are about for the welcoming mouthful and aftersnacks. If there's any gold or silver about, it would be considered polite to at least offer the guests a taste."

"We don't have anything like that to give our guests. Just Naf's sheep and goats, and it doesn't sound like the whole herd would feed them all. How many guests will there be, Istach?"

"Guests imply I invited them," AuRon said. "I didn't."

Natasatch sighed. "The Tyr will go where he will in the the lands of his Alliance. I just wish he hadn't decided to come so soon. We've hardly settled in."

"He said something about bringing the Aerial Host," Istach added.

"Aerial Host. More like Aerial Appetites. Dairuss isn't a rich land. If half the Lavadome descends on me, they'll eat these hills dry."

"Perhaps if you serve him a poor meal, they won't visit again," Istach said.

Natasatch glared at her.

"Perhaps Naf could be convinced to offer a bounty on scrawny old crows. I'd like to set a platter of beaks and feathers in front of my brother. The arrogance."

"Your son will be with them, I expect. We wouldn't want to shame AuSurath among his new comrades in the Host."

"It is an honor to host the Tyr," Istach said. "You should make an effort."

"Is that why you keep our daughter around?" AuRon asked. "To gang up on me like a wolf pack?"

"Very well. Istach, do you have any strength left in your wings?" Natasatch asked.

"A little mutton would help."

"After you've eaten, fly down to Ghioz and tell Imfamnia that we must entertain the Tyr. She's experienced with this sort of thing. I'd like to hear her advice."

"When did you meet Imfamnia?" AuRon asked.

"She flew by when you were out on one of your surveying-the-countryside flights with our good king. Her mate wasn't feeling well and she needed to get out. It was just a social call. She offered her advice in our role as Protector."

AuRon didn't know why that troubled him, but it did. "You could have told me."

She clacked her *griff* in reply.

"Well, if we're going to ask for advice, let's at least fly down to her rather than bring her here. I don't like her poking around Dairuss."

AuRon recognized the Ghioz Protector's resort. NiVom and Istach had settled into the old carving on the mountainside. The face had scaffolding over it and works were being carried out on an enormous scale.

"A feast?" Imfamnia said, upon their arrival the next day. "Why didn't you say so as soon as you landed?"

She shared a quick *prrum* with Natasatch, who said: "I'm still getting used to all the traditions between Protectors. Istach said something about asking permission to land, making sure I didn't alight above you . . ."

"Oh—we're equals and friends, Dearflame. Don't trouble yourself about protocol. We're neighbors. What's more, we're few dragons in a land of many men. We must learn to rely on each other."

Imfamnia guided them inside. Some of the doors and passageways had been enlarged to accommodate dragons. The floors shone brighter than they had even under the Red Queen.

"Mind your claws, please," Imfamnia said.

"I'm to host an Imperial Feast," AuRon said. "The Tyr is coming, along with some of the court and members of the Aerial Host."

Imfamnia's scale rose and resettled as she thought.

"An Imperial Feast, no less. I'm only too happy to be of service to my neighbor. I must call my mate. NiVom!" She sent a human servant scurrying with a nip, his head tucked in between his shoulders like a turtle.

"I'm worried about having enough for them to eat," Natasatch said. "Dairuss isn't crawling with cattle. From what I understand, lambing season is coming up and the herds can't be disturbed."

"When is it to be?"

"Sixteen days' time."

"Oh, food's no trouble at all, then," Imfamnia said. "We'll load a few barges with cattle, and we'll have them at the door of your King Naf's dome in three days' time, with a day to spare in case of mischance. Just don't hold it up in the mountains or anything. Somewhere easy to drive cattle from the riverbank."

"That's very kind of you," Natasatch said.

"What do you want in return?" AuRon asked.

Imfamnia waved a *sii* in the air. "Oh, call it a gift, in honor of your new rank as Protector of a key province."

"You're very kind," Natasatch said.

"Will you be serving gold coin or silver to welcome your guests?"

"Coin?" AuRon asked.

"You grays are always forgetting coin. Yes, coin puts everyone in a pleasantly satisfied mood."

"There's precious little coin in Dairuss. It's a poor province."

"Oh, I'm sure you can urge your thralls—"

"Slaves, you mean," AuRon said. "We don't keep slaves, whatever you call them."

AuRon, don't start a quarrel with someone who is trying to be kind to us, Natasatch thought to him.

"Well, if it's simply a bit of coin holding you back, I'd be happy to loan you some," Imfamnia said.

"I'm grateful for your help with the food, but I must not accept coin," AuRon said.

AuRon! Natasatch thought.

She led them into a balcony room AuRon remembered from his previous visits. The blood and flame had long since been washed away, as had the Red Queen's taste in two-color decor. The Protectors of Ghioz preferred white and gold, accented with a little blue of various shades here and there.

"What's keeping my mate? Dearflame, I must insist on supplying you with some coin. The Red Queen had centuries' worth of coin tucked away. We're always sniffing out new troves. You know the Ghioz of old buried their parents with it."

"They don't object to their ancestors being dug up?" AuRon asked.

"Ghioz? The only thing they regret is that they didn't find the grave first. Even for humans they're unusually bad."

"If there's to be an Imperial Feast I must get my scale into shape." She rapped her tail against a gong and humans began to flow in from crevices like water into a leaky boat, lugging wooden boxes full of tools.

Her scale looked perfect to AuRon, but then, dragon-elles had a better eye for that sort of thing.

"There's just one, tiny problem, AuRon. The Tyr—well, he's banned me from his court. We had rather a misunderstanding about something that wasn't my fault at all; it was my foolish first mate and his friend the Dragonblade. They somehow blame me for letting the dragonriders into the Lavadome."

"I've heard a little about it. Your first mate was Tyr SiMevolant then, I believe."

"Yes, and he was cruel and stupid. But he thought the Dragonblade was just what we needed to survive in a world of men. Have you seen his blade? I was shaking so hard my scale half-dropped out for fear. Yet Tyr RuGaard seems to believe I had something to do with those men taking over the Lavadome."

AuRon rather doubted she had been that terrified. Though she did have a reputation for running from a fight. But enough of the past. "If I'm to be hosting this feast, I'll say who's to be invited and who's not. You and your mate will be my guests. It's the least I can do for your help with the victuals. But I'll have to refuse your offer of coin. The food is generosity enough."

"I won't press you. I knew from the moment I saw you we would be firm allies. Ghioz and Dairuss. With your hardy warriors and our rich lands, we'll have nothing to fear on our borders! I can't think of what's keeping my mate, he must be ill again."

* * *

It wasn't much of a feeding pit. The early-winter rains made it look even more dismal.

He settled on Great Neck in Dairuss as the location of the celebratory feast, and decided to hold it during the afternoon so the dragons would have light to find places to sleep after.

He'd chosen the location for the feast for a number of reasons. First, he didn't want dozens of dragons flying over Dairuss's Golden Dome and unsettling Naf's people. Too many of them were refugees or children of refugees from dragon attacks during the Wizard's old race wars, and panicked, stampeding hominids would scurry about, starting fires and looting each other's homes or spirits knew what else in the chaos.

Great Neck also had the advantage of being easily spotted from the air; it was a distinctively shaped loop of the Falngese river, reminiscent of a swan's curving neck. It was close to Ghioz and had a good landing, and the ridge of the neck gave a commanding view. For ages there'd been sentries posted there to watch the river and lands eastward. It was also the old tribute dock for southern Dairuss when it was part of the Ghioz Empire, so there was ample riverfront for NiVom and Imfamnia's barges of fattened cattle. There'd always been enough commerce and activity, never mind travelers hiking up the ridge for the view that a small town offered to plenty of workers who could be hired to assist with the feast.

Better yet, the locals looked like much of Dairuss: poor, simple country folk in patched-together clothing that looked not all that different from the local sheep. Dragons who otherwise wouldn't listen when AuRon described Naf's kingdom as rustic hill country would accept the evidence laid before their eyes and noses.

He'd overlooked how dragons expect to dine formally—circled around a low feeding area like all the animals of the savannah drinking from the sole remaining waterhole. Servants would rotate with platters, always beginning with the most favored guest—who would naturally be the Tyr—and moving down the social scale. Wistala told him that once upon a time a duel could be fought over being seated last, so a good host usually placed his mate and himself at the final two positions.

They ended up laying down felled trees for the dragons to rest upon, so they wouldn't end up squatting in the mud and flying away with caked scales. Naf's lumbermen worked hard, chaining horses to the big boles and dragging the trunks into line.

Imfamnia and NiVom were kind enough to arrive early, with a few dozen thrall cooks used to prepare dragon cuisine. AuRon thought NiVom looked haggard; perhaps he had been sick of late, though he flew well enough. A big meal would do him some good.

At last the big evening arrived.

His brother did not arrive with as many dragons as AuRon had feared. Wistala arrived with the Copper, a more mismatched pair would be hard to imagine, with Wistala big and broad-winged and her brother thin and limping without scale clean and sparingly polished and hardly a *laudi* on his wings. There were only a few representatives of his court and their mates, some curious Ankelenes exhausted from flying, and a smattering of the Aerial Host, including their commander HeBellereth.

Istach helped him with the introductions. She had a remarkable memory for names and kept close to prompt him as he greeted and announced his guests.

When Imfamnia and NiVom made their appearance, coming up from their barges on the riverbank, arriving late, once the feast had been well joined, all the assembled dragons hushed.

"What is *she* doing here?" the Copper said.

"Perhaps some *oliban*," Wistala suggested.

"What is *oliban*?" Natasatch asked.

A few of the assembly tittered.

"It's a sort of sap from rare trees in the south," an Ankelene named NoFarouk said. "When burned, it is most soothing."

AuRon heard whispers. "No welcoming coin . . . no *oliban* . . ."

"Our new Protector isn't very courtly," HeBellereth said.

"If being courtly is what's required of a Protector, perhaps you should get a new one," AuRon said. "NiVom and Imfamnia are my guests. Dairuss isn't the Lavadome, and whatever she did in the past, she's been a good friend to myself and my mate now."

The Copper's one good eye looked AuRon's way. "This is my brother's Protectorate. He sets his own social conventions. He may invite who he will. I think, however, it would be best if I depart. Please, good dragons, do not consider this an insult to our host or our new allies. But I must choose my society."

The Tyr moved off to contemplate the river.

Just like my brother. Skulking off, AuRon thought to Natasatch.

We musn't make an enemy of the Tyr, she thought back. Then aloud: "I'll see to it that some food is brought to him." Natasatch quit the feeding pit and did her best to order some servants to follow with platters.

With that, HeBellereth rose, and the members of the Aerial Host followed his example.

Wistala came to her feet, said, "I shall return," and trotted off after him.

The feast had turned into a disaster.

"I'm sorry we caused such a rift in your celebratory feast," NiVom said.

Imfamnia laughed. "Well, I never. What, he thought I might attack him? Our Tyr, who has smashed our enemies aboveground and below, retreats at the sight of one ragged exile? And a female at that?"

Ragged? Natasatch thought to Auron. *She's dyewashed her scales to add contrast. Her servants have labored many hours with brushes to get that pattern.*

The rest of the dragons shifted about nervously.

"Protector AuRon," NiVom announced. "I've brought a specialty of my kitchens. In these waxed baskets—a dessert fit for the Tyr, even if he'll have none. Brains in sweet brandy!"

She extended her wings and rotated them down, a sort of a bow crossed with a flourish, to AuRon's mind, beautifully executed.

Part of him couldn't help comparing Natasatch to the former Queen of the Lavadome. Everything NiVom's mate did, she did gracefully.

Wistala settled down next to her Copper brother.

"I suppose I've let you down. Nilrasha would have smoothed all that over much better, or warned AuRon about Imfamnia in the first place. I'm not very good at these squabbles."

"Neither am I," the Copper said. "It's the way many of the dragons in the Lavadome were raised. There's nothing important for them to do, so they pick at each other. Reminds me of the baboons I saw in Bant. They're either hurling dung at each other or picking nits."

"Baboons," she laughed. "Well, AuRon's put together a good feast. You'll have a fine cold breakfast in the morning."

"I suppose I should have a conference with him. Just to see how he's getting on. I'd like to know more about that daughter of his, Istach."

"Why her?"

"Doesn't she remind—well, never mind. She seems a bright young dragonelle and it's a waste to have her just trailing after her parents like a hatchling. Did she come off badly in a fight as a drakka?"

Wistala wondered at this sudden interest. She hoped he hadn't set his heart on winning all of AuRon's offspring—three of the four were already serving the Grand Alliance. "I don't know. I believe she grew up on that island of theirs."

"There's something about this I don't like" the Copper said. "Imfamnia's not a threat. She does incidental damage with her vanity and greed, it's never intended. She just loves being the center of attention and having things her own way. In a way, she enjoys being an outcast. It gets others talking about her."

"I don't know her at all. She was gone long before I arrived at the Lavadome. She's a terrible fighter in the air, I can attest to that."

The Copper lowered his voice. "What was AuRon playing at, inviting her? The little rat tail. He's up to something, I feel it. By stepping away from his feeding pit, it makes me the loser. I should have held my tongue and just pretended she wasn't there."

AuRon's new to all these customs, too. He mentioned something about her helping them gather enough bullocks to feast the dragons. He and his mate didn't want to be embarrassed in his first official meeting with his Tyr.

Her brother looked at her with such astonishment. Wistala suddenly realized that she'd overheard his thoughts. Dragons could only read each other's minds after long acquaintance, though family members could usually pick up on much of what their shared blood was thinking.

"I'm sorry, I didn't mean to break in on your thoughts," Wistala said. She felt his mind dissipate and retreat from hers like water steaming off hot iron.

"I'll have to be more careful around you," the Copper said. "I sometimes think the only reason I survived my youth in the Lavadome was because no one knew my mind well enough to sense what I was thinking."

"Would you like to talk about AuRon? You don't fear he's plotting against you, I hope. I know him, he's an admirable dragon."

"No. If I fall, it won't be because he planned it. More likely he'll knock the arm of the bowman so the arrow misses its intended target and brings me down. He's lucky. Luck's always favored him."

"But he's no Tyr of Two Worlds," Wistala said.

"Thank you, Wistala."

AuRon, still at the feast, listened to the chatter of the females. Most were discussing Imfamnia, either her insulting presence or her elegant appearance.

"Look at her scale tips, they're almond-shaped. Aren't they lovely? Simple and classic."

"I thought scallops were in this year. In honor of the victory in Swayport."

"Scallops? Too much work and it makes you look chicken-feathered. No, a simple almond shape is the style, in my opinion. It draws the eyes up to the face and wing and tail tip."

"I'm going to speak to my thralls as soon as I get back to the Lavadome," the mate of one of the Aerial Host said. "Almond shapes from nose to tail. I don't care if I have to sit in the hygiene trench for a full light and a dark."

The last platters of meat were emptied and NiVom brought up his special dessert, brandied brains in a buttery sauce.

"That's a lot of brains," Istach said.

"Where did you get all those brains?" AuRon asked. "Cattle?"

Imfamnia tilted her head. "Cattle brains? That's thrall-feed. Those are hominid brains."

"Where did you get such a supply?" he asked.

Imfamnia scratched herself behind the ear. "Oh, criminals in Ghioz were some. There weren't quite enough, though, so some of the border soldiers raided the blighters to the east with NiVom. He terrorized them into surrender and our soldiers had their heads off in no time. What's the matter, AuRon? You look like you're going to faint. Blighters have big heads; they're always valued for their brains."

Chapter 6

T he Copper flew through the still air of the Lavadome, his Griffaran Guard to either side. It felt
odd to fly underground without air currents to fight or
take advantage of. To think, for generations there were
dragons who only flew in this still, uninteresting air.

Once you're used to the air and space above the
ocean or mountains, the whirling patterns of stars and
the slow courses and phases of the moon, the Lavadome wasn't quite as spectacular as it once seemed.

But still colorful. The Copper never tired of the streams
of hot liquid Earth running down the unbreakable crystal
skin of the Lavadome. Though the crystal mysteriously
conducted away most of the heat, enough remained that
the heart of his Dragon Empire remained comfortably
warm, at least to dragon sensibilities, and ideal for dozing.

It echoed rather more these days. There were fewer dragon roars from hill to hill as neighbors tossed challenges and invitations back and forth.

It wasn't war, disease, or famine that had emptied the Lavadome, though each had taken their toll during his reign as Tyr. Rather, it was the dragons' success in the Upper World.

The Grand Alliance meant that almost every dragon of the Lavadome could live and bask in the sun if they wished. There was plenty to do in helping their Hypatian allies manage their affairs. If nothing else, dragons made sending messages back and forth between the provinces much easier. A nation that had been fragmenting was coming back together thanks to the dragons, the way laces and buttons joined the garments humans wore over their weirdly upright frames and kept them from falling off.

But some of the changes were for the better. Imperial Rock, long the towering resort of the ruling family and highly placed dragons, was now ringed by two layers of garden. Where once there had been training fields for the Drakwatch and Firemaids, now there was a mixture of fungi and low-light ferns that could survive on the ample light, but no direct sun, that came in through the oval top of the Lavadome where crystal met air in the great volcano crater that surrounded their hidden home.

Tended by blighter gardeners and watered by numerous small pools fed by a newly built extension to the watering and sanitary flows, the greens and whites and pinks and ochres of the gardens soothed the eye in contrast to the brighter reds and oranges of the lava, or the deep blacks and blues and grays of the rocky topography. Off in the distance, near the wind tunnel that sucked air from the Lavadome, a fleck of white showed another garden, the tiny memorial he'd built to his first mate, the sickly but good-hearted Halaflora. They'd launched their public joke of a mating flight from that spot.

Sweet, gentle Halaflora. He liked to think she'd approve of the changes he'd made to the Lavadome. She'd loved growing things. He often wondered about the eggs she claimed to be growing inside her when she died.

He'd never mate again, even if the more vigorous Nilrasha died. The mate of a Tyr was half a widow in any case, for there was little chance of seeing her husband.

The Copper encouraged the remaining dragons of the Lavadome to bring their hatchlings into the garden. Rats and bats lived among the fungi, and the hatchlings had good fun exercising their senses, bodies, and wits hunting them.

Hatchlings were the key.

When the Copper had come to the Lavadome, the "dismals" (as he liked to style them) among the Ankelenes were supposing that dragons were finished in the world. They'd linger on, ever fewer and fewer, scrawny, darksick dragons fighting over scarcer and scarcer resources in the Lavadome. Tyr FeHazathant had begun to turn matters around, selectively supporting certain Upholds, sometimes in secret, sometimes openly.

The grand old Tyr had doted on hatchlings, bringing them to the gardens at the top of the Imperial Rock for viewing. He'd spent a good deal of his precious time as Tyr looking in on the hatchlings of the Drakwatch, and demanding reports from his mate Tighlia about the progression of the newest Firemaids.

Having lived more in the world aboveground, the Copper now understood his interest.

It was a numbers game, like the one he'd played as a wingless drake, with the piles of smooth, marked river stones the Drakwatch used to have to discover, steal, battle over, and carry back to their "home cave." Each hatchling represented a hope for the future of dragonkind. They could never match the breeding power of the hominids, but dragons had their size and wings and wit and fire that, judiciously used, could win friends and strike terror into the hearts of their enemies.

Dragons were also long-lived, and the wise among them could take advantage of their experience. Hominids, especially humans and blighters, tended to make the same mistakes, and be subject to the same weaknesses, generation after generation after generation.

The Copper swooped low over the gardens atop the Imperial Rock. They'd grown in magnificence, thanks to Rayg's new formula of fertilizer and some choice statues courtesy of grateful Hypatia.

Grateful Hypatia knew when it was in their best interest to give up a piece of art.

He alighted, executing a better-than-usual landing thanks to the improved artificial wing joint that had long since calloused properly, to the usual rush of thralls bringing the landing trough and a platter of delectable organ meats. The Copper had developed a bit of a sweet tooth as he aged, and found honey-mead most invigorating after a long flight.

He reminded himself to give Rayg the scrolls and tomes his valuable friend had requested and the Hypatian librarians had been convinced to provide. Strictly of a temporary basis of a few decades, of course.

"Welcome back, my Tyr," old NoSohoth said, executing one of his grave, slow bows. A cross between a majordomo of the Imperial Line and a chief of staff to the Tyr, NoSohoth was as much a fixture of the Imperial Rock as the gravity-fed watering system—and equally smooth and malleable. He survived by bending to the prevailing winds, helping whoever sat in the Tyr's chair to the best of his ability.

NoSohoth was old, but his scale was in impressive condition for an ancient dragon. He'd heard once that NoSohoth had been a mature dragon when Tyr Fe-Hazathant breathed his first fire. Even now it was difficult to distinguish him from a dragon in his prime. Bright silver scale with black at the tips, here and there turned to a sort of bluish white, gave him an appearance unlike any the Copper had ever seen; indeed, he was hard to classify as belonging to Skotl, Wyrr, or Ankelene—which is probably how he had managed to survive the civil wars of his youth. Of course, his diet probably included gold coin thrice daily with a few gems for added minerals. Only slightly clouded eyes gave him away, his vision was going and he sometimes squinted to see objects at a distance. Also, he moved evenly and carefully, perhaps to hide stiffness in his joints.

"News?" the Copper asked.

"Pillithea's eggs have hatched, over in Wyrr hill," NoSohoth said, knowing his Tyr's interest in the next generation. "She was old-fashioned about it and the males fought, but I managed to save the loser. He's in the Drakwatch caves with Mulnessa, widow to Cu-Supfer."

CuSupfer was a member of the Aerial Host killed in the fight with the Rocs over Ghioz.

"Good. She should name him after CuSupfer. I won't have any losers in hatching fights not given a proper, honorable name."

Humans may make the same mistakes generation after generation, but he'd be descaled if he repeated the errors of his parents.

"I believe she has done exactly that," NoSohoth said, with a tone that suggested that if she hadn't, she would shortly at a gently placed hint from a dragon at the Tyr's ear as wealthy as NoSohoth.

"See that both Pillithea and Mulnessa have plenty of Imperial thralls to attend them, under the usual conditions that once the hatchlings breathe their first fire the thralls will be their property to keep or sell as they choose, with the usual messages of gratitude from myself and Nilrasha."

"Done and done. My Tyr does enjoy checking up on me."

"You look as though there's bad news behind the good," the Copper said.

"I'm afraid so, my Tyr. There's problems with the *oliban* trade. Perhaps it's not so critical, now with the Lavadome less crowded, but so many of the trees have been harvested now, the ones left are small and at great height."

Oliban was a sort of sap from rare trees that looked like citrine quartz when properly dried. Burned in the plentiful braziers used for light and warmth deep in the dragon caves, it produced a pleasing, soothing aroma that relaxed dragons. It was traditionally burned whenever dragons met in groups to keep tempers from flaring.

"We must see about replanting it elsewhere, in suitable soil," the Copper said. It never ceased to amaze, the matters that came under his nose. One day the proper burning of a dead egg, the next horticulture. He'd made a study of *oliban*, just as he had *kern* and other products necessary to draconic health and comfort. "The Ankelenes can do a survey of places where it might grow. There's less need for *kern* now, perhaps in Anaea."

His old uphold had rich volcanic soil. Or did *oliban* need sea air to thrive? Something about salt, he'd have to ask the Ankelenes.

"Yes, my Tyr."

"We should have attended to this before," the Copper muttered.

"Hard to think about a few loose tail-scale when there are swords about your throat," NoSohoth said.

"What else do you have for me. Briefly, please, for I am tired."

"Nothing that can't wait until you've rested from your flight and enjoyed a few meals. There's some rather good blind bonefish in the larder."

"I'll spend a few hours in the Audience Chamber. I can try to keep myself awake. I don't want my dragons to think themselves unattended. I'll be on the shelf in one hour; see there's some coin to pass around."

"Just some poor Hypatian amalgams. Next to worthless."

"Well, there'll be some gold from the sack at Sway-port shortly."

"I'm glad to hear it," NoSohoth said. "I rather think the Imperial Treasury spends more on the Empire than it gets in return. If it weren't for NiVom squeezing what he can out of the Ghioz, we'd be destitute."

"We? You mean me, you old hoardbug," the Copper said.

"My Tyr, have I ever denied you grateful coin?"

"No. I'll think about finances later. I'm for a splash, then you can admit the petitioners into the audience hall."

He shook off the thralls busy polishing his claws and oiling his artificial wing joint and descended to his baths. The heat and steam would work faster than any thrall.

The fleshy human female thrall in attendance gave the air a juicy aroma that made him relish his bath. She spread frothy bubbling fats on his scale and scrubbed them off again with a bristle brush. One of his predecessors, SiDrakkon, had made a fetish of the place, filling it so the musky feminine reek made one's head swim, but that was entirely too much of a good thing. One had to come out of the bath sooner or later.

Feeling delightfully clean, he hissed for his monitor-bats.

Aged Ging and her son Fang came in, trailed by a tired-looking Gang. Ghoul had disappeared some years ago in the Star Cave, but then he'd always been the slowest of the three.

"A sup, a sup, my Tyr?" they chorused, like eager, whining puppies.

They whined for blood, of course, and he relented and let them open a vein in his *sii* where he could keep an eye on how much they slurped down. They were the descendants of bats that had been dining on his blood for generations, and they'd grown into monstrous versions of the original clan; they were the size of largish dogs these days, and toothy young Fang displayed a pebbly skin that might be mistaken for his brother's dragon-hide. Fang had cunning eyes and sharp ears, and a nose for sniffing secrets, and a devious mind. The Copper trusted only Fang's weakness and lust for dragon-blood.

The Copper resolved not to feed Fang's offspring dragon-blood. These bats had grown quite freakish enough, thank you.

He'd learned to question them after a feeding rather than before. So eager for blood were they, they'd tell him anything if they thought it would please him into letting them nick open his skin. The Copper would rather hear what he needed to hear than what the bats thought he wanted to hear.

"Any news?" he asked, as the bats burped out their satisfaction with the bloody suckle.

"NiVom and Imfamnia are breeding blighters," Ging, the best-spoken of them said. She had a network of other bats who, the Copper suspected, suckled off her own substantial frame. "They mean to launch a war 'gainst Old Uldam, use blighters against other blighters, it seems."

"Any news passing in the Lavadome?" The Copper liked to think of his conversations with the bats as catching up on news he wouldn't otherwise hear, rather than spying. Spying on the dragons one purported to lead struck him as distasteful.

"The Ankelenes talked a lot against the attack on those pirates."

"Old Ibidio called it bleeding dragons for the humans," Fang said. "Wasting good blood on humans, now. What have they ever done for us but cause trouble? Useless-like."

"He means 'dragons doing the bleeding humans wouldn't do,' " Ging clarified. "Those were her exact words."

The Copper would have to live with Ibidio's second-guessing and disparagement. She had laid the eggs of FeHazathant's second-generation descendants and was of the oldest and most distinguished part of the Imperial Line. "Well, Ibidio's always talking against me to the Ankelenes. As long as it's just talk, I don't mind. Is she planning anything?"

"Naw," Fang said, and the others also shook their heads, hominid style. "That LaDibar, he's the one you have to watch out for. Shifty-like."

"Still visiting the thrall pens and the demen quarter, I hope?"

"Aye, Tyr, nothing brewing there but soup bones. As long as the feed's good, they're happy."

"Aye, jes' like us'n," old Gang said, licking remaining fangs clean of the last bits of blood.

The Copper met with his court the next day, making it clear to them that it was a strictly informal gathering. He ordered a plain meal rather than an imperial feast. They had platters brought into the Audience Chamber, now filled with dozens of newly captured battle banners of Ghioz and collections of skulls and stained hides from the Ironriders.

NoFhyriticus the Gray, a mainstay for sensible advice, was much missed in his new role as Protector of Hypatia. He was an even-tempered dragon, both slow to anger and slow to trust. He was doing well among the humans of the Directory, but the Copper found himself absentmindedly waiting for him to speak at times, so used to NoFhyriticus's counsel was he.

Of course he had HeBellereth, as the Aerial Host was much in need of rest and refitting after the expedition against the pirates of Swayport.

LaDibar was still a fixture. The Copper had tried

making him an upholder, but he pleaded illness that prevented him from making "a proper exertion in duty, as a Protector should." He had a vast storehouse of knowledge in that brain of his, however, so he was still useful to the court.

LaDibar still displayed the revolting habit of exploring his ears, nostrils, and gum line with his tailtip when deep in thought.

CoTathanagar had been reluctantly brought into his inner circle. While the Copper found him distasteful, pigheaded, and ambitious, he knew the ins and outs of Sreeksrack's thrall trade, knew Ankelene politics, knew the hominids, knew which Skotl was forbidden to mate with a Wyrr, yet seemed to get along well with all the clans. Besides, the Copper found it useful to have someone around who, no matter what the job, could supply a name to handle it. And for the most part, those CoTathanagar put forward performed decently enough in their various responsibilities.

And then there were the Twins. SiHazathant the Red and Regalia. But the Imperial Line and the rest of the Lavadome usually just called them the Twins. Others didn't seem to mind their familiarity, but they gave the Copper the shivers. Brother and sister, looking much alike, always at each other's side, eating and sleeping together. Of course, they'd shared the same egg, so by looking at it one way they were the same dragon, but still—an eerie, otherworldly air hung about them.

They were well-liked by the Ankelenes, too. Always

experimenting on their thralls in matters of feeding and breeding and exercise. He'd told them to quit giving thralls dragon-blood; a victory toast among allies or a bribe to bats was one thing, but intentionally breeding a hybrid of something as dangerous as a human—he forbade it.

But they were sensible dragons, fond of feasting, and popular, especially with Ibidio's little faction. She thought them a blend of AgGriffopse and FeHazathant.

Finally, there was Naf. When the Copper first introduced Naf to speak to his court, it had caused some consternation—a thrall addressing dragons as equals!—but they indulged their Tyr, who could be forgiven a blind spot and a soft heart now and then.

He wanted to discuss the matter of the *oliban* shortage.

"Drive the gatherers harder," CoTathanagar advised. "A stout whip hand will get it flowing again."

"Za! From what, twigs and bare stone?" LaDibar asked. "It's whipping and greed that got us into this situation to begin with."

"There'll be fighting here, if we're not careful in rationing it," HeBellereth said, stating the obvious.

"Steaming it rather than burning it makes it last longer. But steaming only works in a small cavern," LaDibar said. "Or if you stand right over the vat."

"It must grow naturally somewhere else."

"The Princedoms of the Sunstruck Sea are said to have it," LaDibar said, examining the contents of a nostril on tailtip. "There are unexplored islands farther south as well, but the weather is so wild at the equinoxes, colonies or a regular trade would be difficult to maintain."

"More difficult than us being at each other's throats light and dark?" NoSohoth asked. Friends of his managed the *oliban* trade and the Copper suspected—no, make that knew—he profited from the Imperial concession.

"We have news of the recent battles at Swayport," HeBellereth said. "Remember that dragon who attacked you over the pirate ship? Four of the Aerial Host tracked him to his refuge. He's outside now, in chains. The new flier, your brother's son, was one of the party that captured him."

What did they expect him to do, order him executed for serving humans in a war?

"Bring him to me."

The black dragon seemed to fill the Audience Chamber.

"You're not about to start a fight in here, are you?" the Copper asked.

"No. Whatever they told you, I came with your dragons and their riders willingly. I wished to meet you without fighting."

"We shall see about that," the Copper said. "Get those chains off him."

Thralls brought pry bars and cutters. A few snips and clatters later, he was free. As free as he could be, surrounded by strange dragons and beneath the waiting talons of the Griffaran Guard.

"What is your name?" the Copper asked.

"Shadowcatch."

"'Shadowcatch, my Tyr,'" NoSohoth prompted.

"My Tyr," the prisoner finished.

"Why were you seeking us?" the Copper asked.

"After our fight in Swayport I asked some questions of some sea-elves I know—don't tell me to reveal their location, I'll keep the secrets of one who's been kind to me or I'll bleed out."

"Sea-elves? I thought Wrimere killed them all," LaDibar said.

"Never mind the sea-elves," the Copper said.

"I've been among few enough of my kind," Shadowcatch said. "Thought I'd join you. Seems like a good bunch of fighting dragons. I'm used to living with my own kind. Having females about, too."

"You thought you'd find us hospitable after you tried to kill our Tyr?" HeBellereth asked.

"That was just war, and I was hired to fight. Nothing personal, my Tyr."

"Of course," the Copper said.

"I say we bleed him out and let the Aerial Host drink to your health, my Tyr. He's an assassin if I ever smelled one."

Shadowcatch's scale bristled but he said nothing.

"You'd like to join us, Shadowcatch? What are your qualifications?"

"I can fight," he said. "I've lived in the Upper World on my own since the Wizard got himself roasted by that NooSho—I mean AuRon. The Gray."

"Ah, yes, the Gray. Many paths lead back to him," the Copper said. Any friend of the Gray might be an enemy to him. Though now he had the advantage of his brother; three of his four hatchlings were serving the Lavadome in one manner or another.

"You like good food, I see," the Copper said.

"The folks who hired me fed me well even if they couldn't always pay."

"An easy life?" the Copper asked.

"You'd be surprised what having a dragon hanging around keeps away. Yeah, I call it an easy life."

"One thing about you impressed me. The other dragons they'd hired. They flew away as soon as they saw the strength arrayed against them."

Shadowcatch ground his teeth, creating a low clatter like woodpeckers all working the same tree. "Trash, those. Half-wit vagabonds from the Wizard's Isle."

"AuRon's Isle, you mean."

"Some call it that."

"When we attacked, they flew away, but you stayed. Outnumbered forty to one or more, if you count the hominids, you stayed."

"Yes," Shadowcatch said.

"Why?"

"They paid me. I gave my word to them. I'd keep it."

"Your word's that important to you, that you'd die for it?" LaDibar asked, as if he was having trouble with the concept.

"Certainty nothing. I have a way of surviving."

There was more to this black dragon than met the

eye. He might be a little fat, and stupid-looking as the thickest Skotl, but there were depths to him, the Copper decided.

"Ever since then I've been thinking I need a bodyguard," the Copper said. "Someone a little more intimidating than *griffaran*. Hominids don't fear anything with feathers as they ought."

"But—my Tyr," NoSohoth protested. "He's an outsider. He tried to kill you."

"As he says, that was just business. And as for being an outsider, it's the same one that led to me being acceptable to Skotl, Wyrr, and Ankelene as Tyr: no clan can trust that he won't move against one of his own. If you took my coin and my food, you wouldn't try to kill me, would you, Shadowcatch?"

"Of course not, my Tyr. Oathbreakers, well, may their bones get ground into wizard dust, that's all I have to say."

"You must tell me more of the Upper World. There's so much to know."

"As long as it's not where the sea elves are hiding, or one or two other oaths I have to keep," Shadowcatch said.

"Very well. Honorable Dragons of the Empire, meet my new bodyguard, Shadowcatch the Black."

The Copper read their expressions like a short scroll. Yes, Shadowcatch was already proving his worth. It was good to have the biggest dragon in the room at one's back.

BOOK TWO

Hopes

"IF YOU LIVE TO SEE ALL YOUR PLANS FULFILLED,
YOU SOLD YOUR YEARS TOO CHEAP."

—*Partnership Articles of the Chartered Company*
(Notes & Additions)

Chapter 7

There had been many changes since AuRon last flew over the city of the Ghioz and the Red Queen's former mountainside palace.

The old monument which had worn three different faces at one time or another, he'd been told, was now being reshaped under a bright new bronze mask. Workers had scaffolding up, creating a metallic snout over a steel frame projecting out of the mountainside. The stone that had once depicted hair had been smoothed and shaped into a dragon-crest.

AuRon found himself staring into the likeness of his Copper brother, multiplied in size many times.

Fluttering red flags showed him his landing spot. He suspected there was ample red and black material for such symbols, left over from the Red Queen's preferred wardrobe and curtaining. He wondered why he found the colors so unsettling. The Red Queen's power had long passed from this age, hadn't it?

As he and Natasatch alighted in a whirlwind of dust from the construction, carrying some of Dairuss's finest sewn-together sheep's hides—they made comfortable and long-lasting rugs—trumpets blared a noisy welcome from the battlements designed to look like decor.

Imfamnia and NiVom stepped out into the sun to welcome them. Ghioz soldiers in their red scabbards and loinskirts marched and countermarched, banners were unfurled, and musicians banged and sawed and blew about their instruments as if they were trying to bring the mountainside down with their noise.

Thralls hurried forward to throw flowers on the visitors. The petals caught in Natasatch's scale but slid off of AuRon, save for one long white bloom that stuck between the growing horns of his crest.

NiVom and AuRon bowed to each other, Imfamnia and Natasatch rubbed their folded *griff*.

"Welcome, fellow Protector," NiVom said. AuRon thought him an intelligent dragon, especially in comparison to his garrulous, flashy mate.

"Oh, Natasatch, how lovely you look. I wish I had your digits, they're so long and graceful. Mine are stunted, awful things, and even if I grow out my claws they still don't look well."

Natasatch gave off a brief *prrum* at the compliment. "Well, I wish my scale shone like yours."

"Get your thralls to properly polish it. Chalk soda

and lemon juice, that's the thing. And if they put a little oil on it afterward, it keeps the tarnish down, dear."

Ear to ear in conversation, the dragonelles proceeded underground. AuRon and NiVom trailed behind in companionable silence.

They sat, according to Lavadome decorum, around a tiny feeding pit with Imfamnia across from AuRon and Natasatch facing NiVom.

The food, rather than being brought up from an underchamber, had to be brought in from another room by a thrall.

AuRon took a quick glance at the Ghioz. He hadn't seen many up close, at least without the din and confusion all about. They were smaller and darker than the men of the north, but had wiry frames that held a good deal of strength, considering the weight of the platters brought in for the guests. Some of the thralls were bearing entire calves and small pigs, roasted with different kinds of gravies.

He had no complaints about the food. AuRon hadn't dined so well—ever. He even sampled the wine, but hardly understood half the words NiVom and Imfamnia used in the description of its origin and reputation. It sounded as though they were describing the quality of a warrior:

"This one's rather new and still a bit stiff; it could have been better treated by the barrel, but you'll find it has strong legs, with the apple blossom carrying the smokey cheese behind . . ." and other such rubbish.

"What does wine care how its barrel treats it?" Au-Ron asked, and NiVom and Imfamnia exchanged looks.

"We're used to eating rough and drinking glacier runoff," Natasatch explained.

"Oh, I do love you outdoorsy kinds of dragons," Imfamnia said, touching Natasatch's tail with her own. "Such stories! Tell us of the north. You must get a great deal of fresh air and sunshine; I can tell by your eyes and scale that you've never had to substitute *kern* for being aboveground."

"They used to give us different kinds of oils in the cave, with herbs suspended in them . . ." Natasatch gave a brief version of her captivity on the egg shelf.

"But where did you come from, originally?" Imfamnia asked her. "You look so familiar!"

"I'm not really sure—I was taken captive very young. I think I remember being underground, but it might have been images from my parents' minds."

Imfamnia went on describing Natasatch's perfections of limb and scale: "Quite youthful-looking; you'd never know you'd mated, let alone sat atop four eggs."

"It was five, we lost one," Natasatch said.

"Five! Oh, if good old Tyr FeHazathant could have seen that. He'd have stuffed you and your hatchlings with cattle."

"We managed," AuRon said. "There's good fishing in the north. The waters around my island are thick with cod."

"Riches indeed," Imfamnia said.

"I understand RuGaard is keeping up the tradition of giving gifts to those lucky enough to sit atop eggs," NiVom said.

Imfamnia cocked her head. "Your brother is an odd sort of fellow. He's no FeHazathant, and not nearly as impressive-looking as SiDrakkon or SiMevolant were as Tyr. He's so clunky and offbeat, it's rather disarming. He's more than he appears."

"You were the champion in the hatching struggle?"

"Yes," AuRon said, which was more or less the truth. He had had some help from the Copper and the egg-horn.

"You still have your egg-horn, I notice," Imfamnia said, as though reading his thoughts. "Is that a family tradition, or . . ."

"It did me great service in getting out of my egg, so I left it in. The skin's almost overgrown it."

"Yes, at first I thought it was a stuck arrowhead," NiVom said.

"There are the wildest rumors going around the Lavadome about your brother," Imfamnia said. "We've been away for years, so perhaps we heard incorrectly, but there is a rumor that he betrayed and murdered his own family."

"None of us treated him much like family," AuRon said. "Except perhaps for one, but she died as a hatchling."

"Poor little blighter, he must have had it hard," Imfamnia said.

"Whatever's in the past, he's a decent enough

dragon now," AuRon said. "Going by what little I've seen of him."

"Yes, his story is altogether remarkable," Imfamnia said. "It's like an elf made it up for a song. To rise from lower than dust and become Tyr."

"If he has truly reformed," NiVom said.

"What's that?" AuRon asked.

Imfamnia tossed her snout to make light of the issue. "Oh, you can never be certain with rumors. Of course no one can say for sure, except perhaps his mate—but his first mate, my sister, a sickly little thing, she died under conditions that were . . . unique.

"My sister never ate but tiny little bird pecks," Imfamnia continued, tearing off a great haunch and swallowing it as though showing a contrast. AuRon watched it pass down, like an accelerated quick trip by a groundhog through a snake. "She had no appetite her whole life. But then she dies, all alone at dinner, supposedly choked to death on a mouthful of meat. Something's not right about that.

"And then he mates an old comrade from the Firemaids—after she's taken her oath, mind—while the poor thing's still moist in her grave."

Perhaps he hadn't reformed so much after all, AuRon thought.

AuRon wondered at NiVom's quiet, tired manner. He looked bloodless, like a dragon back from a winter thin on meals and heavy on fighting, but bore no scars. Perhaps the feasting at Ghioz wasn't as good as his mate claimed.

Their hosts gave them a comfortable old storage cave in the mountain. The heavy doors made AuRon think it had once held valuables; it still smelled faintly of gold and there were some silver utensils that Imfamnia told them to swallow if they chose.

"So much good metal to eat in the Grand Alliance," Natasatch said. "I don't miss the ore from the island one bit. It would just sit in your gold gizzard, taking forever to digest."

"You think we've made a change for the better?" AuRon asked.

"Time will tell. I think the offspring have."

"I'm going for a walk," AuRon said. "Enjoy the silver."

He followed his nose and ears, watched the noisy construction of the dragon-face. His brother had faults, but he didn't believe one to be vanity. He wondered if the image was meant to flatter his brother and disperse suspicions about Imfamnia's and NiVom's loyalty.

Frantic hammering and calls in the Ghioz dialect still echoed from behind the canvas on the brass dragon snout and lanterns cast shadowplay of swinging limbs and distorted bodies bent over work surfaces. NiVom and Imfamnia had their labor gangs working through the night, it seemed. He saw one group of workers, obviously off duty, huddled in the shelter of the scaffolding like pigs in a sty. Speaking of which, the underbrush was thick with dumped buckets of hominid waste and discarded food. He heard rats and other vermin.

There were other camps here and there, with cooking fires and bakeries going even at this late hour. So many workers! They had enough men here to form a small city of them—he wondered how NiVom and Imfamnia were able to afford such a monument to vanity.

His hosts should take more care with their charges; there'd be disease if they weren't careful. He observed red welts on the backs and arms of some of the workers as they lay on their stomachs, the injuries dabbed with some kind of chalky paste.

Whip-rash.

Poor dumb brutes, treated like horses and mules who couldn't be reasoned into performing their duties. Men could reason, after a fashion, though the ability varied from individual to individual. Too much intelligence made them mad, like Wrimere. Naf, perhaps not as bright as Wrimere, was a far more sensible reasoner. Maybe men needed the relief of frequent laughter to purge their brains the way indigestibles purged the bowels. Naf, always ready to bray in that mulish fashion of his or cackle like a sitting bird, had his mind right.

Some of the workers twitched in their sleep as he passed, startled awake and avoided his eye, as though guilty for being at rest. He smelled quick fear in their sweat.

He wanted out of the tumult and reek. It was a fine night, Ghioz apparently had milder winters than the Bissonian Scarpes he'd lived in to the east. Perhaps he could find a spot on the ridge behind the works to watch the stars and think.

He found his way up to the ridge, making use of a dusty road that must lead to a source of lumber or a quarry or smelter or some other camp supporting the alterations to the mountainside, for it was recently and heavily rutted.

As he stepped out upon it he saw a shadow shift on an overhanging tree ahead. The tree, a lopsided hardwood, had been trimmed back to keep the road clear, but a few branches at the top still overhung the road. Near the top, a mass that he took to be an eagle's nest reached out a limb and moved through the canopy to a thicker mass of branches.

AuRon couldn't identify the creature, with a reach like a vulture's wing and smaller back legs, a paunchy body, and a neckless head like an overturned bucket. As it moved it looked at him, two red eyes glowed briefly from the foliage. Then it jumped, breaking through twigs with a crackling sound, and flapped off on leathery wings.

Cautiously, he climbed the tree it had rested on and extended his head to its perch. Claw marks. He tested the air with his tongue, a sharp smell like the worst mammalian urine, that of a cat, perhaps, lingered in the air about its perch.

He suppressed a shudder. Whatever it was, it was the eeriest-looking creature he'd ever seen. He'd have to ask Naf; he'd spent more time in this part of the world.

But the road ran up toward clean sky. Wanting clean air and quiet to think, he followed it.

AuRon smelled blighter on the wind, and investigated, following the scents. He left the road and wandered downhill, crossed a stream and lost the scent, and only picked up on a new ridgeline where the wind had free play. Now he could hear the sound of hammer on metal.

He sensed a dragon above. Imfamnia passed overhead, and loosed a friendly call. She executed a queer landing, dropping her wings, rolling over, and crashing into the branches. Startled birds and mammals fled the collapsing canopy.

She rolled over to land on her feet as she dropped beside them.

"Out for a moonlit stroll?"

"I've seen blighter children jump into a pile of leaves or cornstalks much the same way," AuRon said.

"There wasn't a clearing nearby," she said. "I wanted to warn you away from this gully. It leads to the camp of some of our forces. The Protector's bodyguard, to be exact. It would be tragic if there were a misunderstanding."

"I smell blighters."

"You're aware of the principle of always using foreign soldiery as your bodyguards? They're less likely to betray you."

AuRon had, but wasn't used to hearing Imfamnia speak of matters other than scale care or grooming.

"You spend a lot of time worrying about being betrayed?" he asked.

"When you grow up in the Lavadome, it becomes a

habit." She reached behind with her elegantly shaped claws and began to clean twigs and bits of canopy detritus from her scale.

"Do you know much about the wildlife around here, Imfamnia?"

"I know the rats in our resort come in three colors, all ugly, and the birds make far too much noise before it's decently light out. I'm no Ankelene."

"I saw a big—it must have been a mammal. But winged, and not feathered, with claws—"

"Oh, that's one of NiVom's snaggletoothed bats. He's hard at work breeding them into gargoyles. He found the method in one of those dusty old books we took from the blighters in Old Uldam before that DharSii could get his greedy *sii* into it."

"How does one breed gargoyles out of bats?"

"I'm not sure, something to do with dragonblood and certain choice organs. CuRemom knows more about it than even NiVom, perhaps you should ask him."

"Is that wise?"

"They're loyal as dogs, always in hope of the next drop of blood, but you can't really trust them without evidence. They'll lie like a rug to get the next feeding. Your brother almost got there before us, feeding some bloodsucking cave-bats, but he just lucked into it and didn't breed for effect."

"Why?" AuRon asked.

"For the same reason your brother does, to have spies. Clever of him, using vermin that way. You can never have too many eyes looking out for you, but I hope he stops at four with these gargoyles."

The more he learned of the Lavadome and its ways, the less he liked it.

"I hope my brother's Grand Alliance doesn't turn into a vast version of the Lavadome. Sounds as though it could end badly."

"You're a droopy drake, to be thinking of endings with a new world just begun."

"It's my nature, I suppose. When the sun is shining I wonder how long until the next rain."

Imfamnia gave up on her scale, muttered something about leaving it for the thralls, and went snout-to-snout with him. "What kind of ending do you want, AuRon?"

Growing up in the Lavadome must also give one different ideas about personal space. AuRon lifted his head away. "For me?"

"Yes, and for dragons in general."

"I'd like to avoid an ending. That's why I believe that the farther we stay away from humans, the better. I don't like binding our fate to theirs."

"You think humans are the real threat?"

"My father did, and nothing I've experienced has caused me to change my opinion. The deadliest non-dragon I ever met was a human. He killed many of our kind."

"Are you speaking of the Dragonblade?" Imfamnia asked.

"Yes."

"He was just one man. Any one man only has a brief period of health and vigor, hardly longer than a butterfly's beautiful season in the air. Men rarely see things through; they make some fine starts but it all goes to pieces in a few generations."

"You're an odd one, Imfamnia. You can prattle on for hours about dipping one's claw-tips in liquid silver, then shift to questions of existence."

Imfamnia looked over his leathery skin, from behind the crest to tailtip. "Mate with me, AuRon."

"*What?*"

"Oh, fly with me, then, if you must use poetic language. Take me up."

"Imfamnia!"

"You find me attractive. I can tell. Your neck-hearts go pink. Usually you have to look at a dragon at just the right angle to tell, but your skin makes things so much easier."

"I've no wish to be with anyone but my mate."

"Your neck says differently. You're not a badly formed dragon. You lost your tail at some point, I can tell, and it's come back—though there's still that distinctive notch. I bet that just makes you faster in the air. You could catch me in no time."

"Let NiVom do the catching. He's your mate."

"Being mated to NiVom was strategy. He's obsessed with his plots and plans and tests and breeds. I'm asking you for a little excitement. It's been forever since I've been around interesting dragons. Just your bucolic Upper World accent makes me go all goosey. I can hear the whisper of pines and howling of wolves in it. Those dull warriors of the host, suspicious Wyrr messenger dragons, soft Ankelenes—you've really lived and achieved, I should very much like to hear your song. You back-to-nature dragons are keen on that whole lifesong tradition, I believe."

"What do you know about my song?"

"Natasatch gave me a few details. Now, don't look like a decapitated horse, she's very proud of you, even if she thinks your reclusiveness is a bit stifling. I don't blame her for being fond of you. I see what she means now, with a moon like that above and your snakelike suppleness. I'll wager that you're delightfully flexible, and I hate some big male's scale catching under mine and pulling as we fall."

"I'd never dishonor myself or Natasatch in that way."

She extended her wings and fluttered them. "Honor takes all the fun out of life. Come, we're lords of the earth, and leaders among dragons. Don't let silly old notions tie you down until you've died without ever having lived, like livestock waiting for the culling. Life is short."

"Dallying with mated dragons is a sure way to shorten it even further. *A hot lust for*—"

"You're still talking to me, I notice."

AuRon climbed up one of the trees she'd broken in landing. "Good night, Imfamnia."

He returned to their guest-cave. Natasatch was sleeping lightly and opened her eye at his return. "So, what do you think of our neighboring Protectors?"

AuRon swished his tail in indecision. If he told her about Imfamnia, there might be trouble, there'd definitely be some pain and doubt, and there was a slim chance she'd demand a duel of some sort. "They're free with their food and coin and . . . feelings."

"This is a fine resort they have. I suppose Ghioz is a rich Protectorate. Naf could never afford to build us something like this. I don't think it's such a bad thing to be free with your feelings and quick to make friends."

The wind veered, blowing cold right into their cavern and AuRon dragged a twin set of curtains closed over their entrance. He spat into a fire pit in the center of the room. It warmed within almost immediately, and the smell of dragon-flame stimulated him. "Not if it's genuine. This is all playacting. They might have been elves acting out a mime-battle."

"Oh, AuRon. Ever the crab, worried about the next turn of the tide. Don't be foolish in refusing riches. Let go and enjoy yourself a little."

AuRon almost let out an embarrased Naf-ish mule's bray at *that*.

"I'll keep a foolish constancy," AuRon said.

"Not the words I'd choose. Our Tyr has built a wonderful thing. Dragons can help humans and humans can help dragons. You and Naf will be long remembered as great among your people. Our offspring will see peaceful days."

"Men rarely remember anything once the generation who saw it dies off. They've already half-forgotten

Tindairuss and NooMoahk. Their deeds might as well be fairy tales, and they had a much more impressive alliance that freed a world. All too soon they were right back to fearing and hating us—not without cause, I suppose. One bad dragon can make thousands of men miserable. I wonder if we'll ever work it out."

"Quit wondering and start working to make it happen. Tyr RuGaard could use us. Imfamnia said she'd teach me all about being a Protector. By learning caution from you and charm from her, I'll be formidable one day, I daresay."

"Ever the practical dragon-dame. I don't doubt it, once you get your teeth into a scheme you don't let go. You're the best part of me."

They had a farewell meal the next morning, mostly broths made of animal fats with cold joint jelly so they wouldn't be weighted down with heavy digestion in the air.

There was no honor guard, and the musicians were probably still recovering from the strenuous efforts of their arrival.

"I wish we could convince you to stay another few days," Imfamnia said. "The moon is so lovely this time of year as the air cools and dries. Sometimes it turns quite blue, and I understand that's an omen of change for the better. You should remain with us to enjoy it."

"My lord insists that we return to Dairuss," Natasatch said.

"Pity," Imfamnia said, looking at AuRon, who was already extending and relaxing his wings.

"I believe matters on the northeastern frontier of the Empire are in good standing," NiVom said. He looked exhausted. Was he giving blood to his gargoyles?

"Don't you mean the Grand Alliance?" AuRon asked.

"I like to call things by their real name," NiVom said. "Make no mistake, this is a new Dragon Empire. I hope our long years in the Lavadome have toughened us to run it properly."

AuRon thought his scale looked a little dull. He probably wasn't eating right, chasing around bats and thrashing his slaves.

"What would you do to improve on the present arrangement?" Natasatch asked.

"Stronger lines of authority with the humans. Those who properly submit to our will do well, others will be destroyed. Your brother thinks that they'll act in their own interest, and in the interest of the alliance. Rationality and analysis from hominids? Maybe among educated dwarfs, but from these men of Hypatia? Lazy scut. His belief that humans can act rationally where dragons are concerned could prove our doom."

NiVom paused, as if judging whether his words would bring argument. He sent the thralls away with a slap of his tail against the surface of the courtyard.

One of the workmen far above dropped a hammer in fright at the sound.

"RuGaard chose badly in his selection of allies. Certainly, we should select one nation of hominids and promote their interests, so that in return they'd be hated by the others and be forced to seek the protection of dragons or lose all, but Hypatians! They're blood has bled out and run cold centuries ago. Dragons need vigorous conquerors at their side, not dissipated philosophers. He should have built around Ghioz."

"Vigorous conquerors might be more likely to revolt, don't you think?" Natasatch asked.

"The Alliance seems to be functioning well enough," AuRon said.

"Must we spoil a delightful visit with politics?" Imfamnia asked. "Our guests don't need to leave with their ears ringing. This is a farewell and goodwind toast, not an Ankelene conferral."

NiVom ignored his mate. "To tell you the truth, AuRon, it's Ghioz that's mostly holding it up. Hypatia will take many years to rebuild after centuries of neglect. Tyr RuGaard is a little too impressed, I think, with old monuments and columns to achievements far out of living memory. Our Empire should support us, not the reverse."

"Doesn't it? Naf feeds us well, even if it's just mutton." AuRon said. "Ghioz is famous for its cattle and horses; you should eat more of them. Especially the liver."

"I wanted to warn you, AuRon, war may be coming with the blighters of Old Uldam. No raid this time, but actual conquest. We may need your assistance."

"Why will the Alliance do that?"

"I've an interest in that city. The sun-shard lived there for many years."

"Lived?" AuRon asked. "It's a rock that glows."

"What do you know about the old statue?"

"It gave off enough light to read by," AuRon said.

"You never felt any strange effects? Lapses of time, missing gaps where you found you'd done something and forgotten it?"

"No. NooMoahk used to sleep curled around it. He'd become addled, and challenge anyone in the chamber, thinking they were trying to harm him."

"Or it. Perhaps it was protecting itself."

"A piece of quartz was trying to preserve itself?"

"It's no ordinary piece of quartz, or glass. It may be alive, though not as we know it. Many have died to gain or protect it."

"Again with the sun-shard," Imfamnia said. "It's safe in the Lavadome, though I'd rather use it to impress the blighters. What do we care?"

"What is it for, then?" AuRon asked.

"It has something to do with the Wizard Anklemere, and the Lavadome, we believe," NiVom said.

"Anklemere. I've heard of him again and again. If he was so powerful, I wonder how he was ever beaten," Natasatch said.

"Like many would-be world conquerers, he was so focused on the horizons, he tripped over his own feet," AuRon said. "That's how King Naf tells it, anyway."

"Tell us one thing," NiVom said. "Your sister, Wistala, if it came between her brother and peace in the Lavadome, which would she choose?"

"Wistala and I have been long apart. She clings to her

own ideals about dragons and hominids working together as equals. I know she believes in the Grand Alliance, and is doing her best to further it, but a
Queen-Consort or whatever they're calling her has many
duties. I haven't spoken to her since I became Protector."

"Perhaps you could sound her out on the matter for
us. No need to mention our names, though," NiVom
said.

Imfamnia glared at her mate, and AuRon was sure
he heard *griff* being tightened to keep from rattling.

"She'll certainly oppose Tyr RuGaard if she believes
he's not playing fair by the hominids she cares for,"
AuRon said.

"The Tyr's reign won't last forever. I hope your sister is sensible about it, when the end does come."

"I won't regret it," AuRon said.

Imfamnia relaxed a little. "Please, enough idle chatter
about our good Tyr. There are all these rumors passing
around about him giving up his position to be with his
mate and selecting a successor. That sort of rumor gets
tongues wagging. Remember, AuRon, and remember
for him, Natasatch, this was just idle talk between neighbors. You, NiVom, were up too late working again. I
suggest you rest your mouth and your body."

As if some understanding had passed between
them, Imfamnia called out thralls who tied bags of
farewell presents around their necks. She opened the
bags to highlight a few. Some were delicacies in pots,
others trinkets of copper and brass, for wearing or for
eating.

"I very much enjoyed this visit," Natasatch said. "You know you are free to come and spend a few days with us anytime."

"Didn't I say we would be great friends?" Imfamnia asked. "Perhaps we will come. I want to know what you eat to keep your claws so strong. Mine get worn down just handling fabric, I oath."

The four dragons exchanged bows and the Protectors of Dairuss took wing. The thralls let out a loud cheer as they rose into the air. AuRon guessed they'd been ordered to, under pain of punishment.

They flew home over the course of a day's journey of easy, brief flights, laden as they were by presents and trinkets. They opened one of the pots on a mountainside and enjoyed honey-roasted organ meats stuffed with smoked fish.

They passed the trinkets back and forth. Natasatch agreed that it was junk, but they might as well keep it against a rainy day when metal ran short.

Their little cave, looking out on the Golden Dome and Naf's thriving, smoky city, in the early winter chill, was a welcome relief after the pomp of Ghioz.

They alighted. "Good to be back," AuRon said. He wondered how soon he could get away to speak to Naf. There was much he wished to discuss.

"I smell Istach," Natasatch said. "She must have come from the Lavadome with a message."

In returning to the cave, they woke their offspring. Istach jumped to her feet.

"A dragon, a dragon has come, Father. He wishes to speak to you. He's back in the deep room."

AuRon recognized the odor of a healthy male dragon as he descended. The blazing, almost red-orange scales and the black stripes stood out even in the dim reflected light of the deep cave.

"Greetings, AuRon," DharSii said. "Is this your mate and the mother of your quiet daughter? Honored to meet you, madam. I'm afraid there's a war in the offing, and we may be on opposite sides of it."

Chapter 8

Fount Brass was much as Wistala remembered it. Tucked between two converging mountains like the last pea in a pod, the tin roofs gleamed from far off. Its famous wind chimes and musical water cascades—the water flowed through tubes that created notes through the flow—that gave the city its name could be heard from a hundred dragonlengths away if the wind was favorable.

Inhabited by men, many of whom were wider than they were tall and bowed in leg and arm, who cultivated and knotted their beards with the same care dwarfs took in dusting and watering the lichen within, it was a city of ringing smithies and white-hot foundries venting sulfurous fumes.

They were notoriously independent. They were a

province of Hypatia, but didn't accept Hypatian law or temples, and had fought wars to keep their freedoms in Rainfall's day.

She'd last passed through as a reluctant fortune-teller with a traveling circus. She'd have an easy time telling the fortunes of the men now: If they didn't accept a dragon into Fount Brass, her brother had every intention of cutting off all trade with the obstinate men.

"The slow pillage of a dragon-lord. No thank you," their king, a hulk of a man named Arbus Glorycry, said, bouncing his daughter on his knee. The curly-furred little girl was fascinated by Wistala and watched her every move, wide-eyed.

Wistala wondered if he'd brought his spawn forward as a shield against dragon-wrath or to show courageous nonchalance against yet another of the Tyr's emissaries.

Perhaps a little of both.

"Every other Hypatian province of the old order has accepted the help of a dragon. Why not yours?"

"Where were you when the Ghioz were battering down our towers? Where were the dragons when my daughter's room was burned?"

"Myself, I was fighting in the snow of the Ba-Drink Pass," Wistala said. "Others fought and died in the streets of Hypat, or over Ghioz. Have you not been at peace for ten years? Are there still bandits riding your mountains? Do Ghioz soldiers still walk your streets?"

"They never conquered us," King Arbus said. "As to the old Hypatian order, it fell apart in my grandfather's time, when he knew only the title of Lord Protector. My father took the title of King and passed it to me. Am I to relinquish it to a dragon?"

"We do not interfere with your traditions. Your dragon would act as an intermediary between you and the other lands of the Grand Alliance."

"What good would that do us?"

"Trade. The Hypatians are rebuilding their armies and shipping fleets. They'll need swords and shields and helms. Would you rather have the orders, or shall they go to the dwarfs of the Diadem, or new smithies in the north?"

"Dwarf make! Ha! Twice the price for the same quality, just to say some grubby, coal-oil-reeking dwarf labored over the edge."

Wistala listened to the music of wind and water all around, no two refrains ever the same, no melody repeated, infinitely complex yet soothing in its smooth sameness. "You might find markets for your delightful chimes at the edge of the world to the south, or in the far north."

At that, there was a murmur from some of the King's retinue at the sides of his thick-beamed, tin-roofed hall. Wistala thought the style of the architecture so striking in the manner it echoed the mountains that she considered flying north at once to see if the roof on her eventual resort might be restyled in the manner of King Arbus's palace.

"If we do not join?" he asked.

"I'll make no threat. The world around you is changing. You can remain apart from it, in your fastness and isolation and independence, tending those throwbacks to another age you ride and harness into pulling your wagons. You'll lose sons and daughters to the cities that will grow and thrive and ring the Inland Ocean again like a jeweled necklace."

King Arbus laughed. "I see you're still a fortune-teller."

Wistala breathed easier. When the men of Fount Brass laughed, all was well.

"There's no need to put a dragon in these hills, King Arbus. Only give your word that you and your heirs will offer food and shelter to a tired messenger, and reaffirm the old bonds to the Hypatian Directory, and you'll have title not just here in your city but through-out the Grand Alliance. You'll be welcome in a dozen courts, even deep in the Lavadome, and not just be limited to your own. What say you, King?"

"I thank you for not salting your tongue with threats. I am moved by the truth in your eyes. I suspect you are a dragon Fount Brass can trust. Prove your words with deeds, though, Wistala. I provisionally—provisionally, mind!—accept. If all goes well for three years, we shall call it an Alliance. There! I have given. Will you give as well?"

"In the name of the Lavadome, as Queen-Consort, I accept."

Wistala wondered who she should report the change in Fount Brass to first. The Lavadome or the Hypatian Directory? The Directory dealt more frequently with the men of Fount Brass, but she held a more important position in the Lavadome as Queen-Consort.

In either case, she allowed herself a short *prrum* of satisfaction at crossing the very last item off of Nilrasha's list of issues to which she should devote mind and talent.

Save the unwritten one. Of a conspiracy against the Tyr she knew next to nothing. There were complaints and gossip, but unless her brother and Nilrasha had become unhinged, there was no danger in complaints and gossip.

Wistala decided to return to the Lavadome with the news of Fount Brass. Her brother, glad to have another triumph to celebrate, ordered a feast held in her honor for the new Protectorate—even if it was a provisional one.

"There'll be nothing provisional about the provisions," the Copper said.

NoSohoth saw to it that the banquet pit atop Imperial Rock was decorated with wind chimes, a gift from the King of Fount Brass.

The old silver dragon assigned Wistala the honor of the first position at the feast, so that fresh platters from the kitchen passed under her nose as they were brought up.

So many members of the Imperial Line and the principal hills attended that the dragons had to take turns around the feasting pit. By tradition, the younger ate first and the older ate longer.

Thanks to new Hypatian trade there were entertainments to delight the dragons beyond the usual

songs. Trade with the Hypatians had brought fireworks from across half a world. Rayg had arranged
them on a series of wooden platforms, starting off
with fountains of light and having them grow into
colorful missiles that almost touched the top of the
Lavadome.

"Exquisite," Wistala said to her brother, thumping
her tail with the others. "Who is that human control-
ling the display?"

"Have you never met him? That's Rayg, my engineering adviser."

Wistala hadn't thought of the name in so long it took
her brain a moment to make the connection.

"Rayg . . . Raygnar?"

"I believe so. He was raised and taught by dwarfs, I
believe."

"Rayg. Trained by dwarfs?" Wistala asked, shocked.
This was Lada's child! What was he doing in the Lavadome? For him to have come so far, she had no idea the
Wheel of Fire dwarfs traveled so far in the Lower
World. The last she'd ever learned of him was that he'd
disappeared into the Lower World after King Fang-
breaker's death in the barbarian victory over the Wheel
of Fire dwarfs—an assault and a regicide in which
she'd played no small part.

"How did he ever come here?"

"I hardly remember," the Copper said. "Some traveling dwarfs we captured, I believe. He's smarter than
any of our Ankelenes. He designed and built my wing
joint. Dwarf-training, I suppose, but he's built things

not even a dwarf could create. I keep meaning to free him, but there always seems to be one more task for him to do."

One more trip to make. She'd have to find time somehow to go north and tell Rayg's mother that he still lived. Not only lived, but had grown into brilliant manhood.

But nevertheless, he was little more than a slave.

So when her brother asked her for a private chat in his baths after the feast, she happily accepted.

"It's much reduced from SiDrakkon's day. At one time his bath took up most of the upper level of this end of the Imperial Rock."

"I've heard stories from the Firemaids about all the human women he kept."

"Not my weakness," the Copper said.

Thralls brought in stones heated in the cooking fires until they created an optical illusion of waves above them. The thralls dropped the stones into shallow pools of water, which instantly boiled and filled the bath with steam.

The heat raised her scale and the water beaded up on skin and scale, washing her delightfully clean from nose to tailtip. She felt as though a dwarf's weight in dirt ran off her and into the sluices.

"You've never been in the Tyr's bath before, have you?"

"It's pleasant," Wistala said. "Why doesn't the Queen have her own?"

"The Queen, or Queen-Consort, can use this one whenever she likes," the Copper said.

"I shall. Nilrasha never said how much flying would be involved in being Queen-Consort."

"Her experiences predate the Grand Alliance," the Copper said.

"Of course."

"I think my Protectors are cheating me," the Copper said.

Wistala sighed. She'd much rather brief him on the campaign to get the bandits off the *oliban* trade routes. Or new hatchlings. Or the promotions in the Firemaids, and who had taken what oaths.

No, he had to talk about the Protectorates—and how much gold was coming in.

She prepared her usual speech about how dragons should work out a system where they're paid for the services they provide—keeping bandits off the roads and brigands out of the hills, and flying messages. The problem was the role of "Protector" wasn't codified in Hypatian law.

Her brother had kept the costs, duties, and responsibilities of a Protector vague for a reason.

"Everyone takes a little bit off the tributes we are supposed to be given to keep scale healthy," the Copper said.

Wistala was distracted by motion caught in the corner of her eye.

The Copper continued: "I think that the men—*gaaagk!*"

Wistala felt a hard jerk under her jaw. Strangulation—her vision blurred.

A winged shape, smaller than a *griffaran*, fluttered under her neck and she felt new pressure on her throat.

Her brother had managed to get a *griff* open—the one on the side where his eye was damaged tended to hang half open or move about on its own, adding to the lopsided look of his features.

He extended his wings and used them to deflect other fliers circling his throat with lengths of chain.

Wistala felt the pressure subside and took a desperate breath. Her brother pulled a length of chain away from her throat with his tail—he couldn't reach his own but he could get at hers.

Wistala pulled back—hard—and heard a high, metallic *ting!* as a link parted. Now with the fighting blood running hot in her veins, she lunged and snapped at one of the fliers. She caught it across the back and shook it like a dog killing a rat, flinging it into a corner and going after another.

Leathery flaps covered her eyes. She whipped her neck up hard and heard a satisfying splat as she crushed it against the wet ceiling.

Blinking the sting of the creature's blood from her eyes, she saw her brother still fighting the chains around his throat.

For the first time Wistala had a clear look at their tormentors. They were batlike creatures, furless, with thick, spiny skin. Evilly smiling jaws bristled with teeth and wide red eyes shone under cavernous ears. A thick mat of hair remained on the head, trailing down between the eyes to an upturned nose.

The legs, short but powerful, ended in quadruple claws. Long arms trailed veined webbing; the wings extended down the sides of their bodies to the knee joints.

"*Pah!*" one screamed at her brother, spitting a green globule at his good eye. He lifted his chin and managed to catch it on the *griff*, where it sizzled briefly.

Wistala spat back. Her fire ran across the ceiling of the bath, dropped to a pool, and spread atop it like a flaming leaf, adding to the steam. The creature vanished in the fire, its flaming body plummeted.

Striking with her wing, she brought down another. It tried to right itself on the slippery floor but she stomped down hard with a *sii*.

Just as suddenly as they'd come, they were gone, leaving hooked chains behind. And the bodies of their comrades.

She helped her brother out of the choking chain.

"We'll need someone to extract these fishhook things," Wistala said.

"Thank you," the Copper managed.

Once the alarmed Griffaran Guard, Shadowcatch, and some servant thralls had attended to them, they ordered a thorough search of Imperial Rock for the rest of the assassins.

Their wounds were frightful—the hooks had left holes under the scale. They easily could have lost one or both neck-hearts in the struggle.

"How did they get into the Imperial Rock?"

"Flew—they're dark, we don't have a permanent guard circling in the air. The Drakwatch and Firemaids guard the entrances and lower passages. I expect they just flew in quietly and entered through someone's balcony."

"They must know their way around well."

"Perhaps they explored," Wistala said. "Late, when all are asleep."

"I suppose they could have been mistaken for one of my bats. But not up close. These are out of the ordinary. They must have been hidden by someone in the Imperial Rock. Fed, watered, washed out—until we were together and alone."

"Perhaps they just attacked me to keep me from defending you," Wistala said.

"Then why aren't there three chains—or four? No, they brought two sets of hooked chains. Enough for two dragons. Someone must have seen us go off to the baths together and called them in."

"I see being Queen is not all feasts and viewing hatchlings," Wistala said.

"We'd better see about these wounds," the Copper said. "Some of my own bats can take care of them."

Wistala didn't care for her brother's method of treating wounds—washed out with bat spit, ragged flesh snipped away by sharp little teeth, all to the tune of cooing and animal slurping sounds in between " 'ere, under tha' scale" and "oh, this bit's good, wha's next?" But she had to admire the pleasant numbness and the clean scars.

At last, she had evidence of a conspiracy. But nothing on who might have sent the extraordinarily malformed bat creatures to kill them in the first place.

Chapter 9

NiVom was up to something. The Copper could smell it on him.

His Protector of Ghioz had invited him to enjoy a few days of sunlight in the Upper World "observing a show of Grand Alliance strength designed to enhance our prestige and intimidate possible rivals on our eastern borders," or so the Firemaiden messenger told him.

After the usual courtly pleasantries and cheers welcoming him—and a small contingent of the Griffaran Guard and of course Shadowcatch welcomed him to the only Protectorate that could begin to rival Hypatia—NiVom had some thralls pull away a canvas covering to show him a map worthy of the Lavadome map room itself.

Instead of a map, he'd constructed a model using

sand and paint and some sort of adhesive—sugary egg
yolks, the Copper suspected. It wasn't quite up to the
standards of the the map room in the Lavadome—
rescaled to show the extent of the Grand Alliance, and it
seemed, if NiVom would have his way, soon needing
another improvement—but it showed the topography
from the air in impressive detail, with blighter settle-
ments dotting the Bissonian Scarpes like tiny black beetles. In fact, the blighter positions were beetle carapaces,
now that he looked closely.

"Ghioz has long wanted these mountains. They are
rich in precious metals and ores."

"But this is the heart of the old Blighter Empire," the
Copper said. "Something about the age of wheels and
chariots. I don't remember the history, but wouldn't
they have mined these mountains out long ago?"

"After a fashion. But the dwarfs have a method of
mining using water forced through nozzles. It scrapes
away the mountainside like you cleaning your scale of
dirt with your tongue. Valleys thought long since
cleared of gold have been richly harvested of fresh
nuggets, according to the dwarfs."

Shadowcatch ground his teeth in impatience behind.
The black dragon had no interest in technical talk.

"I wonder," the Copper said, after a moment's
thought. "I've looked at the map. It's a vast stretch of
mountains, and far from Ghioz. How will you possibly
manage it?"

"As you know, my Tyr, I've never been afraid of
hard work," NiVom said.

"Why a war? Ghioz must be rich in goods it can trade."

"We're still rebuilding after the conquest."

"You've had years, NiVom. Let me guess. Imfamnia is spending all the tribute on parties, baubles, and gold paint."

"No, if you must know, we've been working on this."

With that, he called to his linemen, who ran to their places at drag ropes and hauled off, their taskmasters counting the step.

There was a groan, the high bowstring *twang* of lines parting, and the sailcloth covering of the mountain's face fell away.

The Copper looked across the valley, into his own reflection. NiVom had chosen their vantage well. He wondered how the people in the city below felt, under the unblinking stare of a monumental dragon.

You wouldn't call it lifelike, but it was eerily accurate. Except they'd given him two normal eyes—perhaps modeled off of NiVom. It did look rather like him about the eyes.

"Of course, it'll go green eventually," NiVom said. "Copper only looks this way for a few years, unless the tarnish is removed."

"I've no words."

"A thank-you in artistic tribute, for forgetting old grievances and remembering old friendships. Imfamnia herself corrected the model to better match your appearance."

While he was glad of a chance to praise NiVom, he refused to do the same to his mate. She'd be tolerated, nothing more, until she died a natural death. A natural death that couldn't come a moment too soon for the Copper.

Just behind the vanguard of scouts, the Copper marked some unusually big soldiers. Ghioz men tended to be small and wiry; these were great hulks.

"Who are they?"

"That's the Grand Guard," NiVom said. "Five hundred blighters of third generation, raised on dragonblood. Those are dragon-scale on their shield, too, mine and Imfamnia's. A project the Red Queen started and I completed. She called them the Queen's Terrors, but that's a bit too battlefield-poetry for me."

"With whose blood?" the Copper asked, astonished at his own mental calculations.

"Mine. It was taxing. But blighters thrive on dragonblood even better than your demen. And they breed more quickly, allowing for culling and development of promising lines."

The Copper thought about the grim business of "culling." Well, there could be no feast without a few bullocks slaughtered.

The expedition snaked through the landscape, an ever-unfolding pavement of bobbing heads, reminding the Copper of a slow-motion King Gan. The power in its coils was latent until they wrapped around you.

NiVom appeared to be displaying to his Tyr just how soundly he could manage an expedition into enemy territory. From the air he pointed out prescouted campsites, chosen for defensible ground and access to firewood and water, and rivers where canoes laden with supplies were crawling in procession so that the expedition might always have three days' worth of food ready for the eating.

"I doubt even old SiDrakkon could find fault with your preparations and execution," the Copper said, referring to their perpetually gloomy and irascible commander on the expedition into Bant that they'd served together back in their days of Drakwatch service.

NiVom bowed at the compliment.

"But will the blighters give battle?" the Copper asked.

"I venting-well hope so. All this flying for nothing but a march," Shadowcatch said. *Tchhk tchhk tchhk*, added his teeth.

NiVom ignored the outburst. "They'll do what blighters always do. Divide. Some will take to the mountain passes, and they can be dealt with later. Some will throw in with us and look for the Ghioz order to set them above their fellows. Some will grudgingly accept our presence and sneak sand into the corn and flower baskets when they can. A few tribes will band together and give us one good fight. Were they all to unite, of course, that might give us difficulty, but blighters never seem to manage that."

"The same might be said about dragons," the Copper said.

"At other times, of course," NiVom said.

"Let's hope so."

There was something about an army on the march, perhaps all the orchestrated chaos, like an improvised song, that set the Copper's hearts to beating quickly. He had a weakness for this sort of thing, he had to admit. It was so much more invigorating than dull sessions with NoSohoth in the Audience Chamber. Being out under the sky with an army, especially one as disciplined and well-directed as this, was wonderful.

A doubt crept in. This army was well-directed, anyone could see it. Might NiVom be displaying his prowess so that whispers would begin that the Tyr had a rival? There was never any question in the Copper's mind that NiVom was a brighter dragon than he. The only mark against him was a tendency to fly from difficulty or submit to circumstances. Sometimes a Tyr needed the obstinacy of a cave-caught bear to get results.

NiVom chose what looked like bad ground for the crossing into Old Uldam. The river ran narrow and swift here, and there were high ridges on either side and thick vegetation and driftwood along both banks. It seemed like good country for archers and spearmen.

"It looks like we're about to fight our first skirmish, my Tyr," NiVom said. "Our scouts are across the river and into the disputed lands. They say there's a party of blighters sheltering in the woods behind that ridge. I'm sure they see us."

"Do you think they mean to contest the crossing?" the Copper asked.

"We have a footbridge in two pieces. You see it ready there. I can swim out and join them, and we'll be across in no time under a canopy of shields. They won't be expecting that. Then the bridge can be expanded with rafts to bring the carts across. The river is narrow enough here for lines from side to side to hold the bridge against the current; that's why I chose this spot."

"Provided you can hold the far bank. Otherwise your bridge may disappear downriver as fast as those leaves."

The Copper watched NiVom and his men go through the crossing as though practicing a military evolution. He saw a blighter go loping away from the riverbank carrying what the Copper first mistook for a short, leaf-shaped stabbing sword but turned out to be a fish when he saw the blighter tear it in half with his teeth and throw away the tail.

NiVom sputtered and gasped in the current, but with some difficulty and the aid of his tail joined the two ends of the wooden raft bridge with metal pins extracted from behind his ear. Fleet-footed linesmen secured it on the other side to thick trees and brawny axmen moved driftwood out of the far landing under NiVom's attentive direction.

NiVom's Grand Guard crossed first, interlaced shields layered together like oversized dragon scales held over their helms against a rain of arrows that never came.

Archers and crossbowmen followed. Artillerists dragged a cart across and set up some kind of war machine that NiVom claimed could hurl clusters of long, dartlike throwing-spears over the top of the ridge.

The Copper took his word for it. NiVom was a clever engineer.

"That was the tricky part. We shall be safe now. Downriver is a landing for the canoes. We'll move there and be established by nightfall; the rest of the march will be irresistible once the base is secured."

Frantic activity on both sides of the river held the Copper's interest for a little while, but his stomach began to growl. He was just wondering how to properly phrase a request to one of his Griffaran Guard to go and get him a fatty joint from the soup pots, when a bump appeared at the ridge above the crossing.

The bump resolved itself into the outlines of two dragons, walking to either side of a tall blighter carrying a taller banner on a staff.

The Copper recognized the banner—the knotwork-and-goat-tracks design of the Grand Alliance. It gave him a turn for a moment: Was this some scouting party returning?

No, there was no mistaking that gray dragon with the regrown tail. His brother AuRon. And that near-orange-striped fellow, DharSii. He'd turned up unexpectedly again, like the musked stone in a game of Nose-Hunt.

What sort of game was his brother playing?

He forgot his empty stomach, called the Griffaran Guard, and flew to the other side of the river. He alighted just behind NiVom.

Some blighter elders, a few walking with the aid of sticks or staffs, stood behind the banner of the Grand Alliance. AuRon and the DharSii fellow both bowed.

AuRon cleared his throat. "On behalf of the Grand Alliance, we'd like to welcome Tyr RuGaard to Old Uldam and the foothills of the Bissonian Scarpes. You should have sent messengers; we weren't able to prepare a proper reception and a feast worthy of our Tyr."

"Here in the borderlands I won't stand on ceremony. What's going on here, AuRon?" the Copper asked.

"You're looking at the new Protector of Old Uldam," AuRon said. "The blighters of the Bissonian Scarpes asked to join the Grand Alliance. I accepted, as I think you'll find them worthy allies—provisionally, of course. King Naf has already spoken in favor of it. It's up to the Tyr and our friends the Hypatians to further cement the alliance, of course. If you so choose."

The Copper spotted AuRon's daughter, Istach, standing protectively at her father's exposed flank. Every time he looked at her face, his heart gave a thump, thinking Jizara had somehow returned.

One of the blighters extended a bundle of wheat and another a piece of honeycomb to him, yammering something in their tongue as the *griffaran* circled close overhead.

Well done, AuRon. A terrific joke.

The whites of NiVom's eyes showed up against the red at the center, but he kept his *griff* still. Old habits of the Lavadome, no doubt.

* * *

"AuRon, you already have an Uphold to manage. As I told NiVom when this expedition set off, it's too much territory for one dragon to cover. You'd forever be flying. No, we must have someone else."

"Perhaps CuRemom. He's a bright Ankelene," NiVom said.

"No, blighters need someone robust and energetic. CuRemom is energetic enough, but only in his workshop. No. AuRon, what do you say to your daughter Istach taking the position?"

Istach, who seemed to be going out of her way to avoid notice by hanging back behind DharSii, popped her head up like a startled turkey.

"Me?" she squeaked.

"My Tyr, we hardly know her."

"Her parents do, they're just a long day's flight away. They can help her along."

"We came all this way for nothing?"

"It was a splendid exercise," the Copper said. "Surely a commander as careful as you has a path of retreat selected. I look forward to watching you follow it.

"I think, as these blighters seem to hold you in some regard, AuRon, that we should pick as a Protector a dragon related to you. Istach it is."

"A female Protector?" NiVom asked.

"Why not? Many a widowed dragon-dame has served in her husband's stead."

"But this dragonelle is barely fledged. Her mind will be on mating and feasting and society. A collection of mud huts is no place for a dragonelle."

"I think I should manage," Istach said, glaring at NiVom. "As you said, my Tyr."

"Well done, my new Protector," the Copper said, laying his tail across hers.

"I had my first uphold at a young age, Istach," the Copper said. "It's a tremendous experience. Govern an uphold well, and you can be trusted with any responsibility."

"I wasn't any older than you when I was leading these blighters," AuRon said.

"I must have a dragon I can trust. I can trust you."

"But why did you let us go to the trouble of building a bridge?" NiVom asked.

DharSii smacked his lips. "We thought a celebratory feast was in order. Given that mountain of supplies filling those canoes heading upstream toward your landing and on the other side of the bridge, we thought it would make things easier for all concerned to have a bridge in place to bring them across to our cooking fires."

"I've not dined on Ghioz smoked army pork in years," AuRon said. "I'm looking forward to sampling your supply."

The Copper stifled a laugh. It was pleasant to see the Gray Rat bite someone else for a change.

Chapter 10

Wistala was shocked to see DharSii return to the Lavadome in company with her brother.

She couldn't help but see it, as they arrived during a hatchling viewing in the gardens atop the Imperial Rock.

The proud mother, a Skotl, and her mate, an Ankelene, predicted great things from their hatchlings—a mix of brains and brawn. Some in the Skotl clan had warned the mother against mating outside the Skotl line, but had been encouraged from afar by Nilrasha, who always spoke against division by clan in the Lavadome.

She left the hatchling viewing as soon as she decently could, bestowing a gift of cattle from the Imperial Herd to help the sharp young appetites along, and hurried over to where her brother and DharSii shared a welcoming drink from a flower-ringed fountain (Rayg had some success recently breeding flowers that blossomed in the muted light of the Lavadome—when he wasn't working on more important matters).

"Wistala! My felicities on your new role in your brother's tyrancy," DharSii said.

"It's only for a time."

"How much time? I've never heard of a dragon re-growing her wings," he said.

"I . . . I cannot say," Wistala said. Her brother's hunt for a likely candidate to become Tyr was a secret Wistala didn't even dare think about in the solitude of her room. "I am glad to see you allowed to return. Do you visit for long?"

"Returning wingtip-to-wingtip with Tyr RuGaard helps," DharSii said. "Though I'll stay as briefly as possible in some discreet hole near the edge to avoid giving offense to the Imperial Line. The gardens here have changed. They're much improved from the few ferns and mushrooms and lichen-patterning of my day. Will you show me around? I'm too exhausted to do aught but keep you company for a while."

"I've always wanted to hear the story of why you're not welcome in the Lavadome."

"Yes, I'm not quite at the status of exile, but I see my share of quickly turned backs and exposed tailvents on the rare occasion I do visit. I fear it is a long story."

Wistala wanted it to be a long story. She looked forward to forgetting about plots and assassins while she walked with him. "I've no objection to hearing it."

"I suppose, to properly tell the story, I must go back to the dark times after the fall of Silverhigh.

"Dragons scattered. Some, the very young and the very fit, went as far away from their enemies as they could, into the great east or the islands beyond. They made themselves useful to the men there, and when dragon-hunters on swift Rocs came looking for them, they were hidden deep in temples or palace grottos. The grateful dragons did favors in return for this, so legends grew up about how lucky it was to have a dragon in your house. But they hid apart so long they grew estranged, and with no hatchlings they dwindled and died.

"The most indolent and lazy of the dragons sought refuge with a young wizard named Anklemere, who promised them the protection of his magic.

"This is just personal opinion, you must know, but I believe he began to breed dragons. The Wyrr were bred for hardiness and health, meant to travel long distances in carrying messages, and have a mild temperament so that they would not cause trouble. The Ankelenes were selected for their brains. I'm not sure what Anklemere had in mind for them. Of course the Skotl were bred for size and fighting strength."

"So they're different dragons from what we were before Anklemere?" Wistala asked.

"You have a scientific mind. How can you determine speciation? For example, with horses."

"Mating is the easiest rule of claw. If, for example, a horse and a donkey mate, they produce a sterile mule. Other animals, when mixed, can't produce offspring at all, for example a dog and a cat."

"However, if you mate with an Ankelene—"

"I don't think it's likely I'll mate anytime soon."

"In theory—"

"Our hatchlings would be able to produce more hatchlings, so of course we're still the same species."

"Perhaps, if Anklemere had lived long enough, the dragon lines would have become truly estranged."

"Just as well he didn't. We have problems enough."

"Oh, the Wyrr and Skotl and Ankelenes cause enough grief. The slight differences just give them that much more reason for faction and clannishness. Like sea-elves and forest-elves and bog-elves, or all the fall-foliage colors of humankind. I imagine dwarfs fight over something, too."

"Bearded and unbearded females, I've heard."

They shared a chuckle. "But back to your story."

"Yes, well, the smallest number of refugees from Silverhigh fled to the old winter palace in the north. It's a region few hominids dare approach. Volcanic activity keeps the vale itself hospitable enough in the winter, but there are only a few months in summer when men may approach it overland, and even then they have to wade across marshes filled with disease-carrying insects. They say you can find bones of every great hominid empire in those bogs—I've seen a jeweled chariot of the blighter kingdom of Old Uldam myself, when off exploring. I was born to that little clan of dragons, where we first met."

She nudged a wayward paving stone back into place. "Yet you are also known in the Lavadome."

"The dragons made cautious contact—we'd practically died out at the old Winter Palace in the Sadda-Vale. The trolls are a nuisance and have killed their share of drakes and drakka, or the more adventurous had struck off for better hunting. But through Noo-Moahk, back in his younger days before he became addled and obsessed with that cursed crystal, we learned of the dragons in the Lavadome.

"It became a tradition for at least one drake or drakka to be exchanged. In the middle of the clan wars between the Wyrr and Skotl—at first it was just the two of them, with the Ankelenes ostensibly neutral—the tradition was stopped. It only restarted again after the wars were over and Tyr FeHazathant and his mate calmed things down.

"I was both the first and the last of that old tradition. Scabia sent me because she thought me obstreperous, and the Lavadome would knock some discipline into me. In exchange we received NaStirath, who I believe you met in the Sadda-Vale when you were seeking allies to avenge your family."

"Yes, though it was a bloodless hunt. NaStirath was quite possibly the silliest dragon I've ever known."

"Somehow the Lavadome managed to spare him, yes. But he did learn to flatter there. Scabia enjoys hearing him prattle about her greatness."

"So you weren't originally from the Lavadome."

"No, but I grew to love it as if I'd been hatched there. It felt like home, more so than anywhere else I've lived. Mystery and history and secrets, there's more worth finding there than I could discover in a lifetime. But it was only home for a while. I went into the Aerial Host more for mnemonic powers than athletic ability or fighting skill or what have you. If you don't mind listening to me sing my own praises, Wistala, I'm good at finding my way around, even by dead reckoning. I was usually flying scout—this was in the days when the Lavadome was reestablishing upholds that had been lost in the civil wars—and made excellent maps.

"Well, I found myself giving advice to the commander of the Aerial Host, FeHazathan's clutchwinner AgGriffopse. I'd lay out enemy positions, or find a new route to an objective, a few times I even scared up allies— AgGriffopse would base his battle plans on what I'd discovered and we'd usually win without too much fighting. There's a rumor in the Lavadome that AgGriffopse and I were enemies from the very start, but that's not true. He usually sent me back to report his victories, the tradition then was that report running was a mark of high distinction, given only to dragons of sense and ability, because the Tyr would question them and form judgments and give orders based on the reports. I repaid AgGriffopse with my loyalty, always giving him his proper due.

"When he started assisting his father in Tyr duties, I took over the Aerial Host. My name back then—oh, it doesn't matter. I'm DharSii. I like it better anyway."

He watched a new stream of molten rock start down

the side of the Lavadome, bright and almost yellow in its heat. "My command of the Aerial Host is better remembered now than I thought it at the time. While living it, it seemed as though I was making one dreadful error after another. Each victory seemed to cost me dragons, yet when we'd return to the Lavadome we flew around the Imperial Resort to roars of praise. Seems a hundred years ago. Perhaps it was."

"You don't look so old."

"It's the waters of the Sadda-Vale. I think that's why the summer palace was up there; they're filled with minerals dragons need, I believe."

"I could use a few mouthfuls, I think. All this back and forthing and keeping everyone placated—it would tax old Rainfall's patience."

"You must tell me more of him, sometime."

"Finish your story."

"It's not a happy ending, I'm afraid. AgGriffopse and I became, I suppose you would say, rivals. The Tyr liked us both a great deal, I believe. His blood called to AgGriffopse, but I'd like to think that part of him considered me as a possible future Tyr. You always want to look back at yourself in the best possible light, but I find myself unable to do that. I believe I was ambitious, perhaps too ambitious.

"The Tyr had a daughter as well. Enesea. She was silly and headstrong, decent looking enough but a little on the weak side—never flew for exercise, in that she resembles our friend Imfamnia. Not surprising, Enesea being her aunt.

"If ever a dragon courted, so I courted Enesea. I gave her merits she didn't deserve, though I will admit she always made me laugh. In the right way, through wit, not in the wrong way, through foolishness. She enjoyed mentioning other young dragons as rivals, but I believe in the end she would have had me. Not from affection or real respect based on knowing each other's strengths. No, it was status. My position in the Aerial Host made some of her friends sigh and hoot and ripple-wing when I was about, and she enjoyed their jealousy to the fullest.

"I was working myself up to sing my lifesong to her—an old-fashioned proposal is best, don't you agree?"

Wistala did agree, most sincerely, but perhaps Dharsii was blind to just how much she was like-minded.

"But the moment never seemed to come," he said. "One night, after a particularly wine-filled feast, we went for a flight around the river-ring. We were jostling and knock-winging. I was nipping at her tail and she was batting me about the face with her wingtip, young dragon play, when suddenly she threw herself into the cavern ceiling on some sharp rocks. I tried to assist her and she began to roar and call as if I'd been murdering her, and the next thing I knew there were some *griffaran* flying about and a pair of the Aerial Host on exercises were flying to my aid—

"She flew back to the Imperial Rock as quickly as her wings could carry her, bleeding all the way.

"Well, to make a very long and very angry story

short, she accused me of attacking her. To this day I don't know what was in her mind. Did she have a fit of some kind and hurt herself? And when I tried to support her she thought it was a mating embrace—or did she, from the very first, mean to hurt herself and go flying to the Tyr with a story that I'd attacked her?

"I do know this: She closeted herself with the Tyr's mate, Tighlia, and wouldn't see me. Looking back on it now, it seemed clever Tighlia meant to put at least one of us out of the line of succession—if she was very lucky, both, as things turned out—

"AgGriffopse went absolutely mad. That's the only word for it. He challenged me to a death duel. No quarter given until one or the other of us would lie dead. Even if we were each too wounded to finish the other off, the one least able to have his limbs hold him up would be finished by the Ankelene duel-physician.

"So we met in the old dueling pit in the black of night, as was the tradition for a death duel."

"*Your wrath shouldn't win . . .*" Wistala said, quoting the first song her mother had sung to her hatchlings.

"Exactly," DharSii said. "I'm surprised you know it. That's an old song of—well, I believe it dates back to before Silverhigh. A very old song indeed."

"There's some truth in it. That's probably why it's lingered on all these years."

"It could be phrased more felicitously. I suspect we've lost a few words over the years and substituted worse ones. I didn't know anyone remembered it outside the Sadda-Vale."

"My mother did."

"Ahh. Well, yes, AgGriffopse's wrath won. But he also lost, in a way. He stood there, bellowing and stamping out his rage over the insult to his sister—an insult I knew I was innocent of, at least as innocent as a young dragon could be with my intentions of making her my mate. AgGriffopse was a fine dragon, but he did let himself run on a bit. He was yelling to the roof about how he'd tear out my liver and feed it to the fish in the river ring when I took my chance. I lashed out with a *sii* and caught him across the throat.

"The wound wasn't fatal. I know some accused me of poisoning my claws with a venomer's spit, but I'd never resort to such tactics. Besides, if I had, he'd have died within minutes, and it's my understanding that he was recovering and died from an infection or some such— that is, if Tighlia didn't do him in. But don't listen to rumors. The duel was fairly started, he just decided to waste his breath snarling at me rather than fighting.

"He lost blood and consciousness with it, though his neck-hearts were still pumping. As it was a death duel, one of us had to die, and I decided that it would be better him than me."

"But I'd heard he lingered—you didn't finish him?" Wistala asked.

"I didn't have the heart. He had been my friend. Even when we were rivals for the Tyr's admiration, we were still friends. I can't believe that whichever one of us FeHazathant chose to succeed him would have become a bitter enemy of the other. I'd like to think either of us would have rejoiced. But who's to say—dragons don't care to lose. At least, dragons worth the content of their gold-gizzard."

"So, what, it was suspended until he recovered and you'd fight again? That seems—"

"No, nothing like that. One of us had to die. I just decided it would be me."

"You mean . . ."

"Yes, I died, after a fashion. It was all perfectly in keeping with Lavadome tradition. I renounced my name, all my *laudi*, and my position. I went into exile from the Lavadome. The dragon who'd led the Aerial Host was no more, his name was never spoken—I became DharSii, quick-claw, a criminal's nickname. AgGriffopse had won the duel, and avenged the insult to his sister."

"What happened to Enesea?"

"Again, that depends on which rumor you believe. I was long gone from the Lavadome by the time it happened, but some say she went mad and threw herself into the Wind Tunnel after AgGriffopse's death. Others say she was wined into a stupor and told to fly up it. Still others say her body was simply dumped into it after her death. Whatever the cause, she was found at the bottom with a broken neck."

"The poor Tyr. First his son, then his daughter."

"I think he was blind to the evil close to him. Though I hear Tighlia gave a good account of herself at the end. She was the only dragon who resisted the Dragonblade and his puppet Tyr, at the end."

"So, what did you do?"

"I returned to the Sadda-Vale. I angered Scabia by refusing to recognize any name but DharSii, and found NaStirath mated to Aethleethia. They were kind enough to me, but I still felt like an exile among them. But they keened that they needed coin—it's the one mineral the Sadda-Vale lacks. We resort to chipping ores out of the slate there, but they don't care for the work or the taste. I've hired myself out for wars to bring them coin. But never enough, they gobble it down and then it's back to slate chipping."

"You were doing that when we met."

"You think I'd forgotten? You were the first new face there in ages. I've roved the world. But somehow I always find myself returning there, even if the company is a little distasteful. It's one of the few places that still belongs to dragons—not that the trolls don't give us some bother about it, but then a dragon needs a challenge now and then. But I like the sense that it's *ours*. Don't we deserve a few patches of land, too?"

Ours, we—DharSii, don't you know that those words catch me in the throat, too? He was an intelligent dragon, spoke carefully when he did speak. He must be using them intentionally.

"You make me want to fly away with you there now."

"But you have duties to attend to," DharSii said. "Watch your tail in this place, Wistala. And your throat. And your flanks, when you can spare the time."

"I'm the Queen-errant, don't you know?"

"Have you ever heard of a thing called a lightning rod?"

"Umm . . ."

"It's a dwarfish invention for places struck by storms. It's simply a piece of iron placed high, with a wire to the ground. It attracts lightning bolts, rather than the more vulnerable usual rooftop or ship mast. You'll be a lightning rod for discontent. Your dragons are celebrating now, but as soon as bad news comes, a plague strikes, or a battle falls the wrong way, they'll blame you. They always do. A Tyr can engage in all manner of foolishness and still be loved, but his Queen—her slightest misstep is remarked upon and criticized. She's always accused of secretly manipulating her mate."

"RuGaard's not my mate. He's my brother."

"I'm very glad of that," DharSii said. "I've delayed too long already. Tongues will be tasting the air about you tonight and discussing this tomorrow, you can be sure.

"Now, I've recuperated enough to eat a meal without bringing it back up. The kitchens haven't moved, have they?"

"Just follow your nose," Wistala said.

"I was hoping you'd give me a tour, and take a bite with me."

"I was hoping you'd ask," she said.

Chapter 11

Wistala longed to see the sun again.

She was spending far too much time in the Lavadome for her taste. It seemed the Queen, even a Queen-Consort, was expected to preside over every social gathering, on top of her largely ceremonial duties as head of the Firemaids.

Having to listen to the same news repeated over and over and over again, discussed much the same way with the same insipid observations and jokes—it was enough to make you gnaw at your flanks until your scale fell out. Now there was news of the blighters she'd briefly lived with coming into the Grand Alliance, and all the Lavadome wanted to know what sort of gemstones and precious metals could be found in their lands.

"Unless cattle horn is a precious metal and chicken beaks a gem, I don't know that we'll see much wealth from them," Wistala said.

She'd kept her ears open for news about DharSii. He was consulting with the Ankelenes about the crystal statue that had once stood in NooMoahk's cave until the Red Queen of the Ghioz stole it. The dragons of the Lavadome claimed it when they settled matters with the Red Queen in a desperate attack.

Strangely enough, it was when she paid a rare call on the Ankelenes' "hill"—it wasn't a natural feature of the Lavadome but rather an artificial hill made of stone—that she happened upon the first evidence she found of Nilrasha's purported conspiracy.

While climbing the stairs to the Ankelene Hill, she met Ibidio, AgGriffopse's mate and widow. Ibidio was a fixture at Imperial Line events, a sort of Queen-in-her-own-mind who saw to it the traditions of the Lavadome were upheld.

"Ibidio, I've seen little of you for days. Have you been ill?"

"No. I don't care to meet my husband's murderer. I understand today he's swimming in the river-ring."

Wistala suddenly lost interest in visiting the Ankelenes. Her time there always passed like dried, splintered bones through her digestive tract, as she could rarely enter without having some expert question her about conditions near the pole or in the great east or other places she'd visited.

"I might follow your example and go into hiding. I

thought I'd borrow some books and spend a few days reading," Wistala said. "I'm tired of duties and ceremonies."

Ibidio explored her gumline with her tongue. Wistala noticed she was lacking teeth. "You aren't fond of your brother, are you?"

"Fond? No, not fond."

Ibidio cocked her head. "Yet you have dropped scale all over the Lavadome acting as his Queen-Consort. Strange."

"I respect him, I respect what he's built, and what others before him established. I believe in what he's trying to do for dragons."

"Are you aware of the circumstances of my daughter's death?"

"His first mate? I've heard the story. RuGaard said she choked."

"No one knows the whole story, except perhaps for RuGaard and Nilrasha." Ibidio sighed. "I've devoted myself to the subject. Halaflora wasn't a favorite of mine at the time, but since Imfamnia revealed her true character, her memory has sweetened. I'll never forgive her death."

"You believe she was murdered, then?"

"Would knowing the truth change your opinion of your brother from respect?"

"Of course," Wistala said. "I have my own grievances and accusations against him."

"I remember that day in the Audience Chamber. His tyrancy should have ended that day. Would you like further proof of the character of that outcast and Tighlia?"

"I will hear it," Wistala said.

"Follow me."

Ibidio led her into Ankelene Hill, and then down to the storage rooms. They passed through a corridor lined with scroll tubes and into a sort of reading room beyond. There were several smaller rooms off of it filled with materials and implements for writing— dragons had learned the practice from dwarfs, some thought—and Tighlia opened the curtain of one.

A giant, bloated bat and a dwarf had just finished a meal inside.

The bat was unremarkable except for its size and its overlarge ears. Wistala knew that there were some big bats in the Lavadome; the vermin did well suckling on the blood of cattle and dragons, when they got the chance.

The dragons tolerated them, mostly because they'd been part of the fight against the Dragonblade's riders. But she still suspected the dragons of squashing them on the sly.

"Let's hear his story, then," Wistala said.

"Don't be afraid," Ibidio said. "Tell this dragonelle your story."

"Could I have a sup first, your lordship?"

"After!" Ibidio insisted. Wistala thought Ibidio looked a little drained. Maybe she'd stayed in seclusion for more than one reason.

"Well, it was like this," the bat began. "Himself kept a few of us around as messengers."

"Himself who?" Ibidio prompted.

"Tyr RuGaard. Or Upholder RuGaard, as he was then.

"I'd come back from delivering a message. RuGaard wanted to ask something about the construction of a bridge. I was tired, and went right to the ceiling to find a comfortable spot. This horn-blowing woke me up, and I saw RuGaard's human girl blowing on the horn, and both the Tyr an' his Queen standing over the frail dragon, his mate."

"I don't suppose we're going to hear from this girl?" Wistala asked.

"Her name was Rhea. She met with an accident. But this family servant RuGaard gave to Rayg's family, Fourfang, he heard her at her death, talking about it."

"Where is he? Another room?" Wistala asked.

"He's afraid to return to the Lavadome to tell the story. But I heard it myself with two witnesses present."

"The female's story, or this Fourfang's?"

"The human told Fourfang of her death."

"A human woman is dying, and she uses her last breaths to tell a story about a dragon dying years ago?" Wistala said.

"She was afraid of telling the truth. Nilrasha killed Halaflora. She told RuGaard the truth, and he lied for her, stuck a bone in her throat. Vermin."

Wistala heard from the other witness, a beardless dwarf of the sort that seemed to wash up in the Lavadome, to do odd jobs until they built up enough of a hoard to move on to wherever they were going. This one must have been in the Lavadome a long time; he moved stiffly and held his toothless mouth shut.

He only told his story with much prodding and prompting from Ibidio.

He didn't have much information to offer—all he told was a story about working a ferry in the depths of the western tunnel leading to Tyr RuGaard's old uphold. RuGaard and his mate traveled west, and soon after, Nilrasha followed. She asked questions about whether RuGaard seemed happy with his new mate.

Wistala thought the dwarf the next thing to useless. If Wistala wanted to get an idea of a dragon's feelings, the last thing she'd ask would be a wandering dwarf.

"So, a terse dwarf and a thirsty, blood-addled bat are going to bring down Tyr RuGaard?" Wistala felt a little sorry for Ibidio. A dead daughter, a fled daughter, and a third sworn to celibacy in the Firemaids.

"No," Ibidio said. "But I believe I can bring down Nilrasha. She's his real weakness, not the bad *sii* or the lazy eye or the wing joint. Tell us the truth, did he have his family killed?"

"That's a truth not even my brother himself could tell you."

"Don't say a word of this to anyone, if you value your position," Ibidio warned.

"I might say the same to you," Wistala said. She turned and left Ibidio with her hate and her witnesses.

Chapter 12

Imfamnia called a meeting to discuss relations between Ghioz, Dairuss, and the new Protectorate of Old Uldam. This one came from a veteran Roc-rider who had survived the war between Ghioz and the Lavadome and threw in with the new Protectors.

His painted neighbor did keep her messengers busy.

AuRon didn't know of that many pressing issues. Istach was settling into the ceremonial duties of a dragon-Protector, supervising winter feasts and exhibitions of babies and newly matured male warriors and so on. The only thing his offspring had asked him about in her brief reign was a request by some Hypatian mapmakers to survey the mountains—evidently Old Uldam was nearly unknown to them—and a request from some Hypatian librarians to inspect what little was left of NooMoahk's old collection of books and scrolls. She'd never mentioned any difficulty with Ghioz.

Imfamnia probably had some bauble or other she wanted to exhibit in front of Natasatch. Natasatch, both out of politeness and interest, marveled at Imfamnia's collection of glitter that seemed to serve no other purpose than occupying a few moments putting it on and then taking it off again.

Well, AuRon decided, he'd show Imfamnia. He'd leave his mate behind, or send her to the capital in Hypat or the storehouses of the Chartered Company. A silk-train had set up a market in Dairuss and Naf and Hieba had made them a present of some very fine purple bolts, Natasatch's favorite color. Dragons had little use for silk, though, and their scale was rough on it, so she'd keep a little for a divider curtain and trade the rest for a bauble or two. Perhaps Hieba would like to try a dragon-saddle once more and advise her on getting the best value.

Imfamnia arranged a meeting in the old woods where AuRon had given Hieba over to a human logging encampment—strange fate had led her to meet Naf that way. Naf had told him privately that when word came of a girl who made dragon noises coming out of the woods he'd suspected he knew the identity of both girl and dragon, and made it his business to visit the encampment in his rounds as a commander to check up on her. Eventually, they'd fallen in love.

There were still loggers at work, here in the well-watered valley between Ghioz and Old Uldam. Game was plentiful and Imfamnia had arranged a selection of fresh frogs, smoked deer, wild boar in a sweet mustard, smoked-fish-stuffed raccoon in *gar-loque*, groundhog stewed, and an assortment of birds that were difficult to identify with heads, feathers, and feet removed.

"I do so love eating rough," Imfamnia said. "I feel quite like one of those back-to-nature dragons when I dine like this." She swung her head around and poked one of her cooks with a wingtip. "Turn that spit more quickly, there's my man, and don't skimp on the cherry sauce." She sniffed another's bucket and ladle. "Oh stars, you aren't using nearly enough onion in this.

"Roving is *such* an adventure," she mused.

Istach, who'd flown the whole way with a side of bullock to add to the feast, had had her offering rejected. "Not fit for dogmeat, dearest. Never worry, I'll teach you how to hang beef properly."

AuRon hadn't brought anything at all. He was hoping there wouldn't be feasting, so he could plead hunger and the need to hunt to shorten the meeting.

"Where's NiVom?"

"Oh, he's off in Bant, settling things there again. Bant, Bant, Bant, always trouble in Bant. Tribal blighters see a tree struck by lightning and decide the omens are right to start raiding our salt trains again."

The trio ate. Imfamnia snuck in one of the loggers' spits and a copper platter holding barbecued pork, each time trilling out an *oops*: "I'm such a metal hog.

AuRon, you're so lucky not to have scale. Istach, doesn't it drive you absolutely mad, the smell of hot iron? I'd swallowed it before I knew what I was doing. Ah well, they won't miss it. Istach, have some more of that spiced wine, it's a favorite of mine."

AuRon, knowing how scarce smithies were in the frontier, rather suspected they would miss it. Istach politely tongued the offered wine.

There wasn't much to discuss. There was talk of whether to build a road between Ghioz and Old Uldam, and then a second between Old Uldam and Dairuss, or whether to use the existing rivers, which would be longer and slower and seasonably unreliable without an equal amount of work put into dams and portage stations. AuRon was at least suspecting that there'd been some kind of bloodshed between men and blighters that had to be resolved, but apparently there was nothing but the usual complaints of thievery that the dragons couldn't resolve without keeping track of every lamb and loom in their lands.

Istach yawned, being still a young dragon and having flown far with a burden of bullock, and Imfamnia dispatched her to her slumber. She hardly made three dragonlengths into the shelter of a copse before collapsing into deep, regular breaths.

"Ah, to be young again, and just drop off like that," Imfamnia said.

"A hogshead of wine might have had something to do with that."

"Oh, yes, I forget how it goes to the head of those

who aren't used to it. I learned all about wines from the old Queen, Tighlia. She was quite the connoisseur."

AuRon rarely did more than politely coat his tongue with it. It was hard to imagine a more un-dragonish beverage than fermented fruit, but some of his kind were greatly fond of it.

"That was a silly affair with the war we almost had," Imfamnia said, shortly after they agreed to get some Hypatian and Ghioz surveyors to map out a possible path for the imagined road. "It's all your brother's fault, in a way."

"How is that?" AuRon asked.

"This Grand Alliance of his. It's not under a firm hand at all. *Sii* hardly knows what *saa* is doing, and both are constantly stepping on tail. And the Hypatians!"

"I don't know many," AuRon said.

"Well, they're a demanding lot, I can tell you. Fly this message at once! Don't dawdle with the return. Can you bring these medicines north, there's fever in Swampwater Wash and Farmer Pipesuck's pig is ill. Protectors indeed, we're errand runners and lost dog finders."

"Naf just likes to have us show ourselves along the river. Makes the Ironriders think twice about raiding into Dairuss."

"Well! Perhaps we should trade places."

"I've learned enough hominid tongues in my life. I don't want to have to learn another."

"Oh, the Ghioz one isn't so bad, sort of a cross between Parl and Hypatian. If you know Hypatian, it's quite easy to learn, I'm told by the Ankelenes, but then I never was a scholar."

"Well, I should have some water and—"

"AuRon, there was one matter I did want to discuss with you. We get on so famously, I feel like I can trust you. You're just one of these dragons who inspires trust and sympathy."

"Thank . . . you," AuRon managed, worried at what was coming next.

"How would you like to join a little conspiracy?"

"Conspiracy?"

"You're not usually so slow. Yes, a little conspiracy. You must know that when it comes to the ruling of the Lavadome, there are plenty of traditions and practices for obeying one's Tyr, doing this or that properly and in style. But one area that's sorely lacking—and we've suffered for it—is that there's no set tradition for succession.

"Birth is no good. Many a great dragon has fathered unadmirable offspring. Every time a Tyr dies we can't have all these battles and uncertainties and torments, you know."

"I've little experience in the Lavadome, and what I had I didn't much enjoy," AuRon said.

"I'm sorry to hear that. Well, it's very much home to me even if I'm a coinless exile through circumstances beyond my poor powers."

"Yes, well, that's in the past," AuRon said, not wanting to hear again her litany of "nothing was my fault" miseries.

"Of course. I hope someday to redeem myself to the dragons of the Lavadome. I'm not entirely without merit, if I apply myself I'm sure I can one day redeem my name and rejoin society."

"Yes, well, I've never been much for society—"

"Wait, AuRon, don't you want to hear my idea for improvement to the Grand Alliance?"

"I'm all in favor of improvements."

"Well, to be perfectly honest, things aren't going as well as they might under your brother. Yes, the wars are over and the Lavadome is at peace, but most of us expected rather more from the Grand Alliance. We barely see more gold than we did back in the days when we were furtively holding on to a few upholds. Your brother isn't doing a good enough job supervising his 'Protectors.' Dragons are a greedy bunch, and that NoSohoth of his is one of the greediest. The Protectors are keeping all that surface wealth for themselves, when they should be seeing to it that it's brought down to the Lavadome. I mean, there are hatchlings forced to eat iron ores just to keep scale on."

"So, what are you suggesting?"

Imfamnia said, "No harm to your brother! (Unless, of course, you'd prefer some harm to come to him—but I think a little humiliation would quite suffice; he's a dragon who's already risen far beyond the station he deserves and should be taken down a few tailjoints.) We simply wish to have a plan for succession in place, so a new, better Tyr will take over for him."

*　　*　　*

The rest of the conference passed in Imfamnia sounding out Istach on whether she'd like a trained thrall to help shape her scale and train her claws into a more elegant curve. AuRon quit it gladly.

He returned to Dairuss dispirited, and complained that night to Natasatch that he was considering giving up the Protectorship and returning to his island.

"Well, I like it here," Natasatch said. "I feel at home, for some reason, with these social dragons. What is there to do on our island? Snooze out the winters, then argue all summer with the wolves and blighters about the number of sheep that may be taken. It's no life for a dragon."

"It is life. If this contraption my brother the Tyr has set up fails, it'll be another fall of Silverhigh. A good many dragons will go down with it. I doubt we'll ever rise from it again."

Natasatch nuzzled him behind the *griff*. "There's another matter. Think of the offspring. They're doing so well here. Even Istach, who I thought would remain lurking outside our cave like a hungry dog, has found a position—one above her brothers and sister! They're doing so well, because we've been here to help them along. Now, with Wistala acting as Queen, she can be of further use to them."

"I'm not sure Wistala took the position with that in mind. She only wants to make sure everyone's treated fairly."

"What should we do about NiVom and Imfamnia and their 'conspiracy'?"

"If the Lavadome breaks into factions, some will support the Tyr, some will support NiVom and Imfamnia. That seems a reasonable assumption, does it not, my love?"

"Yes," AuRon said.

The air was too still in this cave. If they stayed, he'd have to ask Naf about finding another cave with better airflow.

"We have to make sure we're on the winning side," Natasatch said. "I'd put my hoard on my nest mate. He's a survivor. You can't even kill him with poison, I'd say."

"Thank you."

"But Imfamnia and NiVom are building a network of allies. If she was being honest with you."

"I'd like to hear NiVom's opinion, personally. He's a smart dragon," AuRon said.

"Imfamnia's smarter," Natasatch said. "She doesn't let you know just how smart she is. She plays the birdbrain, but she doesn't act like one."

"So, you think we should side with them?" AuRon asked.

Natasatch paused a moment before answering. "No, my love. We have to be sure we back the victor, correct?"

"Yes. From what I know of Lavadome politics, being on the losing side could be deadly."

"Then we must support both."

"Just how do we do that?" AuRon asked.

"Simple. You'll work with Imfamnia. Do all you can

to ensure her faction succeeds. She likes you, I can tell. She's taken you in on her plans very early."

AuRon didn't like the sound of that.

"I think she likes me too much."

"Well, you're an interesting dragon. Besides, your accent is irresistible, it's not Lavadome at all."

"I often wonder why you feel so at home with that oversized snakepit."

"I don't know. Perhaps my family came from there. I don't know anything about where I was hatched. I was taken away so young."

"You do look a little like some of those dragons, around the *griff* and the jaw. You and Nilrasha, your scale lie very similarly. Maybe you are from a Lavadome family." AuRon wasn't sure he liked where this chain of thought led.

He continued: "No, if I'm going to support someone, I'll support the Tyr. He trusted me here, and by doing so stopped a war with a friend of mine. I'll support him."

"I suspected you would. Well, Imfamnia and I get along."

"Wouldn't it be better to just find a reasonable dragon to take our spot—perhaps one of the offspring—and go back home?"

Natasatch stretched and rolled over on her other side. "The island? I'd rather take my chances here, to be honest. At least there are metals to eat."

"Metals or no, too many plots and plans on the cooking fire for my taste. I had enough stratagems and deception in my life just getting that collar off your neck.

"Besides, by ensuring that one of us is on the winning side, you've guaranteed one of us will lose, too."

"The victor can afford to be magnanimous."

"I've seen victors who use their victory to engage in bloody slaughter, too," AuRon said.

"Oh, that's hominids, they're always gutting each other to make a point. A dragon may humble an enemy, but he'll let them live. Look at Imfamnia or that striped orange friend of yours."

AuRon wondered what DharSii would think of all this. Where was he? He had said something about trading some gathered dragon-scale for coin and paying another visit to the Lavadome. Scale wasn't worth as much as it once was, with so many dragons aboveground these days, but he thought he could get some coin. *Well, no use chasing him down.*

"I think I'm due for a visit to my brother," AuRon said.

"What, already?" Natasatch said.

"It's possible that NiVom and Imfamnia's plans are well-advanced. Maybe if they learn he's suspicious of them, they'll forget whatever it is they're planning."

"While you're doing that, I think I'll invite Imfamnia over for a visit."

AuRon only knew one or two ways into the Lavadome, and a windy tunnel out of it. Long flights didn't fatigue him the way they did other dragons, so he made the trip in two days.

He wondered how much Natasatch would tell Imfamnia. Well, it didn't matter. Not even NiVom and Imfamnia would be able to put their plans into effect, with the head start he had.

He flew straight to the Imperial Rock and spoke to NoSohoth about getting a private audience with his brother on an urgent and secret matter.

The Copper dismissed his Griffaran Guard to wait outside. "Our Protector of Dairuss never was one to start a fight."

"I have finished my share," AuRon said.

"Follow me. It's late, and I know a place we can talk."

He led AuRon down a series of ramps and passages going down through the heart of Imperial Rock.

They ended up in a big, sand-floored cavern. AuRon wondered if it was an arena or a theater of some kind.

The acoustics in this cavern were strange. The sand soaked up the sound of their clawfalls and tail-drags. But when they spoke, the words echoed off the empty shelves and rough cavern roof.

The Copper found a broken metal scale-file on the lowest shelf of the arena, sniffed it for a moment, then swallowed it whole.

"The Tyr doesn't rate better metals for his gold gizzard?"

The Copper let out an acidic belch. "A little iron only makes the rest of the ores more effective."

"Our father said something about that."

"Your father, you mean," the Copper said. "He never sought that title in my case."

"Well, we're somewhere where we can spot listeners ten dragonlengths away. What do you have to tell me in private?"

Choosing his words carefully, AuRon relayed his suspicions about the treachery brewing in Ghioz.

"What's your course, AuRon? Are you trying to divide me from NiVom?"

"I'm telling you what I saw and heard. You'll have to sort out what it means."

"You know what this room is?"

"Some sort of theater or debating hall—that's what I was told as we passed it the first time I came here."

"I killed the Dragonblade here, in a fair fight."

AuRon had heard something of it, but he still warmed toward his brother. "You have my thanks. Our world's a better place for it."

"If you're plotting against me or mine, I'll kill you. Here. Under the gaze of your offspring."

AuRon's firebladder pulsed. "I said I've told you the truth. I don't know what it means. I can't say what sort of dragon NiVom is, except that he's quite intelligent—maybe the most intelligent creature I've ever met. But for all his acuteness, I think his mate's the more dangerous."

The Copper's scale resettled itself. His good eye looked away, into a middle distance.

"What did you come all this way to tell me face-to-face?"

AuRon glanced around the arena. Strange how the habits of a conspirator and an informer were identical.

"Your Protectors in Ghioz, Imfamnia and NiVom. I'm sure they're plotting against you. They're breeding—creatures. You've seen some of them in their attack on Uldam, but I think there are others. Strange bats or gargoyles. I've heard them speak of a change, a new Tyr being put in."

The Copper put a *sii* to a recent wound in his neck.

"I'm curious about this move of yours, AuRon."

"Move? You speak as though my actions are part of a strategy. I am not directing forces for a battle. Your 'Protectors' in Ghioz are your enemies. It's not just the greater glory of your Empire or Grand Alliance or whatever it's called, but they're plotting something."

"You take your responsibilities as a Protector of the Grand Alliance seriously."

AuRon felt better, having unburdened himself. He owed his brother nothing, but it was still the right thing to do. "I take the fate of dragons seriously. There are few enough dragons left in the world. I'm not interested in there being even fewer, which is what will happen if there's a war between us."

There was the noise of dragon voices outside. NoSohoth said in a booming voice, "The Tyr is in private audience. He must not be—"

An aged female's voice: "Oh, none of your delays, you old puff-toad. I will speak to the Tyr. His Queen is guilty of murder and he must answer for the murder of my daughter!"

How had NiVom and Imfamnia moved so quickly? No one could have outflown him.

A group of dragons entered. AuRon didn't know the Copper's retinue well enough to say who was who, but it was led by an aging, but still formidable, female.

"What's all this, Ibidio?" the Copper asked.

"It's about your mate, my Tyr. We believe she is guilty of murder."

Chapter 13

The Tyr ordered everyone up to the Audience Chamber. Anyone might wander into the old dueling pit, and he did not want old bloodstains revealed to just anyone.

The procession of dragons trooped all the way back up in anxious silence. The Copper was grateful for the delay. It gave him time to think. His first instinct, to declare Ibidio a mad dragon, would not go over well in the Lavadome. Ibidio had many friends, both open and in secret.

The Copper faced a formidable assembly. Ibidio might be described as the head of the "First Line" of the Lavadome, the principal root of the Imperial Line. Her experience dated back to the glory days of the establishment of the first Tyr, FeHazathant, after the civil wars were over. With her were his descendants, the twins SiHazathant and Regalia, who shared an egg and a yolk sac before hatching.

LaDibar stood a little behind and in between. The seriousness of the occasion forced him to keep his tailtip from exploring various orifices for once. A few other dragons of the Imperial Line stood safely at the rear of the party.

Only NoSohoth stood a little apart, as if declaring his neutrality and waiting to see his Tyr's reaction.

"Yes, we believe Queen Nilrasha had her murdered," Ibidio said. "If you loved Halaflora, as I'm sure you did, you would want to see justice done."

He had loved Halaflora. Despite her weak constitution, she'd devoted herself to being a proper mate when they lived and worked as upholders in Anaea. After the initial embarrassment of a shared life and even having a mate had faded, he'd found himself looking forward to the time they spent together, and missing her if his duties called him away for more than a day. Beyond that, he was deeply grateful to her. She'd been the first of his kind ever to be, well, proud of him and eager for his company.

Murder!

In the Lavadome there had always been two standards for killing another dragon. One was in a duel—an activity participated in more by males than females—a practice the Copper had tried to end, as the richer and more powerful dragons could hire professional Skotl duelists and thus always win disputes at little risk to themselves. There were few enough dragons and more than enough enemies without killing each other off over insults and livestock theft. But even now, duelists were frequently pardoned if the fight was fair and the grievance just, otherwise. Especially in the case of professional duelists, they were exiled to the surface—though not out of the Grand Alliance, so several still found useful employment aiding a Protector.

The other was deliberate murder. The Griffaran Guard saw to it that murderers were torn to pieces. In the case of a dragon murdering a hatchling, the bodies weren't even burned, they were fed to the Tyr's Demen Legion.

"We even considered charging her with the murder of a hatchling," Ibidio said. "Halaflora was so sickly she might as well have been freshly hatched, and she believed herself with a bellyful of eggs when she was killed."

"I don't accept her cause of death as murder. She choked. Nilrasha tried to save her. I was there, I saw her eating enthusiastically when she should have been downing her usual tiny bites. You might as well charge me with killing her as well, for she choked."

"We have witnesses who say otherwise."

"I see your goal, Ibidio. You'd like me to give up my position as Tyr. You're using my mate as leverage."

"I always thought of you as an interim Tyr until others, more worthy, grew to dragonhood," Ibidio said. "You've wrought great changes, my Tyr, but there will be consequences even the wisest of us cannot foresee.

You've put dragonkind in jeopardy with this Grand Alliance. My mate and his father believed it best to deal with humans in secret, or by proxy, or under carefully selected circumstances such as the men of Anaea. Now you've bonded us to the Hypatians, a corrupt and fallen branch of mankind who've had its day and should have been washed away long ago by the tides of history."

Behind him as always, Shadowcatch began to grind his teeth. *It's a wonder they're not dulled down to nubs*, the Copper thought.

Ibidio's response sounded carefully prepared. He had wanted to throw Ibidio off the track with a counteraccusation, but though Ibidio was well into maturity, she evidently still had a sharp wit. Perhaps he should keep to the subject at hand.

"We know you cared for your mate. There's no thought that you have been involved," Ibidio said. "But as her mother and therefore the most aggrieved, I and the Imperial Line want justice for Halaflora."

The Copper drew himself up. He realized that in only having three sound limbs he'd never be as impressive as others, but he could still raise his neck high. "Had she been murdered, I would have seen to it, and no witnesses or traditions or circumstances would have availed the guilty party. But it was an accident. She believed herself with eggs and ate ravenously. But her throat muscles weren't up to her desire—she choked to death. I felt the bone in her throat myself."

"Perhaps it was stuffed down there," LaDibar said.

"Shadowcatch, our Ankelene has formed a theory. I would like to see it tested. Tear down one of those banners, break its staff and see if you can stuff it down his throat."

Shadowcatch reared up, removed a tattered banner from its bracket. One of the Griffaran Guard cackled in excitement.

"My Tyr, I meant no offense," LaDibar said.

"Accusing my mate of murder will have that effect on me, LaDibar."

"Threats won't save Nilrasha, my Tyr," Ibidio said. "I demand that my witnesses be heard and judged."

"Produce them."

"I'd rather spare you and Nilrasha the agony and embarrassment. I offer an alternative," Ibidio said. "Have Nilrasha fully resign the office of Queen. She may remain where she is, officially in exile. She's unable to carry out her duties, anyway; your sister's attempts to be Queen-Consort prove it."

Why would Ibidio settle for Nilrasha resigning as Queen?

"Produce your witnesses," the Copper said. "I should like to hear what they say."

"You're in no position to judge the believability of our witnesses."

"But I'm Tyr. I've always determined—"

"He should step aside," Wistala said. "Let another question your witnesses. In Hypatia, there are men who do nothing but hear evidence and decide cases."

"Human customs need hardly concern us," NoSohoth said.

"Very well, if you object to me questioning them, perhaps NoSohoth would be willing to perform," the Copper said.

They settled on a date to hear the witnesses two days hence in the old dueling pit, now being called the Voicehall. The name for it came from the new tradition that the Tyr listened to the concerns of any dragon and held questionings of important messengers and decided the fates of those accused of crimes.

While finishing perfectly ordinary business the next day, NoSohoth lingered in the passageway leading off from the Audience Chamber.

"Are you concerned about the questioning, NoSohoth?" the Copper asked.

NoSohoth raised a wing to shield their words from the curtains dividing the passageway from the Audience Chamber. "My Tyr, I would like nothing better than to see this whole matter go away. You have more important affairs to oversee. I hate to see my Tyr enmeshed in this sort of scab picking."

"I'll rely on you to judge fairly."

"My Tyr, if you would allow a faithful old servant to speak his mind for a moment."

"Yes?"

"Ever since your mate was injured, you've been away a great deal, and these old ears, tongue, and nostrils have been filled with managing problems as best as I can until you return to validate my decisions."

"I'm sorry, NoSohoth. You're absolutely right."

"I've been serving the Imperial Line through all four Tyrs and before, when I stood guard atop the Imperial Rock during the civil wars. I am weary and need a rest, my Tyr. I was thinking of retiring to become a Protector and spend my remaining seasons sunning myself in the Upper World."

"Oh, of course. I should hate to lose your services. Perhaps Anaea, it's sunny there and there's only two busy times, at planting and harvest."

"I was thinking Hypatia, my Tyr. I understand the climate in the capital city is very mild."

Hypatia! The Copper wondered just how tired old NoSohoth was. He'd been skimming a percentage of much of the trade that came into the Lavadome for ages. His hoard must be fabulous, wherever it lay.

"Hypatia. That's not exactly a Protectorate to while away one's time in the sun, you know. You'll be at the heart of the Grand Alliance."

"And it is in the keeping of your friend NoFhyriticus. A dragon has a rare sense and even temper, I will admit."

"You have both those qualities as well, old friend."

"My Tyr flatters me."

The Copper could see the reason behind NoSohoth's desire. A Protectorate as rich as Hypatia—he could fill his resort's bathing pools with silver if he wished.

"Don't speak of flattery. You deserve it."

"I'll train a replacement, of course. I was thinking, perhaps, of devoting myself to selecting and training one to take my place after the hearing of this accusation of murder."

"You doubt their evidence?"

"I've only heard rumors, my Tyr, but it strains credulity."

"You deserve a reward for all your services past."

"And future, my Tyr."

"Yes, and future. When we've put this ugly matter behind us you may begin your preparations for becoming a Protector."

"Of Hypatia, my Tyr?"

"If that is what you want, that is what you shall have," the Copper said.

He wondered if he'd just outbid Ibidio in this contest for justice.

It was impossible to sleep, impossible to think—the Copper wanted to fly to Nilrasha and tell her about the predicament, but the questioning would be over by the time he could return. He lurked in his chambers and bath, like SiMevolant of old, brooding. No wonder he was so dour and sought refuge in the aroma of sweat emanating from plump human females.

Could he send a swift messenger to Nilrasha, seeking her advice? No, she'd tell him to sacrifice her to preserve his status as Tyr.

It seemed unfair that she couldn't answer the charges with her own voice.

The arrangement with NoSohoth was cold comfort. Too much could go wrong. It may all depend on the digestion of the audience when the witnesses were heard. He'd have to see about sending some bullocks from the Tyr's herd around to the principal hills.

A thrall announced that his Queen-Consort wished to see him.

"Very well, show her in."

He had no interest in listening to Wistala's latest complaint about one of the Protectors taking too many cattle or making a meal out of a bronze statue.

His sister entered, followed by Rayg. What was she doing with him?

"My brother," Wistala greeted him. "DharSii has returned. He's trying to learn more about the crystal statue taken from the Red Queen."

His bats had told him that DharSii was in the Lavadome, mostly visiting with Wistala. As for that crystal . . . Rayg had been experimenting with the crystal for years. For all its size, it didn't seem to do much. He'd done much better with the smaller jewel AuRon had brought into the Lavadome when he delivered the Queen's ultimatum.

DharSii wanted permission from him to descend with Rayg into the depths of the Lavadome, Wistala explained.

"Unless he's interested in a show of lights, I don't understand what he thinks he can learn."

"I've been studying what happens to the lights when we try to interact with the crystal," Rayg said.

Interact? What, could a piece of stone live?

He needed to get his mind off of the upcoming questioning. "I'll come. I'd like to see what DharSii is up to with my own eyes. I hope the great dandy doesn't mind getting his *sii* dirty."

"The Ankelenes are slowly coming around to my opinion," Rayg said.

"What's that?"

"It's easier if I show you."

They met DharSii outside, and the Copper waved off the usual formalities, though he did offer the visitor a mouthful of coin. DharSii declined.

"I'd rather keep my thoughts clear."

They descended through Imperial Rock, down into the livestock pens and storage rooms, and finally to slippery chutes coated with waste from dragon, thrall, and livestock. The Copper hadn't been this low in the Lavadome since learning the few passageways into the depths during his time in the Drakwatch. The only things that thrived in this noisome mess were worms and brightly glowing cave-moss. Thick masses of dwarfsbeard hung from the ceiling like hedges.

Rayg led them through a series of dripping passages. Unpleasant waste pooled and reeked.

They passed along a natural watercourse that churned the muck out of the Lavadome and down. Here they picked up a cleaner trail again.

Then they came to sort of a twisting passage that

dropped like a root, with a root's branching divisions. Rayg, hanging on to a rope thrown around the Copper's neck, stayed on his feet.

The party began to see pieces of crystal running through the stones. Cavern increasingly gave way to crystal.

"We're on Anklemere's old road," Rayg said. "After he was killed, dragons took out his stairs to make room for us to pass."

They came to sort of an overlook. The Copper thought the cavern looked like an unusually angry sea, the whitecaps frozen forever into blue-white still life.

Lights like tiny drifting jellyfish ran inside the crystal caps. The lights waxed, sparked, waned, and flickered out like fireflies dying in the time it took to draw a long breath.

"What is this?" the Copper asked.

"It looks like fairy fire," DharSii said. "But brighter. We get it in the sky in the far north."

"It reminds me of stars," Wistala said. "What is it?"

"Not even the Ankelenes know," Rayg said. "Some believe that this is where the heat from the Lavadome is channeled and dispersed, the way wet drips off a mammal's fur.

"I can tell you one more thing. These lights—they've become more active. They start and burn out faster, and there are more of them. According to the Ankelenes, the only variation before was when the lava was more active. They would burn brighter, longer."

"Magic?" the Copper asked.

"Magic is a cheap explanation for the inexplicable," Rayg said. "A dragon's fire may seem magical to many humans, but it's just an oil fire with a little sulfur mixed in. With a few more chemicals it's difficult to identify, because they react so strongly to air."

"Rayg's practical," the Copper said.

"Let me see him create dragonfire in his workshop," DharSii said.

Rayg pulled up a chain from his overshirt. The crystal AuRon had worn, an unfortunate "gift" from the Red Queen for his emissary duties to the Lavadome. It glowed behind a metal lattice, like a tiny owl in a miniature cage.

"Why the bars?" DharSii asked.

"If I let it touch my skin, I become—overexcited. I can't sleep. Or even sit down. For a few minutes it's exhilarating, especially when I'm working on a problem. An hour is exhausting. A day would drive me mad."

"What's the longest you ever had it on?" the Copper asked.

"Three days. I think. It could have been less. One of your bats found me on the floor of my workroom with my nose bleeding. After that, I quit touching the crystal except for a few minutes at a time, by putting a finger or two through these bars."

"They're obviously connected," Rayg said.

"Similar material, similar structure. Similar origins?" Wistala asked.

"I believe you're right, Wistala," DharSii said. "You

have an Ankelene's mind in a Skotl body with a Wyrr temperament."

Wistala's scale rippled at the praise. The Copper remembered their mother's scale rising and falling that way when Father spoke to her.

He wondered. DharSii was a well-enough-formed dragon with a good mind, but he struck him as one interested only in his own affairs. He wasn't likely to make much of a mate, nor would he, the Copper suspected, mate unless it were somehow to his advantage. Perhaps he did wish to return to a position of importance in the Lavadome. If that was all, the Copper couldn't help but think less of him.

DharSii cleared his throat. "There are records of the Lavadome dating back to Anklemere. It may be older, we just have no proof. The crystal NooMoahk had in his library that the Red Queen seized goes back to the days of blighter dominance, if not before.

"I would suggest it's an engine of some kind, but beyond anything we could possibly comprehend."

"Ever since the Red Queen sent NiVom, Imfamnia, and myself to retrieve the object the blighters call the 'sun-shard' I've been curious about what she thought it would do. NooMoahk's library yielded some pieces of information.

"I believe there are three important pieces to this enigma. One is the Lavadome entirely, the second is the sun-shard. The third is a smaller crystal. They might be compared to your body—the Lavadome is the muscular meat, the sun-shard is the heart, and the third is the mind."

"So where is the third?"

"It went from Silverhigh to Scabia's Sadda-Vale. From there, she told me that a dragon named AuNor took it. He was fond of looking into it—according to Scabia it gave some visions . . . others nightmares."

"AuNor!" Wistala said. "My father's father?"

"The same. He passed down the traditions of the Silverhigh Star to you and your brother . . . or at least he began to."

"What is the Silverhigh Star?"

"Order of the Silverhigh Star, is the proper name," DharSii said. "A league of dragons devoted to improving dragonkind and its place in the world. *From good dragons, better* was one of their sayings."

"I've never come across anything about an Order of the Silverhigh Star among the Ankelenes. Though I've limited my studies to the physical sciences, for the most part," Rayg said.

"Its influence was waning even before Silverhigh fell," DharSii said. "Your mother sang one of its songs to her hatchlings."

"If you find your missing piece of the puzzle, what will you do with it?" the Copper asked.

"Unite the pieces. Very carefully."

"So it will belong to the Lavadome."

"It belongs to all dragons, I believe," DharSii said. "I would like to examine your home cave. With Wistala to guide me."

Home cave. Bitter words.

"My home cave is the Lavadome," the Copper said. "For now, it's also Wistala's. She has duties here."

"Let me try to change your mind," DharSii said.

"If there's nothing more, Rayg, I will leave."

Rayg ignored him, staring at Wistala in thought.

The Copper turned tail and began the long climb back to Imperial Rock. He heard Rayg's quick footsteps behind.

Wistala and DharSii lingered behind.

Wistala couldn't take her eyes off DharSii. He stood there amidst the fairy lights, looking as though he were standing in a thundershower of fireflies.

"I'd like to know more about your order," Wistala said.

"It's a matter of few words, or a great many," DharSii replied.

"Tell me." As far as he was concerned, she could listen to him forever.

"The Order was committed to learning from others. Hominids, avians, whatever. All the natural world holds a lesson."

"That's true. I learned courage from an old horse," Wistala said.

"According to the philosophers of Silverhigh, dragons taught others to speak and record their thoughts. But sometimes I wonder if it wasn't the reverse. There are so many odd words in the dragon vocabulary that are of little use unless you're dealing with hominid concerns. Terms having to do with architecture, or agriculture. Dragons in their natural state don't grow food and sniff out shelter more often than they build it. You'd think we'd only have three words for a cave, much as the bears do."

"When would you like to leave for my home cave?"

"What about the Tyr?" DharSii asked.

"Talking about the past upsets him. That part of our shared past, I should say."

DharSii planted his feet. "I'd rather talk about the future. Wistala, I'd prefer to have you as a mate."

Wistala thought she'd imagined his statement. He'd like her to be his mate? "That's it? I'm a preference? No song, no mating flight, no—"

"You're a sensible, intelligent dragon. You really want to sit there and listen to me sing about my life? You know the particulars—the important ones, anyway."

"That's it," she repeated, feeling the heat in her words.

DharSii looked puzzled. Perhaps he expected her to quietly agree, then have a long talk about the ideal Protectorate for a home cave. "These old traditions sound better than they live. My bellowing, you flying off and trying to outrace me. It's silliness. I'm sure two intelligent dragons can come to a reasonable decision."

Wistala spoke without thinking. "Reason, reason—everything with you is reason. Give me a reason to be your mate!"

DharSii stamped in confusion, looking at her first

out of one eye and then the other as if to make sure his visual abilities were functioning properly.

"So we're not to be mated?"

The Wyrr temperament he'd just praised disappeared. "Not without a proper courtship, no. Furthermore, I have my duties as Queen-Consort. I don't know where Lavadome traditions stand on such matters."

"Vent the Lavadome. There are dozens of dragon-elles, in the Firemaids and in the hills, for your brother to choose from. Any of them could preside over ceremonies and sniff hatchlings as well as you. I don't want us to be following old traditions that have outlived their usefulness. Let us start our own."

"I swore oaths on my honor when I became a Firemaid. I cannot mate without breaking that oath. Nilrasha broke hers and look what happened. They think her capable of murdering a sister dragon."

DharSii blinked and took a deep breath. She might as well have told him that his teeth needed a polish. Curse him, was he a wind-up toy, built by dwarfs? Didn't a recognizable emotion exist in that great horned head of his?

"We'll talk more. Let me see about helping you find this missing piece of the puzzle, or engine, or whatever this is."

With that, she fled upward, afraid that if she stayed any longer she'd forget those oaths and her duties to a nation of dragons.

*   *   *

Wistala wanted to fly, wanted to touch the sun. DharSii wanted her to be his mate. But instead of flying, she had to find her brother to ask him to accompany Dhar-Sii on his search.

She found Shadowcatch with a great bucket of wine guarding the entrance to his chamber.

"Shadowcatch, I must see the Tyr."

"My Queen, I suppose I should tell you that I'm to kill you," Shadowcatch said, slurring a little. He was a great eater and an ever greater drinker of wine, and the Tyr had recently given him some barrels of brandy-fortified syrup, the tribute of grateful elvish winemakers on the Ku-Zuhu coast whose fields and cellars were no longer being raided by Inland Sea Pirates.

Wistala couldn't have been more shocked if the world had turned upside down.

"My own mate's bodyguard, an assassin?"

"Don't misunderstand. I've no intention of killing you now. Your mate's been so kind to me. I was hired by the Wheel of Fire dwarfs to hunt you down and kill you. But seeing as most of 'em are lying dead on the battlefield, I doubt anyone will be asking for their up-fronts back."

"Why tell me?" Wistala asked.

Shadowcatch looked discomfited. "I'm not a clever dragon like some here. But I know when a fight is on the way. I can just tell, the way some dragons look at me, they're guessing which way I'll jump if there's an attempt on your mate's life. I wanted to tell you about the dwarfs hiring me so you'd know that you could trust me. But at the same time, if I don't kill you, I feel like I'm breaking an oath."

Wistala thought furiously. "What were the terms?"

"Kill you, bring back your head to prove it, and then I'd get the rest of my coin."

"Was there a time limit set on the job?"

"No, though they wanted one. But I told them with the whole world for you to hide in, it'd take a while to track you down."

"Then let's put off the day of reckoning. The way things are shaping up, I may very well end up dead in any case. Should fate overtake me, you're welcome to my head and your reward."

The Copper watched the questioning from the unusual perspective of the audience ledges.

The old dueling pit under Imperial Rock was roughly oval, sand-bottomed with lines of ledges that could accommodate many dragons, depending on how willing they were to be squashed. When very full, thralls pulled chains that worked winglike flaps moving in and out of the two exits, one leading to the Lavadome and the other up into Imperial Rock.

A unique, rising ledge projected out into the arenalike sand pit. When it was used for dueling, a neutral dragon would oversee the duel from that vantage, ready to intervene in the event one of the duelists received aid from a nonduelist or fought with non-natural weapons. Now the promontory held the Tyr as he listened to witnesses and heard evidence and held debates over important issues when he wanted to hear other opinions.

Now NoSohoth reclined on the Tyr's ledge, and looked as though he enjoyed his view. There were enough spectators so that every fan-chain was employed, every *oliban* brazier was lit, and still the air was thick with stale air and dragon-musk.

The Skotl and Wyrr clans gathered on either side of the arena, with the Ankelenes scattered about. Drakwatch and Firemaid drakes and drakka were grouped around him and Wistala.

The Copper hoped he'd live to see the day when Wyrr and Skotl wouldn't divide in this manner—they were all dragons, after all, and had enemies enough without dividing.

He'd heard rumors about the supposed witnesses, everyone had. Even his bats hadn't been able to learn anything about their location or who was hiding them. He suspected they were among the thralls somewhere, but as Tyr and Nilrasha's mate he had to remain above the controversy.

NoSohoth did an impressive job once Ibidio brought in her witnesses. The first was a down-at-beard dwarf who claimed Nilrasha stalked Halaflora as the just-mated couple traveled west to Anaea.

First NoSohoth quizzed the dwarf about how he came to be a ferryman deep beneath the surface. An Ankelene translated for those who didn't understand the dwarf's rough Parl.

"We were a labor team brought down to build a

bridge for the Hypatians. A digger friend bought a map to a secret gold mine in what you-all call the Lower World. So we bucked off cutting stone for bridges and sought fortune. We tried to find it—got lost. Starving, we were, had to earn a living somehow."

The actual story required a good deal of prompting from NoSohoth—dwarfs were notoriously recalcitrant about their histories. Many in the audience grew bored and one or two slipped out for air.

Then NoSohoth asked: "How did you know the dragonelle in question was Nilrasha?"

"She said so, your dragonship."

With that, NoSohoth nodded to a thrall and three Firemaids entered.

"Could you please show us which one labeled herself as Nilrasha."

Ibidio spat a torf into the sand of the pit and the Copper heard *griff* rattle.

"Err . . . the one in the middle, I think. The light wasn't good."

"The light wasn't good," NoSohoth repeated.

The next witness was an aged bat the Copper didn't recognize, beyond his size and toothiness, thanks to being fed dragon blood.

NoSohoth's questioning was brief. He spoke to the bat in a loud, stern voice and the bat crumbled.

"What would you be likin' me to say, sir?" the bat cried.

"I think we've heard enough from him. Take the poor old sot away, he's confused."

Some of Ibidio's allies hissed and clattered their *griff* at that.

"What does the Lavadome believe?" NoSohoth asked the assembled dragons. "Who will call Nilrasha a murderer?"

"Murderer!" Ibidio roared. A few other voices joined in, some loudly, some with half a voice. The number of voices grew.

NoSohoth looked at the Copper, alarmed.

Wistala muttered something about this process being subject to manipulation. The Copper thought it an immense improvement over the Tyr just passing judgment based on whether he liked the look on the accused's face and the lay of his scale or no, but Nilrasha's honorable name, and possibly his Tyrship, lay in the balance . . .

"Innocent!" shouted Wistala, which wasn't according to tradition of trial by questioning.

"Innocent!" she roared again, also not according to tradition—if practice of such recent vintage could be called tradition—but the Firemaids joined in.

"Innocent! Innocent!"

Some of the poorer dragons from Nilrasha's home hill took up the call. NoSohoth joined in. Soon, the shouts of "Murderer!" dwindled and fell off.

"Thank you, Wistala," the Copper said.

"She blames herself, you know," Wistala replied.

"For Halaflora's death?"

"She told me she tried, but she was too late. I believe her."

The Copper had long wondered about exactly what had happened that night. Sometimes he'd doubted Nilrasha's version—privately, that is.

He couldn't find words. Someday soon he'd have to ask Nilrasha to forgive his doubting her.

"Poor Halaflora," the Copper finally said. "Well, my Queen-Consort, if you must chase the ghosts of the past, I give you leave. I hope DharSii finds what he's looking for."

Chapter 14

W istala had forgotten how close the cave of their
birth was to the gap in the Red Mountains that
admitted the Falngese River. No wonder Father had had
trouble with men and dwarfs. While the mountains
themselves weren't settled, trade routes at both the north–
south and east–west routes passed nearby.

DharSii had heard the story of the attack on the egg
cave and the murder of her parents with cool distaste.
He'd undoubtedly heard other such stories about
dragons hunted right to the egg shelf, but she'd hoped
for a stronger reaction. Of course, he'd been withdrawn
since the suggestion of mating in the twinkling depths
of the Lavadome.

The cave smelled as though some bears had taken
up residence in the upper chamber, but at this time of

year they were out getting fat on berries, honeycombs, and fish. Which was just as well; she didn't care to fight bears, as they contented themselves with their own needs and left even the smallest hatchlings alone. Only bats bothered to venture deeper. The smell of their excretions felt like a welcome.

The cave moss still glowed green, and the bats were, if anything, more numerous. She'd forgotten how small natural bats were. The oversized dragon-blood-sucking monstrosities of the Lavadome needed a different name.

Luckily, scavengers—both hominid and on four legs—had long since cleared away the last scrap of bone and scale.

"What are we looking for?" Wistala asked.

"I'm not sure, exactly. A piece of the puzzle. I know it's small enough for a hominid to carry easily. Aklemere called it his 'perspicacitor.' "

"I've never heard that word before. Is it a name?"

"You might interpret it as device that extends sight or brings understanding. It worked with the larger piece, the sun-shard, as the blighters called it."

Wistala remembered the cave being so much larger. Why, the egg shelf wasn't even a tail-length off the floor, yet she remembered it as a clifflike precipice.

"It would help more to know what it looks like than what it's called."

"Round or oval, and clear as glass when not in use. It may have been hollow, I don't know—he wrote of images forming within. If it were hollow, it could be much larger."

"With facets, you mean?"

"I believe so, since he states it was of the same material as the sun-shard. The only reference I've read describes it as round or oval and clear."

Wistala couldn't remember anything like that in the egg cave. Father had given her and Jizara very small gemstones to play with.

"I only had a quick glimpse of Father's hoard. I'm sure whatever was in here, the dwarfs took."

"Show me, please."

She pointed out the once-secret shaft. The boulder concealing it had been long since removed. He searched the little cave off it, then dropped a *torf* of flame to see how far down the shaft went.

"It's not too deep. I'll check it out."

Wistala waited, her memories keeping her company, while DharSii plunged and sputtered and made noises that sounded as though he were rolling in mud. He came back up covered in black goo and stinking, glowing faintly from patches of cave moss. . . .

"That was unpleasant. Nothing at the bottom but some bits of what I think was a saddle and some bones, well covered in muck and cave moss."

"DharSii, if you do find what you believe to be the final piece in your puzzle, what do you intend to do with it?"

"It depends on what the secret turns out to be. Perhaps it's a weapon of some kind, but I doubt it. Anklemere wrote that, having tamed the dragons, there were no more enemies to fear. He often wrote that he had all this power, but was trapped in a cage no mind, no matter how acute, could open. The sun-shard and the Lavadome and his perspicacitor were his 'key to the cage.' I'm learning to despise metaphor."

Wistala had a hard lump in her gut telling her she'd forgotten something important. She called up every memory of her time as a hatchling in the cave, even mind pictures passed down from her parents. Nothing.

"Were there any other secret spots, perhaps something very inaccessible?"

"The pool? That's where RuGaard used to come in and out. No! The tunnel, I remember the tunnel where Mother had us escape."

She felt her throat close up as she remembered Mother's last, desperate call—*Climb, hatchlings, climb!*

Wistala climbed onto the egg shelf and sure enough, the recess that hid the tunnel was still there, marked only by some water flow. Father would never have been able to get his horned head inside, but he might have been able to feel his way around with snout and tongue. She could use her eyes.

She searched the little chimney.

"Here is a sign, on this loose rock. I think if I put a little light in here you may just be able to make it out." She spat a *torf* of fire on the opposite wall, where it burned, throwing an orange light on the scrapings.

DharSii maneuvered his head as she pointed with her tail. "Yes! The Star of Silverhigh."

It was a simple design, a little unevenly done. Five

sii marks, evenly spaced out, coming together at the center. It reminded Wistala of the Wrimere's old "Circle of Man" emblem, save that it wasn't enclosed in a circle, and there was just the slightest curve to the claw slashes, a little like the Wheel of Fire's standard. Perhaps both the Wheel of Fire emblem and Wrimere's had been modeled on the Silverhigh Star.

"Well done, Wistala," DharSii said. "That's about the right size."

A piece of her thrilled at the compliment. Another part wondered that he only truly became animated when something of interest to him could be found. Whenever DharSii looked at her he just stared at her as though she were an unusual boulder formation.

She nosed around. "Yes, this stone moves. I'll pull it out, I think I can get my tongue awoun' yeeth . . ."

The stone moved. She spat it out.

"Yes! Got it."

"Is there anything in there?" DharSii asked.

"No," Wistala said, her wings and tail sagging. "It's empty. Wait, there's a little bit of—I don't know, moss like dried seaweed in the bottom."

She removed her head from the hole, with something like a brown string clamped in her nostril, and spat out the stone and the remainder out on the egg shelf.

"That might be—"

"Elf hair," Wistala said. Though the leaves were long-shriveled, there was no mistaking elf hair. "I don't remember elves attacking. There were some outside the cave."

AuRon had been caught by elves soon after they saw Father return. He'd said—

"Wait! Hazeleye!" Wistala said. "She was an expert on dragons, spent many years in NooMoahk's cave. I met her. She was very old and frail. I expect she's dead now. Perhaps it's her hair. I always wondered why someone who apparently loved dragons would go along with murder and enslavement."

DharSii drooped. "Another wasted trip," he muttered. "How many just this year?"

"The question is, was the hair an accident, or a token that she'd searched here?" Wistala continued. "Elves often leave a strand of hair as a signal to others. Rainfall used to mark his honeycombs he'd checked, or garden beds he'd planted, or the oldest sack of horse grain with his hair once it began to come back."

She picked the stone up and put it back. That was how Mother and Father had left it; that's how the egg cave would remain. Except for a little bit of stained stone, that star was the only evidence that her family had ever lived in this cave.

It was a good cave. Water and light and air and well out of seasonal changes of temperature. It could be improved, of course.

"What does the Star of Silverhigh signify?" she asked DharSii, to get his mind off another dead end.

"One point for each of the gifts of the Four Spirits," DharSii said. "And a fifth point for the mysterious gift. Our ability to change what we touch."

"How do you mean?"

DharSii wandered around the cave, inspecting. She supposed he was just being thorough. "No member of another race comes away from an encounter with a dragon unchanged. Some hate us forever, others want nothing more than to be around us, observe us, be protected by us, even if it means a lifetime of shoveling up waste and hauling it to the nearest dung heap.

"Of course, I'm sure you've noted the effect of dragon-blood and heard of the strange powers of our dead bones and teeth and so on."

"Yes. When I was in the east I almost ended up as part of someone's medicine supply. Aren't most of those legends, though?" Wistala said.

"Not all. The Tyr himself has been feeding bats dragon-blood for decades. His original strain of rather overlarge, greedy cave-bats has grown into an entirely different species of quasi-bat. NiVom in Ghioz, who's been breeding with more care toward developing certain traits, has created gargolyes almost as large as old Anklemere used to keep."

"I should pay a visit to Ghioz and see what he's up to," Wistala said to herself.

DharSii continued: "We must use that gift wisely, our power to change what we touch. The problem is, destruction is too easy. It has a terrible beauty. A burning tower falls and in one glorious moment, we forget all the effort and care it took to lay the stones for a tower that will even stand up straight."

"Where did we get that gift, I wonder?" Wistala asked.

"Some old songs say the sun gave it to us, so pleased was she with our ability to tame the blighters. Others say the moon snuck it in to ruin us, for once a creature has tasted dragon-blood and enjoyed the benefits, the desire grows in them for more. Around Hypatia much of that lore has been forgotten, but it still exists in the east. That's why there are practically no dragons there, though they figure so strongly into their culture."

He finished his circuit in silence. Wistala waited, lost in memories. "Did anyone else return to the cave?" he finally asked.

"My brother," Wistala said. "I met him here. I gave him that droopy eye, too. Father, too. We tried to warn him but we were too small. He couldn't hear us. He left again, fighting."

"If it was a treasure of your parents, he might have carried it away," DharSii said.

"You don't know our father," Wistala said. "He was in a rage. I don't think he had the presence of mind to look at anything except the bodies of Mother and my sister."

"Still, there's a small chance."

"Very well," Wistala said. "I'll take you to where he died."

She left the cave with small regret and tumultuous feelings. It would be a good place for eggs, if she could ever banish her memories. Once they reached the surface, she guided DharSii north.

The promontory with the old blighter altar was very much as Wistala remembered it, except the obelisk stones with their cryptic old runes no longer loomed quite so high. She re-experienced the ache brought on by the long, long climb down to the rushing white water turning its near-loop around the outcropping in her trips to get water for Father—she even smelled the rank rot of the old driftwood tossed up by floods with dwarfsbeard growing on it.

"This may have been a dragon-throne," DharSii said.

Wistala didn't know what he was talking about, but rather than ask DharSii to explain yet again she just cocked her head.

"Before the founding of Silverhigh, after the dragons had tamed the blighters, they worshiped us. Again, I suspect your parents knew something of the Star Order if he chose this as a place to land and die."

"He had a little help with the dying," Wistala said. "I led hunters right to him. Unwittingly."

"Did he ever mention anything about a crystal?"

"No. Never. I'm sure of it. I hardly knew what the word meant until I saw the crystal ball—wait. Intanta. She had a ball. She claimed it was part of the old sunshard. Why didn't I remember— Oh, I'm a fool!"

DharSii stared hard at her. "You're many things, Wistala, but you're not a fool."

"This Intanta traveled with a circus, it belongs to a dwarf named Brok now—she and her gang of humans never mixed much with the rest. They were—shady, I suppose you would call them. I think they cheated people and stole. But she had this crystal. It was most strange. It helped a woman—Rayg's mother, in fact—with the nausea she suffered while carrying child. It also comforted her during birth."

"I wonder if Rayg knows more than he's saying. He's studying the sun-shard," DharSii said.

"I hardly know him," Wistala said. "I doubt Lada would even recognize him. She's old now, too, worn down with work as a priestess."

"Then this Intanta is surely dead. Do you suppose the crystal is still with the circus?"

"Intanta's people had left when last I met the circus. Her granddaughter, Iatella, inherited it, I believe. She read my fortune with it when she was just a little girl. She told me AuRon was still alive when I thought him dead."

"I wonder how it ended up in the hands of that human? You say they were a strange tribe?"

"I always had the feeling they traveled with the circus, rather than as part of it. They dressed oddly, even for humans. Lots of metallic pieces on their clothing. They sewed layers of coins onto bandannas and belts and such."

"Like they were imitating dragon-scale?"

"Perhaps, I thought they just wanted them to rattle together when they walked."

"Just as Silverhigh still has its loyalists who still keep the faith, so too are the men who served it and later rebelled, passing their traditions on. It appears," DharSii said, "I have a new quarry to hunt. Thank you, Wistala, you've given me hope."

"I should return to the Lavadome. I have promises to keep."

"And oaths that must never be broken," DharSii said, a touch of fire in his voice. "We part for now, Wistala. If you think of anything else, or learn more from Rayg, you can leave a message with Scabia at the Sadda-Vale. Coin is no doubt growing short and I must return with more."

He gave a brief bow to the altar Father had lain bleeding on, spread his wings, and launched himself off the precipice Wistala had fallen down all those years ago. Dogs with teeth had locked into her, tearing at her flesh. DharSii caught an updraft, turned, and swooped over her, gently running the end of his tail down her fringe. With that, he was gone once again.

BOOK THREE

Charity

"THE ONLY SUCCOR A DRAGON GIVES FREELY IS DEATH."

—*From Hazeleye's notes on dragons*

Chapter 15

W istala slept in the luxury of the Tyr's chamber. Her brother was away; she felt she deserved the rich bed of the finest damasks, so tightly woven to the cushioning they were guaranteed not to catch on scale.

Also, there was less of a chance that a messenger would seek her here instead of the Queen's chamber. Nilrasha was a fine dragon, but she had garish tastes; there were far too many skins and interesting bone sculptures of various animals and hominids for Wistala to relax. It was like trying to sleep in an abattoir.

Exhausted from travel, from revived grief in visiting the deathscapes of her parents, and from calls to her attention from NoSohoth so frequent that they invaded her dreams.

The Firemaids and Drakwatch are having a mock battle beneath the griffaran columns you must judge, my Queen. CoTathanagar wishes an audience, he has heard there must be a second messenger for NoFhyriticus in Hypatia and is wondering if the position has been filled yet. There are three new hatchlings in Wyrr Hill you must view. The Tyr's Demen Legion is appointing a new captain and the dwarfs are attacking the Lavadome from the river ring . . .

Dwarfs? Attacking from the river ring?

She opened an eye. Strange roars and calls had broken out from the Audience Chamber.

She rolled out of bed and became tangled in the curtains—curse them, some chamber-thrall must have drawn them; they were open when she'd settled down. She staggered out into the passageway leading to the Audience Chamber, dragging purple material.

Still shaking the cobwebs from her head, she entered the Audience Chamber on the Tyr's platform, a little above the confused throng of thralls, messenger bats, *griffaran*, and dragons.

NoSohoth came through the other door as she entered, looking his usual prim self, every black-tipped scale in place. Did that dragon ever sleep? Or did he just have the ability to instantly transform into wide-awake and arranged.

"I've a Firemaid messenger for you, my Queen," NoSohoth said.

Wistala knew her features, but her name escaped her at the moment. She was a young Firemaid, supervising the Firemaidens in their first real duties. Wingless Firemaidens typically had the easiest posts in which to learn their duties, at the entrances to the La-vadome. The occasional escaping thrall was the big-gest challenge they ever had to face.

"Dwarfs—they came up the Nor'flow. Already across . . . the river ring . . ." she panted.

"Dwarfs!" several in the assembly gasped.

"Wheel of . . . Wheel of Fire! I remember . . . their flag from the . . . pass. Where Takea . . . fell."

Wistala fought with the remains of her brother's curtains. A long way to come for the Wheel of Fire. Even overland, it would be a hard trip. They'd come underground, where three dimensions had to be nego-tiated and obstacles couldn't just be hacked away. They must have used the river.

"Where do we meet them?" NoSohoth asked.

It suddenly occurred to Wistala that as leader of the Firemaids and as Queen-Consort she must direct the defense. Battles were dreadful, detestable things, but how much more dreadful was defeat?

The responsibility fell on her like a net. She was oathed as a Firemaid to protect the hatchlings of the Lavadome and as Queen-Consort to be at the forefront in defending the dragon-realm. *Master your emotions, Wistala!* she heard Rainfall say. *Confidence flows downhill like water.*

They might have an hour, especially if there was fighting in the tunnels leading from the river ring. There was always a Firemaid or two on guard at the tunnels. If they could hold the tunnel mouths, the La-vadome would be secure.

Even if the dwarfs made it to the tunnel mouths, the Lavadome was huge. It would be hours before they could reach Imperial Rock on foot, even trotting.

Only dragons could make it there that quickly.

"Send word to all the hills—evacuate, back to Imperial Rock. Leave home and hoard to the enemy, we must unite here and win or be cut to pieces in parts," she told NoSohoth.

She sent another dragon to alert the Drakwatch, some thralls to drive cattle into Imperial Rock in case the dwarfs besieged it, and a drake to Ankelene Hill to warn them to shut and bar the mighty portals at the entrance to their hill.

SiHazathant and Regalia arrived together, as always. No sense separating them.

"You two, go to the Aerial Host. I know most of it is in the Upper World, but there are a few sick, and He-Bellereth is somewhere. He just gave a report yesterday. Send whatever they can to the river ring holes on the north side, try to hold the dwarfs there."

NoSohoth was still standing around, stupefied. "Didn't I tell you to evacuate the hills."

"Yes, Queen-Consort. But—well, this hasn't happened in an age. They won't like leaving their hills. There are eggs—"

"They'll have to be brought here. Fly the eggs here, bring extra carriers, put them in carry baskets like wounded drakes."

She suddenly remembered the name of the Firemaid messenger. "You, Aruthia, go to the Firemaid hill. Get everyone you can, have them go to the other hills and gather eggs and hatchlings and bring them to the Imperial Rock. They should trust the Firemaids."

"The Ankelenes won't leave their hill, too many valuable records there," NoSohoth said.

"I'll send them the Tyr's demen legion. They should be able to hold Ankelene Hill, even against dwarfs. They have those great decorative gates, now's the time to test them. We can aid them from Imperial Rock. The dwarfs might not know how big the Lavadome is, how high we can fly. I know I never imagined . . . well, get going."

She didn't know as much as she should about dwarf-fighting. Actually, it wasn't so much the dwarfs you fought as their infernal machines. Obviously they'd used some kind of contraption to move south against the hard-flowing current of the Nor'flow.

The only other thing she knew was that dwarfs were much better on the defense than the attack. Her father always told her that chasing down dwarfs in a tunnel was the most dangerous hunt a dragon could overtake. They could look like rocks until they leaped out of concealment, swinging an ax for your throat.

But get them in the open, and they're not so hard to squash.

Oh, Father! I thought I was done with the Wheel of Fire. Do feuds never cease?

Wistala gave more orders for any of the young dragonriders in the Aerial Host, plus such of their women as wanted to take up arms, to be readied to defend the lower galleries and windows in the Imperial Rock.

Then she went up to the top level. From there she could see and direct the defense of the Lavadome.

She learned she was fortunate in one matter. He-Bellereth and two of his dragons of the Aerial Host had returned to the Lavadome with small injuries from their brushes with pirates on the Sunstruck Sea. She saw Ayafeeia whispering to him.

"If there's going to be a battle, Wistala, you should be properly suited. We must have you looking the part," HeBellereth said.

"What do you mean?" Wistala asked.

"Follow me, my Queen," Ayafeeia said. "We still have a moment to prepare, and the engagement in the tunnels is not yet decided. Let's hope it's all for nothing, and the Firemaids hold them."

"I'd rather help at the tunnels."

HeBellereth was breathing hard, twitching to get into battle. "You're the Queen. Your place is here. Ayafeeia, see to your Queen. I'll go and reinforce the tunnels to the river ring."

With that, he rushed to the gardens and launched himself into the red light of the Lavadome.

Ayafeeia led her down to a chamber beneath the old Imperial Residence. Wistala had only visited it once before. It was a storehouse for gifts from the upholds, trophies taken in war, first lost scale of Imperial Line hatchlings—that sort of thing. Within the cramped chamber were a number of barred cages holding the most valuable items.

Veeeeee—Ayafeeia whistled through a nostril for thralls, and some fat old servants of the line appeared.

"The Tyr's armor," Ayafeeia ordered.

The thralls pointed and Ayafeeia nosed open a barred stall. In it were gleaming pieces of dragon-armor.

"Most dragons don't like armor in battle—we have scale and the additional weight slows you down. Besides, you can't fly with this heavy plate. It was built for FeHazathant but I believe you'll fit in it, with your framing and musculature."

The thralls and Ayafeeia extracted the pieces. Someone had kept it polished and oiled the leather straps. It was beautifully arranged and decorated; perhaps some dwarf had helped fashion it.

They put it on. Wearing something against the scale felt odd to Wistala. She felt herself a prisoner of the armor. But it did cover her head, chest, hearts, and flanks admirably—though her crest was squashed.

"I don't know," Wistala said. "It's supposed to be for the Tyr."

"You're Queen-Consort, and the Lavadome is under attack. You want dragons to see you, don't you?"

"Not being able to fly makes sure of your courage," Wistala said. "Your leader can't fly away when he's wearing this."

Ayafeeia snorted. "She's wearing this. You look good in it, Queen-Consort Wistala. Let's not delay, now that you're dressed for the party, go up and see and be seen."

Party. Wistala stifled a snort. Ayafeeia avoided the socializing Imperial Line, despite being of Tyr Fehazathant's line. The only parties she had a taste for were battles.

Wistala made a light clattering sound as she walked wearing the armor *ching-ching-ching-ching*—the sound reminded her of coin rattling in a purse.

She went to the top of Imperial Rock, reflecting light from the polished armor on the passageways around her.

"Your orders, my Queen," Ayafeeia asked.

"You know more about warfare than I do. Should we fight them in the hills, or concentrate on defending Imperial Rock?"

"We're better off staying mobile, striking and flying again. If you stay in one place, they use war machines on you. Spirits, are they in the Lavadome already?"

Wistala saw one of the Aerial Host flying in loops at the edge of the Lavadome, above the north passageway down to the river ring.

Dragons, drakes and drakka, many carrying eggs or with hatchlings riding on their backs, streamed toward Imperial Rock. The Drakwatch, guarding the entrances, urged them on.

The dwarfs came in waves. Wistala had to admire the precision of the attack.

War machines fired clusters of sparking missiles into the air at the flying dragons. They spread as they rose, like dandelion seeds blown by a strong wind. A Firemaid dove, dropping fire, and a fountain of sparks shot up around her. She rolled over and fell.

Flying wildly, the last of the Aerial Host she'd sent to defend the holes swooped left and right, avoiding the fireworks.

It wasn't HeBellereth.

HeBellereth fallen, the Lavadome overrun—and I'm responsible, Wistala thought.

The dwarfs, in open ranks, formed a crescent around Imperial Rock. From the height, they reminded Wistala of ants among the beetles of their war machines.

They'd taken captives. Thralls mostly, but also a few drakes and drakka. They had them bound, carried on poles, heavy axmen to either side.

"Parley!" a great fat dwarf with a booming voice shouted. His beard glowed redly.

Wistala and a few others cautiously looked over the edge of the gardens. Parley, when by appearances they were charging toward victory.

But appearances could be deceiving. Wistala was reminded of her first battle with the Firemaids, when a last, suicidal charge by starving demen had been turned back in the Star Tunnel by a few disciplined dragonelles and drakka. These Wheel of Fire dwarves had a ragged air about them, their shields and helmets were patched and dinged, and hardly a beard among them glowed. Only a dwarf who'd suffered a prolonged period of poverty let his beard go dark, without even sugar-water to keep the lichens they cultivated in their thick beards thriving.

Was this attack also a last, desperate gasp of a dying nation?

"We come only for Wistala, who betrayed our king to his death. Give her to us, and we release the captives!"

That may be, but bearer-dwarfs and slave blighters hammered and notched together war machines just behind the first rank of fighters.

"Give us Wistala!" a chorus of dwarfs called.

"Wistala! Wistala!" they chanted. One of the war machines fired a helmet full of burning coals that exploded when they struck Imperial Rock.

"Do it," a court dragon named CuRemon urged. "All they want is you. Trade your life for all of ours."

"You think the dwarfs would stop with me?" Wistala asked.

"We'd only be one dragon less in finding out," a drakka said.

"Stop that, now," NoSohoth said. He turned to Wistala. "Don't listen to them. The Tyr doesn't negotiate with invaders—unless it's terms of their surrender."

The dwarf crescent was spreading. And thinning.

She tried to pick out detail on the dwarfs but had only a vague impression of heavy armor and beards. They moved deliberately, trotting, but they must have been very tired. What faces they could see were thin and haggard.

They'd come a long way, quickly, fighting hard against the current, and then they'd battled their way into the Lavadome. Dwarfs were famously indefatigable, but if she could break up their attack somehow—

"NoSohoth, I'll lead the demen in an attack on their left. When we engage, have the Drakwatch attack."

"But that'll leave no one to defend—" CuRemon sputtered.

"No one? The Imperial Rock is full of dragons, Wyrr, Skotl, and Ankelene. They'll have to fight for once. Even dead, some of them are so fat they'll plug up the entrance until the dwarfs drag them out."

"You hear me," she told the spectators atop Imperial Rock. "You look like dragons and speak like them. Let's see you fight like them, for once in your pampered lives!"

They grumbled, but a few made for the passageway down. Odd that they were more outraged at the Queen-Consort upbraiding them than a band of invading dwarves wrecking as they came. Maybe her parents had a point—if the tales about their origins were true. Dragons shouldn't allow themselves to get too civilized.

Hurrying to the other side of the Lavadome, she spread her wings and—

"Wistala, don't, it's too heavy!" NoSohoth shouted.

Remarkably, her wings didn't fold on her. Of course, she always had been a strong dragon. She glided down toward the Ankelene pyramid. She tried a few experimental beats—she might be able to hold herself up, even in the Tyr's armor.

The Tyr's demen legion were arrayed around the Ankelene Pyramid, defending the archives and workshops and healing nooks.

She called on the demen to gather.

"This is the day, demen legion," Wistala said. "The enemies of your blood stand before you!"

"Yes, the dwarfs, who slaughtered your females and children in battle after battle." Wistala knew little dwarf/demen history, only that their wars were long and bloody, with entire communities slaughtered in raid and counter-raid. Life was as hard as stone in the Lower World.

The demen started up an eerie hissing that wasn't quite a whistle, and clacked their spines together. On a demen it was hard to tell where limb and carapace ended and armor and weapons began. Wistala thought it sounded like a swarm of insects.

"We fight, we drink blood?" their general asked.

What had started as a victorious drink of blood every now and then had grown into a need terrible and desperate. Wistala wondered how they'd ever sate their appetites after a battle again. The idea was to lose less dragons, not more.

"You can drink from my own veins," Wistala said. "Form for an attack!"

LaDibar and a few other Ankelenes stood at the top of the stairs leading to their hill. "If you take the Tyr's legion, who—"

"Arm your thralls and make your own flame," Wistala ordered. What had happened to dragons over the years in the Lavadome?

"Follow me," she said, trotting around to the west side of Imperial Rock. Instinctively, she flapped her wings and the next thing she knew, she was aloft.

Perhaps a heavier male dragon couldn't fly with the Tyr's traditional battle armor on, but she could. Hard flying with the armor—it cut the wind and made it harder to push through the air with the proper lift.

She circled back and the demen cheered.

A knot of dwarf-warriors, coming around to encircle Imperial Rock, saw the oncoming demen. She couldn't read their expressions, but they were clearly shocked to see demen formed up and ready to fight for the Lavadome.

One of them raised a metallic tube, with smaller vessels and cylinders attached, capped with a bellows-like structure.

Wistala couldn't identify it and certainly didn't wish to see its effects. She folded her wings and dropped, spitting fire that fell only a little faster than she did. Her nostrils were well-scorched by her own flame.

The war machine sparked and sputtered as it burned, shooting thin projectiles in all directions.

The dwarfs fell into a defensive line and the demen washed over them like an incoming wave. The first demen in line locked limbs onto the dwarfs' shields, the second braced himself low to keep the others from being shoved forward or pulled back, and the third ran up and over the backs of the second and first ranks.

The dwarf line disappeared under a carpet of demen as they rushed up and over. The dwarfs fell back.

A dwarf-leader called on his signalman to wave a banner. Wistala swooped down and struck hard with her tail, sending both rolling and cracking like a pair of dropped melons.

White sparking streaks surrounded her and Wistala felt a stabbing pain. Her wings were holed in a dozen places. She came to earth in a mushroom field, sending the growths up in a shower of fertilizer.

She'd been struck by nine or ten shafts like heavy crossbow bolts. They stank of sulfur. Luckily none caught her under the throat or in her wing joints. Three pierced her chest armor and ground a claw's width into her scale. If it weren't for the Tyr's armor—

Dwarfs charged from three directions, axes and spears aiming.

Still stunned from her hard landing, she reacted more slowly than she should have. She lashed out, put a wall of flame in front of two. They came through anyway, ignoring the pain of burns, and buried their weapons in her flanks.

She struck back with tooth and claw, smelling blood, sending her opponents into the next life in pieces.

Her vision red, roaring and fighting, she saw the dwarfs setting up a larger war machine, something shaped like two crossbows stacked atop each other.

The war machine disappeared, immolated by twin streams of dragon fire.

SiHazathant and Regalia came around in a tight turn, riding each other's air.

"Now, Firemaids! For Tyr and home-cave!" Regalia cried, leading her brother in for another pass.

Later, Wistala was told that while the demen struck

the dwarfs' right, the Firemaids struck from behind. The remaining dwarfs shifted to support their center, and that's when the Drakwatch advanced, advancing behind and through their own flame.

Wistala's perception was correct: the dwarfs were exhausted; the attack was a last desperate gamble to avenge themselves on a dragon who'd humilated them twice. According to dwarfen legend, the Lavadome was beard-deep in gold ingots and stolen jewels, but there's no accounting for folklore.

AuRon's son AuMoahk, who was studying remedies and medicines under the Ankelenes, sniffed at her armor and wounds. "We should put some salve on your nostril burns. In the Aerial Host those are called 'warrings.'"

"It wasn't the fight they were after so much; it was all that dead dragonflesh on the ground," old Rethothanna said. "Look at 'em go."

Wistala thought his legion looked like ants stripping the corpse of some small lizard.

The Ankelenes and Rayg took great interest in the detritus of battle. They examined the tree-trunk-like boats, driven by ingenious underwater wings that revolved and steered by fans that allowed them to come up against the flow of the great underground river.

"HeBellereth still lives!" a white-eyed member of the Drakwatch squeaked.

"Did I win you enough time?" HeBellereth asked.

He was in ruins. Scale riven in too many places to count, a small lake of his own blood surrounding him.

He'd used his wings to shield his throat from ax blows. They were as broken as felled trees and in tatters. He'd no more fly again than Nilrasha would. He'd also lost over half his tail. It lay farther down the tunnel like a beheaded snake.

Wistala managed to find a few words to answer. "Yes, you did, great dragon. Your deeds will become legend in the Lavadome and the Upper World."

"Glorious," HeBellereth said. "Those dwarfs really put up a fight. I'm ready . . . for a good long nap."

HeBellereth shook his head. Wistala realized he was trying to raise his neck but was unable. "You'll need to replace me. My slipwing, BaMelphistran, is a good dragon—assuming some pirate arrow hasn't killed him, that is. In his place I'd put young FePazathon, he's a cool head for a Skotl. Oh, and a new messenger, I suppose. That young AuMoahk might do. He's bright as an Ankelene, and eager. He carries Gunfer into battle and they're fast friends."

Wistala wondered. AuRon wasn't overly happy with his family becoming entwined in the tendrils of Lavadome politics. To put one of AuRon's on the path to leadership of the Aerial Host should make him proud, but . . .

Demen had fallen to their knees and were lapping up blood with eager hoots and whistle calls. Others gathered, drawn like ants to honey. One clacked his jaws and approached HeBellereth's severed tail.

"You'll keep away!" Wistala roared at the gathering demen.

They backed away from her fury. Wistala almost spat fire at them—but then her empty firebladder only produced a rather thin, smelly liquid and the effect would be more comical than intimidating.

HeBellereth was a tough old dragon, and incredibly, he didn't die. But he lay in the tunnel he'd defended with his blood for days with support flowing from two directions, being brought water from the river ring and food from the Lavadome. An honor guard of the Drakwatch stood there at all times, listening to his breathing and licking out his wounds.

When he took his first halting steps to drag himself out of the tunnel, Wistala confirmed his orders in the Tyr's name for the new arrangement in the Aerial Host at a celebratory feast of fresh beef and pickled dwarf hands and feet. He could hardly deny the new position for AuMoahk out of vague suspicion. Apparently the young drake had distinguished himself adventuring on the Sunstruck Sea with his rider, so it would be doubly strange to not recognize achievement.

She watched NoSohoth paint new *laudi* and messenger insignia on the youngster.

However AuRon might feel about it, Wistala's brother's offspring were doing well in the Grand Alliance. Perhaps too well for their own good. Already there were whispers that the Copper was starting his own line to supplant the old and venerable Imperial Line.

* * *

AuRon looked forward to an evening with nothing more serious on his mind than deciding whether to have leftover mutton or fresh chicken for his evening meal.

Dairuss sweated under the late spring sun. Sheep were being shorn, rows of crops planted, the winter's craft goods and woodwork were being hauled to the markets and boat landings for sale or transport, and Hypatian salt was cheaper than at any time in living memory.

Until their white-scaled neighbor decided to drop in. AuRon watched NiVom circle his resort, now with a comfortable wooden outside sleeping area added so he and Natasatch could sun themselves as they napped.

NiVom landed, dancing on *sii* and *saa* with impatience.

"AuRon, I've just heard some news. There's been a catastrophic attack on the Lavadome. Dwarfs, I believe. Dozens are dead, especially among the drakes and drakka. Our Tyr has failed us, with tragic results, and we must act. Will you fly with me?"

"I'll fly with you anywhere, NiVom, but if it's to fight against my brother—I won't do it."

"Dearest, we've spoken about this," Natasatch said. "I've told Imfamnia we're with them. You have our support, NiVom, if the other Protectors believe another Tyr could do better."

AuRon stiffened. How much of this was playacting, how much was real? Well, they'd take their roles. "My mate has her own mind about politics, as you see."

"Well, AuRon, you're still welcome to come, either way. I've asked some other Protectors to meet in the Lavadome. Perhaps you can talk some sense into Tyr RuGaard."

"You mean to attend to matters in the Lavadome, or use his sense to relinquish the throne?"

NiVom sniffed the wind. "The fastest way may be to fly straight to the south entrance. I can't predict what the other Protectors will say, but many have told me privately they believe it's time for a change. With luck, there'll be no fighting. Too many Tyrs have fallen in a bloodbath. I'd like this to be different. Spilled blood always leads to bad blood."

Fine fellow, that NiVom, AuRon thought. According to Imfamnia, he'd been intended to be Tyr at some point, but other, ambitious dragons had fomented a plot against him. Perhaps he should have been Tyr. Why the Spirits put the burden on his brother's uneven shoulders he never knew.

The choice of mutton or chicken would have to be left with Natasatch.

"Farewell, my love. Do your best for King Naf until I return."

"I would tell you to be careful, my love, but I know you. You'll take the safest road again. I hope it leads you back to our door."

Chapter 16

Wistala had all manner of important news to relay to her brother.

First she had to track him down.

At the Lavadome they told her he'd gone to see Nilrasha in her eyrie. Nilrasha said she'd just missed him; he'd visited for a few days to forget his worries, but then had gone up to see NoFhyriticus in Hypat.

Wearily, Wistala flew north, glad that she enjoyed the exercise of flight.

The Tyr's banner was flying over NoFhyriticus's resort in Hypat. At last!

Hypatian workmen were still building it, of course, though in size, if not in height, it now equaled the Directory. All this for one dragon!

It resembled four pyramids joined by long, column-filled walkways wide enough for two dragons. In the center was a vast courtyard, open to the sky, with a feeding pit leading down to the kitchens. Each pyramid housed a sleeping chamber for a dragon or two, and bedchambers and workrooms for servants. Terraced gardens built from bricks of destroyed structures from the Red Queen's siege of Hypat surrounded the resort. The gardens were fed by two vast pools, probably both freshwater, judging from the plants lining the rims.

The lushness of the gardens let her guess where the servants spread the dragon-waste. No need for mushroom and low-light tubers to feed livestock here.

She was greeted by a young drake who served as NoFhyriticus's assistant. As he bade her inside to Tyr and Protector, thralls announced her presence.

Rich curtains adorned the walls of NoFhyriticus's resort, polished lamps threw light on scrubbed floors. Pools filled with fragrant flowers added their notes to the heavier dragon smells.

"Ah, my Queen-Consort," the Copper said. "You're just in time for dinner."

"Your resort is coming along splendidly, NoFhyriticus," Wistala said, trying to find polite words as he showed her around. They could use some of this stone in the north to build watchtowers against the barbarians, or on the proposed wall to cover the Iwensi Gap where the Falngese turned west to flow into the Inland Ocean.

"It serves its purpose," NoFhyriticus said. His gray

skin was painted in elegant Hypatian designs, his claws painted like a Hypatian Directory banner. "The Hypatians always come away impressed. It projects an air of stability and permanence."

It projects an air of indulgence, Wistala thought. And close-packed humans. How many servants had he picked up over the years?

Thralls, thralls, thralls. Thralls to part curtains, thralls to light and extinguish flames so they traveled on an ever-unrolling carpet of flickering light, and an entire train of thralls each carrying three fat cushions atop their heads, so when they finally sat down and rested they did so with joints, head, and tail protected from contact with harsh flooring by combed sheepskin and thick coconut matting.

"Many mouths to feed," Wistala remarked.

"What, am I hosting more than my Tyr and Queen-Consort tonight?"

"No, I meant your servants."

"How do the Hypatians feel about you keeping so many thralls here?" the Copper asked. "You must have the population of a town."

"Oh, I am bringing in a few gardeners and such to help with the feast, seeing as we have visitors of distinction. Usually I'm only attended by a dozen or so."

NoFhyriticus discussed matters in Hypat intelligently enough as they dined. He was even aware of trouble in the north from the barbarians and recent Ironrider raids on Wallander, though King Naf of Dairuss and his Protectors had driven them off.

Ripe young human females dressed in the sheerest of fabrics began a vigorous dance to a band of musicians playing in a high alcove. Once hot and puffing, they reached for elegantly shaped vases and began pouring warm streams of oil on each other's bodies as they moved. The smell of the runoff filled the room.

"The dance is entertaining enough—you can't fault these humans for their flexibility, but the sweat on their adornments and in the oils makes for a pleasant atmosphere."

"I'm sure you can afford the best dancers in Hypatia."

"Only when my Tyr visits. Otherwise I enjoy the simple life." He let out a long belch.

"Where did you get all this coin?"

"The Ironriders attacked another caravan, and that young dragonelle Protector of yours, oh, in those mountains with the blighters—Ulam, no, Uldam is it?"

"Istach," the Copper said, growing animated. "I expect great things from Uldam. It's rich in cattle. It will make a good bulwark against the eastern kingdoms and the principalities on the Sunstruck Sea."

"Well, for now she did a fine job chasing the Ironriders away. The merchant prince of the Silkway gave me a partial share of the proceeds in thanks. Silks are much in demand with all the wealthier daughters of Hypatia, and the summer festival season is coming up. He had some never-before-seen colors that commanded fantastic prices."

"That's humans for you," the Copper said, taking another tongueful of gold. "Wasting their gold on frippery. They should buy a few more sword-arms to see off the Ironriders, rather than dressing their daughters like market dancers."

"We can't just have our Protectors taking what they want," Wistala said. "It causes resentment."

"Wistala," the Copper said, "the more the Hypatians prosper, the more we will. Their achievements of late are largely thanks to the dragon half of the grand alliance."

"Still, we should be modest in what we consider our due," Wistala said.

The Copper waved away another platter of food. Wistala thought the bearers looked underfed: What cruelty it must be to carry such a weight of meat with your own belly empty. "We have to give them a generation to get used to us. Maybe two generations. What is that, thirty summers up there, or thirty-five?"

"About that, my Tyr," NoFhyriticus said. "Yes, Hypatia is growing rich again. The Princedoms of the Sunstruck Sea are sending their sons to Hypatia to learn at its libraries. Its fishing and trading fleets sail the Inland Ocean uncontested—and if that great canal ever gets cut, they'll reach the wild western sea. Hypatian halls supporting Hypatian couriers and Knights of the Directory could be built even in the far north again, if you'd encourage it. You've inaugurated a blessed age."

"It's important that the Hypatians thrive," the Copper said. "They need to know their position in the world depends on dragons. Thanks to dragons Hypatian messages travel faster than their enemies, their armies can reach farther, their wrath felt even in the great east, if it should come to that. They will grow dependent on us, and eventually we'll have a vast nation of thralls to do our bidding."

Wistala would have dropped a scale in shock.

"But what about all this talk of the Grand Alliance. Allies should be equals," Wistala said.

NoFhyriticus chuckled. "You told me your sister was fond of the hominids, but I had no idea. Wistala, smell the facts: No two allies were ever equal. Sun and moon, horse and rider, frog and lily pad—each may benefit from the association, but there's no equality to it. Hominids must remain below dragons, or we'll just begin to dwindle again. We can't outbreed them, and outwitting them by hiding only works for so long. We must groom a few of them to exist only at our sufferance, like the Tyr's legion or his bats."

The Copper sipped a little wine. "We'll start small, of course. Ceremonial tributes are already common. Soon we'll start asking for regular fees from the great merchant houses. The ones who pay will enjoy our protection and see their non-Hypatian rivals pillaged. The ones who don't pay—well, ships may be lost to mysterious circumstances, or caravans will find their dragon-protection suddenly called away in the middle of the Ironriders Sweep. Capricious fate will teach them the caution of buying our close assistance.

"Before long only those who pay the Dragon's Levy will see success. Once we have them used to paying levies, we can then see some of that wealth diverted to the Lavadome and the Protector's resorts."

"It seems more than enough has already gone into this resort. Greed kills, NoFhyriticus. Well, if this is the future you have in mind, I want no part of it," Wistala said, bristling.

"Wistala, settle down," NoFhyriticus said. "After dinner we're to see some new trade goods brought over from the western side of the Inland Ocean. The humans there have discovered rich new quantities of gold and gemstones."

The announcement thralls began voicing a new arrival. Yefkoa of the Firemaids came in, following the tail of the Protector's assistant.

It appeared after-dinner plans would have to wait.

"My Tyr," she panted—Wistala thought that Yefkoa always flew as hard as she could to maintain her reputation. "Ayafeeia bids me tell you that NiVom's come into the Lavadome. AuRon is with him. He's been meeting with the leaders of the seven hills and been to Imperial Rock. She fears something is amiss."

Chapter 17

The Copper, flying hard across the Lavadome with Shadowcatch and Wistala behind, had no idea which way he'd jump until he landed.

They arrived late, with the Lavadome asleep and the oval at the peak of the dome dark. Perhaps it was his overactive imagination, but the Lavadome seemed hushed, holding its breath. Usually a young dragon or two was up flying.

On the one *sii*, if Ayafeeia and Yefkoa were telling the truth, he'd just put his mate's life in jeopardy. But the Copper wondered if his brother could be playing some sort of deep game, trying to sow division between the Tyr and his Protectors. Or make him look like a paranoid fool.

He hoped it wouldn't come to fighting. First, he'd

assemble the Aerial Host. Then he'd replace a few of his Protectors with loyal members of the Host.

He found himself hoping his brother was as nefarious as he thought him. He wouldn't mind settling things once and for all with the Gray Rat.

"Come with me, you two," he said. "By the spirits, I hope you're wrong."

Wistala and Shadowcatch followed behind as he wobbled his way toward the Tyr's hall. He descended into Imperial Rock.

The Griffaran Guard, who should have been waiting above the Tyr's door, was absent.

"NoSohoth!" he called as he went inside. "Where is everyone?" Even CoThathanagar, who was always lurking about, looking for a new commission for a friend or relative, had vanished.

He found NoSohoth in the throne room. NiVom, his scales shining white, stood under four *griffaran* with several of the court dragons, including LaDibar of the Ankelenes, BaMelphistran of the Aerial Host, and a couple of the Skotl and Wyrr patriarchs. His brother stood a ways apart, warily eyeing the *griffaran*. A few of NiVom's dreadful gargoyles occupied a Griffaran Guard perch as well, clinging to each other with claws and wing hooks in an ugly ball.

"I represent an alliance of my own," NiVom said. "There are some dozen of us, Protectors all, who believe your rule has grown rather—erratic of late. There's a rumor going around that you mean to groom AuRon's daughter Istach to take your place. We won't have it. Many of the dragons left in the Lavadome agree."

"We'll see. Call the Aerial Host," the Copper ordered.

BaMelphistran stood still.

"You just lost your leadership and your good name, NoSohoth! Send for AuSurath."

No messenger moved. The Griffaran Guard stood still, without an actual attack on the Tyr's life requiring action, they had no reason to become a part of the conflict.

The Copper felt a brief dizziness, as though the polished stone beneath his feet had suddenly fallen away and he was suspended in space. He lashed his tail to keep from fainting.

"It's already too late," NiVom said.

"Meaning?" the Copper asked.

"We've just recognized a new Tyr."

Behind him, the Copper heard Shadowcatch's teeth grinding louder than ever.

"You, I suppose," Wistala said.

"No, I've no ambition to sit atop Imperial Rock. The twins, SiHazathant and Regalia. They're handsome, popular, and performed heroically during the Wheel of Fire attack. Best of all, they're of Tyr FeHazathant's blood. They're consulting with Ibidio now on which Protectors are backing them. Most of them are."

"Even Istach of Old Uldam?" the Copper asked.

"Yes."

Well, *it's the smart move*, the Copper thought. *Istach would do the smart thing.*

"What about you, brother?" the Copper asked Au-Ron.

His brother looked from the NiVom's group of dragons to the Copper's.

"To tell the truth," AuRon said, "I'm indifferent to who sits on top of this dank rock. But I don't care for how this is being done—threats of bloodshed, meetings in the dead of night, everyone waking to find a new Tyr in place. Even my barbarian tribal neighbors in the north would call it rotten. Suppose we gathered all the dragons of the Alliance and put it to them?"

"That sort of thing was tried before, in the age of Silverhigh," LaDibar said. "The dragons just selected whichever demagogue promised them the most coin for their gold-gizzards."

"Most of the dragons in the Lavadome can't be trusted with their own waste," NoSohoth said. "It's up to the leaders to decide, dragons with responsibility and foresight."

"You, too, NoSohoth?" the Copper asked.

"I am not following one faction or the other, Ru-Gaard. I've always served whomever is named Tyr, to the best of my ability."

AuRon snorted, then ambled over to stand beside his sister, behind the Copper.

"I'm with you, my Tyr," he said.

"We can't do this again," an elderly Wyrr leader behind NiVom said. "Civil war. I lived through one, just in my youth. Smashed eggs, bodies strewn across the hills, starvation. It's horrible. Spare us that, RuGaard.

You'll be remembered as one of the great Tyrs who knew when to step aside."

NiVom stepped forward. "It's up to you, RuGaard."

"Why are you pressing for this, NiVom? I thought you wanted to be Tyr."

"We've worked out a new structure for the Dragon Empire. The Tyr is to remain in the Lavadome, the heart of the Empire. I'll take charge of the Protectors in the Upper World. Right now the Protectors are badly coordinated, each is acting for his own interests and those of his lands, rather than for the Empire as a whole. That's going to stop. I say again, what will it be? Civil war? You'll have the weaker side."

"I'll have the Firemaids," the Copper said. "Ayafeeia warned me of this plot."

"The Aerial Host will side with the twins," BaMelphistran said.

"Then there's an alternative?"

"I'll give you the same one you gave me, all those years ago. Flight. Leave the limits of the Dragon Empire and never return, or you'll forfeit your life."

"Then try to kill me and be done with it," the Copper said. "I'm not leaving my dragons. I know there are some still loyal to me."

"Not only will your life be forfeited, but so will your mate's."

"Nilrasha! She's not a threat to anyone. She plays a part in no faction."

"Save your dwindling one."

"I'll stand by him."

AuRon could never say why he spoke up thus. Years later, when asked, he simply replied that the words were out before he knew he had said them.

SiHazathant and Regalia entered the Audience Chamber from the Tyr's door. A more perfectly matched set of dragons would be hard to imagine—their red and green became deeper and more brilliant the closer they stood.

"All hail, Tyr SiHazathant and Queen Regalia," NoSohoth said.

NiVom's faction roared, the Copper's stayed silent and still.

"I'm glad to see you here, RuGaard," SiHazathant said.

"We've no wish to be enemies," Regalia added. "You've done great things for dragonkind. But your hearts and mind are only half in the Lavadome. Your care for your mate does you honor, but a Tyr must devote himself to all dragons, not just one."

"Will you recognize me as your Tyr, RuGaard?" SiHazathant said, getting to the point in the manner of old FeHazathant.

"I will not fight you," the Copper said, tiredly. "Just let me return to Nilrasha. She deserves better than this. She sacrificed her wings for our cause."

"So it is to be exile," Regalia said. "Very well, go in peace. Who goes with you?"

"And I," said AuRon.

"But your mate—" SiHazathant said, looking at NiVom in doubt.

"Natasatch is one of the Protectors backing you," NiVom said. "She wishes to remain in her position as Protector."

"It will be a bitter exile for both of you, AuRon," NoSohoth said.

"Natasatch is perfectly capable of acting as Protector of Dairuss. Perhaps better, for she's an armored dragon. One well-placed Ironrider arrow would slay me."

"We'll allow her to visit you on your island now and again," NiVom said. "But if you insist on not recognizing SiHazathant as Tyr, you must not be allowed to return to the Empire.

"My Tyr must have his bodyguard," Shadowcatch said, heavily. But then he did everything heavily. "I shall follow Tyr RuGaard wherever he goes."

"I will go with Tyr RuGaard as well," Wistala said.

For the first time, NiVom looked doubtful. "You're leaving as well, Wistala?"

"I'm his Queen-Consort."

"That's an informal tradition. There's no need for you to leave."

"Other than the duty I owe my brother. I abandoned him to his fate once. I won't do it again."

"Very well. The banishment applies to you, as well, then."

"I am a Hypatian citizen by position," Wistala said. "I'm not sure you can banish me from Hypatia. But I take it I am free of my oaths to the Firemaids?" Wistala asked.

"That is for you to resolve with your conscience."

"I'll not wait here," the Copper said. "I hope you enjoy a quieter reign than I did, SiHazathant."

"Thank you, RuGaard. BaMelphistran, see to it that he leaves in safety and security, and is supplied with whatever he wants that will aid him on his journey. Do this if you value your position as head of the Aerial Host."

The Copper took one last look at the Audience Chamber, full of banners won in victories. He'd been at many of those battles. He'd miss the clucks and squawks of *griffaran* over him.

"Why did you join me?" he asked AuRon as they returned to the plaza atop the Imperial Rock to take off.

AuRon blinked. "It's one way out of your crossbreeding of human and dragon society. I now have an excellent excuse never to return."

"What about your mate?"

AuRon shifted his feet, as though trying to decide what to say. "She has a tooth for this sort of life. It's not for me. She thinks of the Alliance as her home, not my island."

"It looks like your island will have to do for me. And Nilrasha, though she'll have to make the journey on foot. If you'll have us, that is."

"You may find it quiet, after the Lavadome."

"I should very much like a little quiet. Let's get a mouthful before we take off. I want to get to my mate's cave before the news of this reaches her."

Chapter 18

To the Copper, AuRon was entirely too cheerful about leaving the Lavadome.

NiVom, with his gargoyle escort, relished watching him fly into ignominity, flapping along with the artificial joint doing its job—just.

They took the swiftest exit they could, the south door, even if it meant a longer flight north to Nilrasha's eyrie.

The lands they flew over, the rough terrain south of Ghioz, made for poor eating. Nothing but thorn and cactus and foul mudholes. Game was scarce and the journey slow until they reached the Horsedowns.

Men here were scarce, tribal, and what there were more or less worshipped the dragons. They happily let the dragons eat horses and ponies.

Their escort fed themselves on wild horses, and allowed the exiles only their scraps. AuSurath proved his loyalty to the Lavadome by only giving them what dragons usually considered offal.

While AuRon was too proud to ask his son for more, Wistala was under no such obligation to go. "You expect us to fly on gristle and hooves, nephew?" Wistala asked.

"The loss of a few pounds will do you good," AuSurath replied.

Finally Shadowcatch, irritable because of all the flying, ambled over and picked up a horse half and glared at their escort, daring them to do anything about it. The Copper ate a few bits as a polite thank-you, but had no appetite. Even the juicy horse tasted like ash.

Nilrasha's eyrie no longer looked picturesque and cozy. If anything, it seemed horribly remote and lonely. Anything could happen to his mate here, far from witnesses.

She had a visitor, although it wasn't one of her favorites. Old Ibidio, mother to Halaflora and Imfamnia and Ayafeeia, leader of the Firemaids. The old battle-ax never thought the Copper and Nilrasha were worthy to dwell in Imperial Rock, let alone preside over it.

Nilrasha looked worried and haggard. Entertaining Ibidio for who knows how long had taken its toll. Did she know?

"My love, you arrive with quite a procession. I don't think my refuge will hold them all," Nilrasha said.

NiVom had the flying escort circle the eyrie. Wistala

and AuRon landed. Shadowcatch put his bulk on a precarious grip at the landing ledge. He closed off Nilrasha's cavern like a door.

"What brings you this far north, Ibidio?" the Copper asked.

She rattled her *griff*. "I hoped to get some truth at last."

"I suspect you wanted to see the look on my mate's face when she heard the news."

"What news, my love?" Nilrasha said, clearly nervous.

"I'm no longer Tyr. The twins will rule the Lavadome. NiVom and his mate will take charge of the Upper World for them."

The rims of her eyes and nostrils went white. "What's to become of us?"

"Exile, I'm afraid," the Copper said.

Ibidio thumped her tail. "I came to see to this personally. Nilrasha, you have one chance to save your mate from disgraceful exile."

"Now, just one moment, Ibidio," NiVom said.

"Shut up, NiVom, or I'll see to it that the twins choose another dragon to oversee affairs in the Upper World." Ibidio turned back to Nilrasha. "Confess to the murder of Halaflora and face punishment. Then we'll allow your mate, an innocent in your schemes, to remain among us."

What did poor Halaflora matter now? The Copper felt his temper flare. If he could just spit fire properly, he'd flame the old buzzard's face.

"Don't say anything, Nilrasha. Ibidio, isn't seeing me dethroned triumph enough for you?"

"It's bloodlines that matter," Ibidio said. "I've had enough of rule by unknowns. Such a court! This Ru-Gaard, a usurper, a foundling who mates a nobody from Milkdrinker's Hill and then brings in a dragon who believes herself a Hypatian to presume to rule as Queen. Arrogance!"

"You think you will do better under the twins?" the Copper said. "You're a fool if you think so, Ibidio. It's the Red Queen's old bargain. NiVom and Imfamnia will rule the Upper World. The Lavadome will exist only at their sufferance."

"They can be managed. The Ankelenes have the crystal. We'll keep an eye on them. Imfamnia may be a greedy, vain ninny of a dragon, but she at least comes from a noble line."

"You nostril-clenching gargoyle," Nilrasha roared. "With your precious bloodlines and family traditions! You've always resented me. RuGaard was perfectly acceptable as Tyr; you put him forward! Until he mated with me, that is. Then you started your whispers. Viper, you've spat your last poison!"

With that, Nilrasha charged, mouth agape.

Shadowcatch threw himself in front of NiVom, who was moving in to protect Ibidio. Old Ibidio, who'd probably never opened her mouth in battle since she'd breathed her first fire at the end of hatchlinghood, froze in fury. Nilrasha struck her like a charging elephant and they clawed briefly, frantically, at the edge of the parapet before disappearing over the side.

"Nilrasha," the Copper shrieked, launching himself into the air. His throne didn't matter. The only thing that counted was his mate.

Together, the combatants plunged into the valley, bouncing off the sheer side of Nilrasha's eyrie. Ibidio's wings weren't up to supporting both.

He folded his wings and dove. If his artificial joint gave way, so be it.

He heard a crashing of timber below. Startled black-and-white birds took to the sky, marking their fall.

The Copper opened his wings, daring them to give way and stop him from striking the valley floor next to his mate. But Rayg's engineering supported him.

He found Nilrasha, bleeding from torn-away scale but otherwise miraculously uninjured, atop the broken body of Ibidio. Sightless eyes stared in different directions.

So passed the mother of his first mate.

"I can't even die right," Nilrasha managed between gasps. She licked him across the snout, exposing a broken fang.

"You're just lucky," the Copper said.

NiVom and his gargoyles came down at a safe pace, followed by Shadowcatch and the Aerial Host escort.

"Well, Nilrasha, I suppose I owe you a thank-you," NiVom said. "Ibidio and her clique would have given me some difficulties. You've just strengthened my hold on the Lavadome."

Nilrasha spat blood at him.

"Why don't you just kill us and get it over with?" the Copper asked.

"No, RuGaard. I want you to go live with cold memories, in hiding, as I did. As nothing but a memory, you're bound to improve. The dragons will forget your limp and your stupid expression and only remember your victories. But you and your wretched mate aging in exile, growing ever weaker—that'll take the glamour off your name."

"Then at least give me leave to live quietly with my mate, here in her eyrie. I can hunt and fish for us both. I'll never enter the Lavadome again, or so much as offer advice to a young member of the Aerial Host."

"No, Nilrasha's too clever. She's been your brains for years. You two might get up to something. The best safeguard of your good behavior is your mate, here, where I can keep an eye on her—and you as far away as possible. The other side of the world would do nicely."

"You would forcibly part mated dragons?" Nilrasha asked.

"Your mating, if those ridiculous ascents you attempt could be called a mating flight, is of dubious provenance," NiVom said.

"Now hear this, dragonkind. You are stripped of the honorable name RuGaard. From now on you're just 'Batty' to us. It was good enough for you in the drakwatch caves, it'll be good enough for the future. This is my bargain, a better one than I got: as long as you remain outside the Dragon Empire, you and Nilrasha will come to no harm. But set *sii* back on our lands and I'll see to it that she's thrown from her resort. Only this time, I'll make sure she lands on something sharper than Ibidio."

Chapter 19

They flew in stages, resting frequently in the cool sea. It was not a quick trip—their escort frequently demanded that they stop and argue the correct course so as not to pass too near the Hypatian coast, or to circumnavigate some island belonging to the Empire by map rather than actual occupation. AuRon thought it petty of their escort, and it reminded him of the Wizard Wrimere's prickly vindictiveness. The escort left them near the great neck, turning home for Hypatia.

"Fair winds guide you to rest," one of them said. The Copper, prodded, received a final thank-you for his promotion into the Aerial Host.

"Foolish of you, Father," AuSurath said. "You'd

think a dragon with no scale would be more sensitive to the direction in which the winds are blowing."

He was silent and thoughtful the rest of the flight.

AuRon experienced the moment every dragon father must, when his son breathes fire into his face—metaphorically, of course, here in the windy skies of the Inland Ocean.

Wistala said little on the flight. AuRon had heard much of her exploits. He believed this was the first time she'd been really defeated.

His brother flew mechanically, as though strings controlled his movements. Or perhaps it was just the false joint midwing.

Once they made it to the island, after a few days they'd decide what to do. AuRon found himself wishing he could have DharSii available—he was a strong, reasonable dragon who'd be a stout ally and a clear-headed counselor.

To AuRon, the Copper seemed increasingly numb to all that had happened. He spoke less and less at greater and greater intervals, and when he did speak it was only a commonplace, such as that he was tired or hungry. AuRon suspected that were it not for Wistala and Shadowcatch nudging him along from either side, he would have just flown aimlessly until he dropped from exhaustion into the sea.

Wistala tried to reassure him about Nilrasha, that she was still popular with some of the Firemaids and dragons from the less exalted hills; therefore NiVom had very good reason to keep her alive.

"I did my best for them. I truly did," he kept repeating.

That's the problem with the ambitious and ruthless, AuRon thought. *They're thunderstruck when they meet someone even more ruthless and ambitious than they.*

"The Tyr gave his word," Wistala said. "As long as we leave the empire in peace, we're not to be harmed. More important for you, brother RuGaard, Nilrasha will stay comfortably in her eyrie. For you, brother AuRon, Natasatch will maintain her honored position, Naf's kingdom will be at peace under the wings of its Protector, and your offspring will continue their careers in security and honor."

"I just feel as though he has us by the throat, and we don't have so much as a claw into him," the Copper said.

"Are you sure this is NiVom's doing?"

"What do you mean?" Wistala asked.

AuRon, once again, tried to put vague suspicions and feelings into words. "Imfamnia. His mate. I can't help thinking there's more to her than we know. She's so cursedly sure of herself."

They arranged the last lap in the hopes that they might arrive at the Isle of Ice with the sun setting, then spend a quiet night in AuRon's cave. With strength renewed by sleep, they'd see about finding some food in the morning, if Ouistrela hadn't eaten all the sheep.

But the Copper flagged again and a spring storm threatened, so they rested on an uninhabited piece of rock. There were crabs and other shellfish to be had in the clear, cold water. Even Shadowcatch, who'd never quite broken the habit of having his food brought to him by humans, managed to come up with a few.

As matters turned out, it was just as well they rested.

They arrived midday. AuRon and Natasatch's cave looked quite primitive. The dragons were used to smoothed corners and holes bored for venting and drainage there. But still, it felt safe and warm for the travelers, and they settled in for a long nap, albeit in a cave sized for two dragons rather than four.

A faint howling of wolves woke AuRon from sleep, slightly squashed between bulky Wistala and even bulkier Shadowcatch.

He roused his fellow exiles with tail slaps.

"The wolves have some news for us?" Wistala asked.

"They're far off, I can't pick up what's being said, the echoes are confusing the sounds. It's a danger call," AuRon said.

AuRon hadn't had reason to creep to his own front portal in all his years on the island, but this time he did.

Staying in the shadows, he peeped out. Ouistrela stood there, a male AuRon didn't recognize beside her. Hard to believe Ouistrela had taken a mate.

There were men, shaggy barbarians of the north by the look of them, behind and before her, the ones to the front with evil-looking spears, the ones behind with great bows and heavy dragon arrows.

"Ouistrela, what's all this? You're standing on my doorstep with armed men?"

She was bristling for a fight and clearly enjoying her moment. "I'm here to evict you at last, AuRon. You and your pitiful band."

He sensed the others falling in behind him, tensing.

"What right and what cause allow you to tell me to leave my own cave?" AuRon asked.

Glittering green alighted next to her. Imfamnia!

"You have visitors, I see," AuRon said. "Imfamnia, we're keeping our side of the bargain. We'll live here quietly."

"I'm afraid not, AuRon," the once and future Queen called back. "Remember that clever trick you pulled in Uldam? NiVom and I did. You're looking at the new Protector of the Isle of Ice. Ouistrela will find the duties light and the meals hearty. The Isle of Ice is part of the Grand Alliance. It is you who broke the arrangement, not I."

"It's a trap," the Copper said. "Fly for your lives!"

Wistala and Shadowcatch led the way, by virtue of their bulk and heavy scale, shielding AuRon and the Copper.

A ropy mass fell atop them from the upper rim of AuRon's cave.

Nets! No ordinary fishing nets, either, but dragon-nets of chain and barbed hooks.

Falling on them like an oversized octopus, the nets

engulfed Wistala and Shadowcatch. AuRon worked one side with *sii*, trying to untangle them, listening as arrows sang through the air.

The heavy net may have held one powerful dragon. But two, such as Wistala and Shadowcatch, tore it to pieces. Pieces of it encumbered them still, but they stood on *sii* and *saa* ready to fight.

"You!" Ouistrela said, spying Shadowcatch.

With that, Ouistrela launched herself at the black.

Her fury spoiled the aim of the blighter and human archers. Some loosed anyway in their excitement and struck their own leader.

The heavy, unknown red stood stupidly, not knowing if he should join the contest below or wait for the archers to bleed their enemies.

"Idiot!" Imfamnia shrieked, backing away from the fighting. "*Griffaran*, tear their throats out!"

"AuRon, ware! *Griffaran*," the Copper called.

Colorful, taloned lances swept down from the heights. Five.

"Only you have a chance against them," the Copper said.

One against five? AuRon admired his brother's definition of "a chance."

Wistala was shielding AuRon with her muscular bulk. Arrows and bolts and heavier projectiles bounced off her armored skin the way rain ran off a cliff face. He could achieve little on the ground—he jumped into the air, beating his wings madly to gain speed and altitude.

The *griffaran* swerved, coming at him from either side.

Oh, will you!

AuRon felt his wings and spine protest at the backbend, reversing course like a cracking whip.

The *griffaran* had evidently never flown against a scaleless dragon before. Their heads came together with a satisfying *konk!*

The third overshot. AuRon got on his tailfeathers. Rage at Imfamnia's betrayal made running a line of fire down the bird's back easy.

It screamed as it burned and fell.

AuRon turned to race after Imfamnia, who was putting as much sky between herself and the fighting as possible.

A hard punch struck him across the back. He looked back; a *griffaran* had its claws dug into his middle back. It extracted a set of bloody talons and reached for the wing joint, ready to tear out his wing—

A flutter of feathers and *whoosh*—the *griffaran's* head was off and the body, dragged by the wind, fell off behind him in a shower of blood.

AuRon, astonished, saw another *griffaran* drop its comrade's head.

His brother and sister needed him below. He turned and dove, coming in behind the archers trying to score a hit on Wistala or Shadowcatch without striking Ouistrela.

It felt good to at last to loose his flame. He flapped hard with his wings, arresting his dive and creating a whirlwind of pebbles and dragonfire. The archers shielded their faces and either tried to burrow into the hard earth or fled.

The red dragon, not eager to fight, was jumping up and down and exhorting some human spearmen to close. AuRon whistled to him. When the red turned his head, AuRon struck him across the snout with his tail.

His strange *griffaran* savior raked the red across the throat. The red yelped and bounded away, calling on dead *griffaran* to save him. The *griffaran* fluttered down to come to the aid of the Copper, who was alternately breathing fire and kicking rocks at a line of spearmen trying to close in.

The red ran for his plump life, knocking archers left and right. If that red was representative of NiVom and Imfamnia's backers, perhaps his brother should have stayed in the Lavadome and fought.

Shadowcatch and Ouistrela grappled and tore at each other still, swishing tails and batting wings, keeping the barbarians from closing in on the little party by the easiest route. Straining *saa* loosed boulders that rolled and bounced down the mountainside in front of their hatchlings' old cave. Madly whipping tails sent showers of pebbles into enemy eyes.

The biggest boulder of all was green and metal-protected. The clattering bangs of light war machines firing their spear-sized projectiles sent Wistala into a rage.

Ouistrela, much torn about, saw that her support from the Grand Alliance had vanished. With a contemptuous flap of her wings, she backed away, throwing fire this way and that.

AuRon watched the Copper dragon fight. His brother continued to amaze him. The Copper was no great fighter—his limited vision, dragging limbs, and general off-balance awkwardness put him at a disadvantage against any dragon near his own size. The Copper wasn't stupid—he had his faults, but he wasn't stupid—he must be aware of his disadvantages in combat.

Yet he threw himself into battle regardless. And he didn't fight with the fury of a dragon with his blood up, he didn't throw himself upon the nearest enemy and lose all his wits in a red madness; he fought craftily and cannily, using wing and tail to both strike and defend.

The barbarians, lacking the support of the dragons they counted upon, quit the fight, running in little groups with shields held over heads and spears up to ward off aerial attack.

They needn't have bothered. AuRon had no flame left, anyway. Long flights on short rations tended to dry the firebladder. He settled for making threatening dives to hurry them along.

AuRon turned back to what was left of the fight. Shadowcatch was in a poor way, his wings had bites and tears in them. But he still raged, smashing dead men and broken spears into splintered pulp. Wistala looked a little like a ragged porcupine, with numerous arrows and spears stuck in her. Very little blood ran from the wounds, however, so AuRon expected there would just be the painful work of extracting broken-off tips. His brother had a number of men gathered like a herd of sheep in surrender, begging for their lives with upraised palms.

"Gather all the dropped shields and weapons left lying about, put them in a pile here, then you may return to your boats, or however you came here," he said in rather faulty Parl, holding head high and standing square. AuRon repeated the instructions in the northern tongue and they fell to their knees and cried out in gladness at the dragon's mercy.

AuRon thought his brother carried off that lordly, implacable air rather well. Better than he himself could have, at any rate.

Yes, the Copper had courage. Courage and heart and the ability to keep his head. It had taken him far and won him a mate AuRon admired. He also wondered about RuGaard's first mate. Clearly she'd seen in the ungainly young dragon with the slack eye a quality others missed.

Your wrath shouldn't win.

Maybe AuRon could have done better by his brother. Snuck him food from the egg shelf. He'd been a greedy little hatchling, even stealing what he could from his sisters.

In his way, he'd done more for dragons than AuRon had. AuRon admitted to himself that he'd gained them a safe refuge, hard for men and elves and dwarfs to find, and even harder to attempt to control. His brother had made it a world where dragons were no longer hunted.

Then there was his sister. Wistala, who didn't set dragons above the hominids as the Copper did, or apart from them as AuRon would have it, but beside them, cooperating as best as she could. Had she been wrong? Too idealistic? Blinded by memories of a kindly old elf who'd taken her into his home?

AuRon couldn't fault her.

Each of them were products of birth and circumstance. Each had found a way to make their outlook work. Only time would tell who was right.

The question was, which approach would last?

The *griffaran* who'd turned on his companions settled on the Copper's back to rest and rearrange his feathers.

The *griffaran*, a grizzled veteran with feathers that were thin and dull, but with a painted beak showing bright markings of rank, executed a bob before his brother.

"Who are you?" the Copper asked

"Named Miki!" the oldster squawked in a *griffaran's* usual punchy Drakine. "Years ago. Many! Others forgot! Not me!"

"What happened years ago?" his brother asked.

"You saved an egg. From demen. 'Twas me!"

Miki shot out his story like a dwarf rock thrower war machine, in quick bursts of words. He'd been raised to be loyal to the dragons, and especially loyal to the Tyr who had saved him.

"Great RuGaard Miki Tyr! Always! Protect Tyr!"

"Thank you," the Copper said.

"What now?" Wistala asked. "If this island is part of the Grand Alliance, they won't let us stay here."

Shadowcatch inspected his torn wings. "I'm not going anywhere for the moment. I don't suppose there are any thralls around who are good at stitching?"

"Even united, we can't hold a hole against the Aerial Host," the Copper said. "They'll simply fly in demen and dwarfs and who knows what else."

The surrendered barbarians dropped the last shields in a pile and the Copper waved them off with his tail.

"Wistala and Shadowcatch, you'd better let your gold gizzards make what you can of this," the Copper said.

"So much for a peaceful exile," AuRon said.

"Well, the civil war was at least brief," Wistala said, crunching a shield down into an easy-to-swallow size.

"It's only begun," the Copper muttered.

"Where can we go?" Shadowcatch asked. "This isn't a big enough island to hide us. Not many caves, as I remember."

"They've made an enemy today," AuRon said.

"Two enemies," Wistala said.

"Three," the Copper added, his good eye alert and intelligent for the first time during their trip.

"Five," Miki squawked, either assuming Shadowcatch made four or employing the wrong word of Drakine.

"In any case, we need to go somewhere safe, where we can to lick our wounds and have a moment's peace to think. Hypatia is barred to us. From the Isle of Ice they'll be able to watch all the shores of the northern part of the Inland Ocean."

"The Great East?" the Copper asked.

"I've been there," Wistala said. "Dragon bones are a much-prized item for their medicines."

"Old Uldam is big, with many valleys and caves," AuRon said. "My daughter might be willing to hide us, at least for a little while."

"That's a long way off," the Copper said.

Wistala lifted her head and dropped a piece of chain at a sudden thought. "I know a place. Food, it is remote, there are even a few dragons there. We may even have a friend."

"What's that?" the Copper asked.

"The Sadda-Vale," Wistala said. "It's ruled by an old white dragon-dame named Scabia. She said something once about being distantly related to us. Our grandsire may have come from the Sadda-Vale."

"I thought that was a legend," the Copper said. "Some bit of Silverhigh everyone's forgotten."

"There are still dragons there. DharSii, for one. He lives there at least some of the time."

"If we are to leave, we should go soon," AuRon said. "Imfamnia might be back with more *griffaran*, or those gargoyle creatures."

"I can't make it," Shadowcatch said. "My wing's torn up."

"Can you swim?" AuRon asked.

"I think so."

"If you can make it to the shore in the east, there's a tower—"

"Yes, I know it. The Dragonheight. That woman's place. I know her, she's gotten me jobs in the past. She'll stitch me up in a trice. Didn't occur to me to swim all that way, though. Hope I don't sink."

"Will you be all right?" Wistala asked.

"I can buy you some time. Make them think we're hiding on one of the outer islands. I can make enough racket to make them think the whole Lavadome's squatting in those sluice-caves. Do a bit of bellowing at anything that comes close. Besides, I could do with a little fresh crab. That's the one problem with the Lavadome, no shell-carriers. Keeps the digestion clean."

AuRon forgot his unhappiness for a moment. Shadowcatch's thoughts rarely moved far from his stomach or fighting.

"More might come than you can handle," AuRon said.

"You know me, NooSh—er, AuRon. I'm not a bad fighter when the blood's up."

"If you must, hide out at the north end of the island. The wolves have seen you with me. They'll stand guard while you sleep."

Wistala watched the sun drop toward the horiozn. "Let's all be seen swimming or flying for that island, then. I'm sure we're being watched from somewhere."

They crept down one of the glacier-runoff streams and slipped into the water for the swim to the island.

Salt water felt good on everyone's wounds, and they took a few minutes to lick one another other clean, pull riven scale, and extract arrowheads—which could then be swallowed for a little needed metal. The Copper had shoved a few shields and helmets under his bad wing.

"Hope this contraption holds out for the rest of the trip," he said.

"DharSii might be able to figure it out," Wistala said. "He's very clever. Between us and the blighters she keeps around we might be able to keep it functioning."

"I'm not likely to make many more trips," the Copper said. "I'd hardly dare. A whole Empire wants me dead."

"Let's leave the worries for another day," AuRon said. "Join us if you can, Shadowcatch."

Wistala gave him instructions on how to find the hidden valley, east of the Red Mountains.

"Please come," the Copper said. "It doesn't sound right without you grinding your teeth behind me somewhere. It's difficult to think without the noise."

"I'm tempted to stay and settle things once and for all with Ouistrela. But as far as I'm concerned, Tyr RuGaard is still my lord. I'll come if I can get my wings catching air again."

With that, the three dragons took to the skies, with Miki flying close beside the Copper.

Chapter 20

They flew in a tight grouping, flying over sand-hills tufted with patchy grasses, with AuRon at the angle. Game trails followed the water found here and there, but they couldn't catch much that offered even a partial mouthful. The bigger game herds were probably still on their way north.

Wistala wondered if they even would have made it, traveling in the north in that bleak and bitter spring, without AuRon flying at their head. He cut the air for them, and they rode with the advantage of the draft he'd created.

Miki suffered terribly from the cold. They took turns lighting dragon-fire so that he could warm his thin body. The only thing that kept the old *griffaran* going was a promise of bony fishes taken from the deep lake of the Sadda-Vale.

At one of their warmth-and-water breaks, RuGaard offered to take over the lead position to give AuRon a chance to rest.

"I'm not dragging scale," AuRon said. "I don't mind anything except that the rest of you are a little slow."

They all chuckled at that. Perhaps the family had learned to laugh after all.

They flew high over the mountains surrounding the Sadda-Vale at the cost of exhaustion, but with the journey almost at an end.

Wistala thought Vesshall in the Sadda-Vale hadn't changed in the intervening years any more than as if she'd just left the previous night. The stone latticework over the entrance, the great dome carved out of living rock, the steaming pools of the lake beneath giving wisps of heat up into the sky.

Perhaps the Sadda-Vale was a sister location to the Lavadome. Unchanging year in and year out.

Not such a bad place to live in exile. Hot and cold natural pools for swimming, the vast, deep lake, architecture unlike anything she'd seen in the wide world, and plenty of game. A troll hunt with three or more full-grown dragons would be an interesting challenge rather than a risky hunt. She'd have to remind her brothers about the trolls.

Though today it was mist-shrouded. Nevertheless a few blighters were employed sweeping leaves from the vast courtyard before the entrance.

They dropped their brooms and fled at the sight of the new arrivals.

DharSii was the first to amble out of the entrance with its ancient writing. He startled when he recognized them.

"We seek refuge," AuRon said.

"And fish. And worms," Miki said in his bad Drakine.

DharSii cleared his throat. "*Ha-hem*. Welcome, Wistala. It's good to see you again. Greetings, AuRon. Tyr RuGaard, you fly with a small escort. Has there been trouble?"

Scabia the White shuffled out, dragging her tail, but the aged dragon still had bright and alert eyes. "We've met before, Wistala of the line of AuNor."

"Yes, briefly."

"A young dragon seeking help in her battles in the wide world," Scabia sniffed.

DharSii looked uncomfortable.

"So, how did your contest in the world of hominids turn out? A smashing success, no doubt."

"I am no judge of my own success."

"Now you've returned."

"As you see."

"I can't imagine what your party seeks that is in my power to grant."

"We seek refuge with you from a hostile world. We are all exiles from the Grand Alliance."

"DharSii, is this the confounded arrangement you were speaking of?"

"Yes, Scabia. The Lavadome dragons and the Hypatians are now allies."

"It'll end badly. Such arrangements always do. Well, I expect you're hungry. I can see the ribs on that poor scaleless dragon with the regrown tail."

"We'd be grateful for your hospitality," Wistala said.

"You never struck me as the grateful type. But perhaps your experiences have taught you better manners than to go running off from your hosts in the dead of night. Well, it's a cold day, and I don't care for the Upper World."

She led them all down into the great hall Wistala remembered, with its many lofts projecting from the side and pools of rainwater on the floor. It still smelled musty, like secrets hardly worth keeping.

As the others ate, Scabia settled down beside Wistala.

"It's good to have another dragonelle around," the aged white said.

"We may stay some time, if you'll let us. We all could use a rest."

"The Sadda-Vale can support many more dragons than it does. It has in the past, in any case. You can win a place for yourself and your companions permanently, as *uzhin*."

"You still need eggs for your daughter?" Wistala asked. Scabia's charity always came with a price, and she'd asked, years ago, that Wistala mate with NaStirath so that her barren daughter Aethleethia would have hatchlings to care for.

"Yes. I'd still like you to produce them. The superiority of your characteristics, your size and strength, suggest that you would lay fit, healthy hatchlings. Why, you might have eight or more eggs in a single clutch. You could be the foundation of a new age in the Sadda-Vale."

Scabia's eyes gleamed. Was she looking forward to a new age, or back at past glories?

"The price is mating with NaStirath."

"He's not so bad, Wistala."

"But—mate with him?"

"Take it from one who has mated many times. It is over before you know it."

She wondered how far she could dare tax Scabia's charity and desire for another generation in the Sadda-Vale. "I'd much rather mate with DharSii," Wistala finally said.

"DharSii? Surely you joke."

"He's a closer relative of yours, isn't he?"

"Yes. But he's a striped dragon. They're always difficult, often sterile. I don't believe mating with him would be productive. Striped dragons never fit in, no offense intended against either my *uzhin* or your scaleless brother."

"My brother has stripes, and has managed to produce offspring. One clutch of four eggs."

"Probably striped as well. If that's all he's managed to have, he'll be the last of his line. DharSii is out of the question. You must lay the next eggs in my hall, with NaStirath."

She stared at the empty floor.

"Besides," Scabia continued, "there are attributes of DharSii that I wouldn't wish to see passed on. He has forever humbled himself by working in harness for hominids. I would not have any line of mine sullied by a slave."

"He worked for hominids to bring you coin."

"A real dragon finds coin, takes it, demands it of his inferiors. He doesn't run errands like a dwarfen shopkeeper."

"You think NaStirath his superior?"

"I wouldn't trust NaStirath to burn down a barn full of oil-soaked cotton. But he is of an impressive length, his bone structure is exceedingly fine, he displays a better-than-average wingspan. I've never known him to be sick a day in his life."

"The way he idles, I wonder how you could tell if he was sick."

"What will it be, Wistala? You wish to live in my vale, you will accept my rule. Produce eggs for my daughter to raise as her own, or find another cave for your poor exiles. If you can."

Wistala knew what her choice would be. It was there, half-formed and painful, like a toothache just setting in. She was but one dragonelle, thrown out by her society, but she held in her tender jaws the lives of two brothers, their families, and a handful of loyalists to an exiled regime.

"I will do as you demand."

"You and your friends will find us generous hosts.

There is nothing to fear from the Lavadome, relations between our two societies are of long-standing."

"I hope that proves true," Wistala said.

"The rule of Scabia is not to be trifled with."

There was nothing to do but get it over with. If it had to be done, it might as well be done quickly. Her Copper brother was making himself miserable, and AuRon lay in his loft and slept like a jungle snake with a deer in it.

But they roused themselves to attend her "mating."

Scabia even managed to climb a little spit of land that looked out on the unusually misty lake. Blue clouds high above looked like a stormy sea.

"Wistala," NaStirath said. "Don't look so down-at-hearts. Think of it as a silly game, to please your relatives. You may not admit it, but you're a sprig of the great tree Scabia tends, in her way."

She took one long, last look at DharSii. If ever a dragon looked miserable enough to drop scale, it was he.

"I don't suppose I get a song," Wistala said.

Scabia snorted. "Don't be ridiculous. You're not his mate, my offspring is."

"Well, off with it, you two," Scabia said. "I've waited long enough for some eggs in this cavern."

DharSii, evidently unable to watch the rest of the ceremony, moved off in the direction of the lake.

"Don't stand there twitching like a thunderstruck rabbit," Scabia said. "Into the air. I'll be watching, remember."

"Oh please, must you?"

The Copper spoke at last. "Scabia, if my sister has agreed to . . . to create some eggs with NaStirath, she'll do it. Save her the embarrassment of knowing she's being watched from the ground."

"Oh-h-h, once upon a time all the hominids of the world read their augurs whenever dragons mated."

"Let them have their privacy," the Copper said. "I've been on the receiving end of such curious stares. I didn't care for it."

"I'll see that you get your eggs," Wistala said. "I don't want us watched."

"Oh, very well," Scabia said, darting suspicious glances at the siblings. "I suppose I can trust *you* to see this through, NaStirath?"

"The sooner it's over, the better," NaStirath said. "Not that anyone asked my opinion, but I don't care to be watched either."

"When you start having sensible opinions, I'll start asking for them," Scabia said. "Well, get on with the matter. I must go to my offspring."

DharSii was lost in the mists coming off the lake. Au-Ron and RuGaard both dropped their heads in bows that were meant to be both grateful and encouraging, she imagined. Odd that their gestures were so alike, with decades of different experiences behind them.

"Flying is not my favorite pastime," NaStirath said. "I hope you don't expect me to perform up where the air's too thin."

"Be assured, I'll fly gently," Wistala said.

"I'm no more looking forward to this than you are," NaStirath said. "I live here on Scabia's charity as well, you know. Though mine comes in dearer coin, being mated to her insipid daughter."

Wistala let loose a deep breath. *It won't be so bad. A battle is worse, and you've survived many of those. A brief embrace, a fall—*

That's an idea. Don't open your wings again.

No, my brothers need a refuge.

"Look," NaStirath said. "This is all a joke. Think of it as a joke. I assure you, it'll be over soon enough, and we'll all be laughing."

Wistala wasn't so sure about laughter anymore. Perhaps her parents had a reason for giving it up when they went into the wild.

So this was to be her mating flight. Taking off from a windswept plaza into a cloudy spring sky over the Sadda-Vale, on a day as cold as DharSii's heart and as gray as her brother.

She spread her wings and took off, tempted to fly, fly hard east until either her heart burst or she crashed in exhaustion.

But no, she wouldn't do that.

"Well, if you're going to follow, follow," she said, taking off.

NaStirath launched his bulk into the sky behind her. He was a goodly-sized dragon, one of the very few larger than her in length and wingspan.

Might as well make NaStirath work a little harder for it, Wistala thought.

She fought to gain altitude. NaStirath shrunk to a madly flapping miniature behind, bellowing something about giving up on a joke going far enough.

No, the joke hadn't gone nearly far enough. Or high enough. She put her whole body into getting a few more beats out of her wings, willing her heavy frame to rise. Muscles toughened by the ground-armor responded.

NaStirath gained his second wind. She heard him coming up behind. What would his blundering grasp be like?

They'd gone high enough. Surely even NaStirath could manage the job with this distance to fall.

She felt a nip at her tail.

That idiot is too much.

She turned her head to give him a taste of flame in his face.

DharSii!

How had he followed her here, in the clouds, and where between the Four Spirits was NaStirath?

She swooped, glided, and DharSii fell in beside her.

"What is this? Don't tell me you're going to fight NaStirath for me, or convince me to flee with you."

"Neither," DharSii said.

"So what is this?"

"Didn't NaStirath tell you? It's a joke. We're playing it on Scabia."

"But what about the mating with NaStirath and her precious next generation?"

DharSii twitched a *griff* at her. "Oh, she'll get her eggs. I'll see to that, if it takes a generation's trying."

His wing close around hers. Wistala shivered with excitement at the touch. For the first time in an age, it seemed, she felt like laughing.

Drakine Glossary

Drakine

FOUA: A product of the firebladder. When mixed with the liquid fats stored within and then exposed to oxygen, it ignites into oily flame.

GRIFF: The armored fans descending from the forehead and jaw that cover sensitive ear holes and throat pulse points in battle.

GRIFF-TCHK: an instant, an immeasurably short amount of time.

LAUDI: Brave and glorious deeds in a dragon's life that make it into the lifesong.

PRRUM: The low thrumming sound a dragon makes when it is pleased or particularly content.

SAA: The rear legs of a dragon. The three rear true-toes are able to grip, but the fighting spur is little more than decoration.

SII: The front legs of a dragon. The claws are shorter

and the fighting spur on the rear leg is closer to the other digits and is opposable. The digits are more elegantly formed for manipulation.

TORF: A small gob from the firebladder, used to provide a few moments of illumination.

Hypatian

VESK: A Hypatian mark of distance based on the amount of distance light infantry can cover in an hour: about three and a half miles.

Draconic Personae

AETHLEETHIA—Daughter of Scabia

AUSURATH—AuRon and Natasatch's red offspring

AYAFEEIA—Leader of the Firemaids, daughter of Ibidio

BAMELPHISTRAN—Assistant to the Aerial Host, later leader

CUREMOM—Ankelene with idea for selling dragon parts

FEHAZATHANT—Former Tyr, now dead

IBIDIO—Elderly female dragon, mate to AgGriffopse, Tyr FeHazathant's only male offspring

ISTACH—Striped daughter of AuRon and Natasatch

HALAFLORA—Tyr RuGaard's first mate, now dead

NASTIRATH—A dragon of the Sadda-Vale. A very silly dragon indeed.

NATASATCH—AuRon's mate

VARATHEELA—AuRon's daughter

NoFarouk—A dragon of the Tyr's court

NoFhyriticus—Gray Protector of Hypatia

Ouistrela—Cantankerous old female on the Isle of Ice

Regalia—Green twin

Scabia—Ruler of the Sadda-Vale

SiDrakkon—Former Tyr, successor to Tyr FeHazathant, now dead

SiHazathant—Red twin

SiMevolant—Former Tyr, successor to Tyr SiDrakkon, now dead

SoRolatan—Former Protector of Dairuss

Yefkoa—A swift-flying Firemaid

Read on for an excerpt from the stunning
conclusion to the

Age of Fire

series by E. E. KNIGHT

Dragon Fate

Available from Roc in trade paperback.

Wistala, newly mated dragon-dame, might have been living an idle, romantic dream, save that she was eyesore from searching mountainside crevices and frostbitten about the nostrils.

She was out hunting trolls with her secret mate DharSii in the chill air among the peaks of the Sadda-Vale. They'd been up before the sun.

There were things she'd rather be doing with her mate, of course. Swimming in the steaming pools at the north end of the Sadda-Vale, for a start, rather than fighting winds that threatened to freeze her blood. The remote fastness of the Sadda-Vale, resting like a twisted skeleton on the vast plains east of the Red Mountains, had a pleasant microclimate in the snake-track vale between two short mountain chains, a gift of the mild volcanic activity in the area—along with an occasional earthquake.

Ancient ruins filled with highly stylized artwork, much of it featuring dragons, their prey, and cowering hominids, still waited to be explored. Their were secrets to be discovered in abandoned old tunnels and sub-chambers, icons to be discerned in high corners, ancient relics of dragon history.

DharSii, a powerful yet thoughtful dragon whose scale color reminded her of the tigers she'd seen in jungles to the south, had some interesting theories about the old structures of the Sadda-Vale and she wanted to hear them again, this time while looking at the art and iconography that had inspired such ideas. Wistala had developed her taste for pedantry while doing what her fellow librarians called "outwork." She'd seen hints here and there of an ancient golden age of dragons and DharSii shared her interest in that time.

When conversation became too dull among their fellow dragons of the Sadda-Vale, they liked to escape mentally to other times and places. Those were her favorite hours, as they broke down the last few bones of dinner and swallowed after-feast ores laboriously cracked out of the slate-fields. Sometimes the conversations went on until the next morning and they revived themselves by taking a swim in the steamy waters of the pools beneath Vesshall.

Instead, this particular morning they flew parallel to the western spine of mountains sheltering the vale. The mountains, like old, worn-down teeth, were full of crags, holes, and pockets. The peaks and ridges caught the wind and sang mournful tunes to unheeding clouds and fog. Above them, bitter winds blew hard and cold enough to freeze one's eyes open in the winter. On the other side of the clouds, she knew, the stars at night were brilliantly clear with spectacular fireworks of shimmering, flame-colored lights dancing on the horizon like maddened rainbows—if you could brave the chill. But in their shelter, the heated waters of the Sadda-Vale created pools of warmth and the omnipresent clouds and fogs.

DharSii dipped lower, seeing something on the slope. Just a shadow. He led her higher again, so their hunt might be concealed by the clouds.

Her brother AuRon should be with them. He was a skilled stalker. His scaleless skin, though vulnerable in battle and badly scarred because of it, shifted from color to color according to where he stood even to the point of imitating shadows and striations in the rock face. But as soon as winter had broken above the Sadda-Vale and flight over the plains of the Ironriders became possible without fighting blizzards, he'd gone aloft to travel south to visit his mate. Natasatch, mother of his hatchlings now serving a new Tyr of the Dragon Empire, acted as "protector" for one of the Empire's provinces. Which really meant humans fed, housed, and offered coin to AuRon's mate.

AuRon, who'd incautiously drunk too much of Scabia's brandy-wine, once slurred something about "political necessities" separating him from his mate.

Her brother AuRon had to be cautious on these visits and use every camouflage of wit and skin. An exile and in danger of death every moment he was with his mate, AuRon's ability to become invisible at will, and his many friends in the Protectorate of Dairuss, where he knew the king and queen from old, allowed him brief visits.

But Wistala feared that every time she saw him depart, it would be the last.

She returned her wandering mind to the hunt.

The air this morning had a hopeful, alive smell. Fresh winds blew from the south, bringing the smell of the coming spring.

She noticed a herd of goats, tight together rather than grazing, the dominant males alert and watchful, all looking in the same direction and sniffing the breeze. Had they clustered at the sight of DharSii and Wistala? It seemed unlikely, goats rarely searched the clouds unless a shadow passed over them and there were thick, steely clouds today. Hardly a day went by without mists and drizzle as warm, wet, rising air met the cooler streams above.

Good for the grasses the herbivores loved, but the patches of fog and wandering walls of drizzle also gave concealment for prowling trolls. You had to get lucky to see one in the open, they could squeeze themselves into crevices that seemed hardly thicker than a tail-tip at the sound of a dragon's leathery wings.

No, the goats were alarmed by something else. Had they caught the scent of a troll?

Her other brother, the copper-colored RuGaard, formerly Tyr of the Dragon Empire and Worlds Upper and Lower, wouldn't be of much use on a hunt. Thin and listless, hardly eating, drinking, or caring for his scale, he lived a lightless existence at Scabia's hall, hearing without really listening to her old tales of the great dragon civilization of Silverhigh from ages ago. The only time he showed any sort of animation these days was when AuRon brought news of his own mate, Nilrasha, a virtual prisoner in a tower of rock thanks to the stumps she had instead of wings and a guard of watchful *griffaran*.

Or when Scabia told some old tale of desperate vengeance. Then he grew attentive and his *griff* twitched as he stared at Scabia through lidded eyes.

RuGaard frightened her at such times. She could almost feel the violence in his thoughts.

Thank the spirits she had the comforting presence of DharSii beside her at such times. Caught between the quiet, reserved AuRon, creepy in his ability to disappear into the scenery and his own thoughts, and RuGaard's gloomy brooding, she needed a companion to provide mental, and a bit of exhilarating physical, escape.

There were flowers in green meadows in the colder altitudes just above the ground that could support trees. Spring had come at last.

Spring. Her hatchlings would be aboveground this spring.

Wait, not her hatchlings. They counted Aethleethia

as their mother, even if they could barely comprehend a mind-picture from the lazy ninny.

The offering of her hatchlings had been Scabia's price for giving the exiles from the Dragon Empire refuge at Vesshall in the Sadda-Vale. Her daughter Aethleethia was unable to have eggs of her own and both were eager for hatchlings in their hall. Almost as soon as she laid them—the other dragons thought their father was Aethleethia's mate NaStirath, a foolish dragon of proud lineage, who had mated with Wistala to produce the eggs—she'd lost her clutch.

She, DharSii, and NaStirath had conspired to hide the truth that DharSii was the true sire. Though one of the males did bear stripes as dark as DharSii's, the suspicious Scabia had been placated when Wistala pointed out that her brother AuRon was also a striped dragon.

No matter who they counted as mother, the three males and two females would be ravenous, and if they were to have anything besides the bony fish or carapace-creatures and snails of the lake to eat, she and DharSii would have to find and kill the trolls that had been raiding sheep, goats, and caribou from the mountain slopes and patches of forest in the valleys.

DharSii and Wistala had discovered the remains of troll-eaten game on one of their flights to get some privacy from the other dragons of the Sadda-Vale. A troll could easily eat as much as a dragon, and according to DharSii if the food supply was truly superlative, it would reproduce.

Scabia's blighter servants had been frantically

breeding cattle, sheep, and goats and releasing them into pasture ever since Wistala and her exiled companions arrived. There was ample game for a whole family of trolls, though the solitary trolls didn't form anything that might be recognized as family.

So now they were on the hunt for what might be called the most dangerous vermin in the world.

Wistala liked a hunt. She liked it doubly well with a dragon she loved and admired. She'd long since learned she could admire something without loving it, or love someone without admiring them, the combination of the two went to her head like wine. DharSii—"Quick-Claw" in the dragon-vernacular—when on the hunt spoke and acted quickly and efficiently, with none of the stupid roaring and stomping a typical male dragon, NaStirath, say, indulged in upon spotting the prey.

"Troll tracks," DharSii said, waggling his wings.

She followed him down to a felled tree on a steep slope. She had to dig her claws into the earth deep to keep from sliding.

A long, muddy skid-mark stood on the lower side of the fallen tree, the mosses and mushrooms devouring it were smashed and smeared where the troll had placed a foot, and it had slipped on the soggy mud beneath, sliding a short way on the slope. They could see broken branches on another tree a short distance downslope where it had arrested its slide.

Wistala sniffed.

"Scat, too," she said. She followed the bad air to a

mound of troll droppings, though the less said about it the better for all concerned. For all their strength of torso and limb, a troll's digestive system was rather haphazard, sometimes expelling food barely absorbed. This mass of skin, bones, and hair was disgustingly fresh and hardly touched by insects yet, a beetle or two crawled about on the waste waving their antennae as though celebrating their good fortune.

"Looks like its making northeast, toward our herds," DharSii said, counting the widely spaced tracks heading down the slope. "This is fresh enough that I'll hazard it's still climbing that ridge."

Almost a long mountain in itself, the ridge DharSii spoke of was cut by deep ledges, almost like colossal steps, running at an angle down toward the central lake of the Sadda-Vale, where its bulk forced one of the lake's many bends. On the other side of the ridge were herds of winter-thinned cattle, hungrily exploring meadows springing up in the path of snow retreating to higher altitudes, along with the usual sheep and goats.

"I'll try and follow the tracks, stalking or flying low," DharSii said. "You get up into the cloud-cover, so you can just see the surface. If it knows it's being followed it will make a dash for cover, we may be able to corner it. I know that ridge well, there aren't many caves but there are fissures it will use."

If DharSii had a fault, it was arrogance. If there was a risk to be run, he assumed he'd be the better at facing it. Gallant, but vexing for a dragon-dame who enjoyed a challenging hunt.

"Why shouldn't I follow the trail? Green scale will give me an advantage in low flight, if the troll's climbed the ridge already and looking behind and below."

"I know this troll. This track is familiar. Long-fingers, I call him. I've tried for him several times, and he's tried for me almost as many. I know his tricks, you don't, and he's nearly had me even so. One of us must put an end to the other sooner or later. He'll be expecting me to be hunting alone, and he may take a risk that will draw him into the open. Then you may strike."

"As you wish, you old tiger," Wistala said.

"I'm scarcely above two hundred. Hardly old," DharSii said. "Mature and distinguished."

"Just don't distinguish yourself any further with more scars," Wistala said. "Scabia's blighters sew skin closed like drunken spiders, and we've no gold or silver coin to replace lost scale. I'll be above."

"*Ha-hem.* I'll return hearts and scale to you intact," DharSii said.

Wistala snorted and opened her wings. She flapped hard to gain altitude and the concealment of cloud cover.

She flew out over the choppy water of the lake, then circled around to the other side of the ridge. After hearing that this troll and DharSii were old enemies, she'd feel terrible if she got lucky and spotted Long-fingers out in the open and vulnerable to a dive. But given the chance, she'd end the hunt quickly. DharSii was prickly about his honor but he'd understand. Trolls were too wily to let one live when you had an opportunity for a kill.

She hung in the sky, drifting, surveying the terrain below, feeling as though she'd been in this air before, hunting. Once upon a dream, perhaps. Or some old memory handed down from her parents and their parents.

She scanned the ridge, and the more gentle lands beneath, green hills rolling like waves coming up against a seaside cliff. More goats. Some sheep feeding on the north side. Perhaps if the hunt was successful they'd celebrate with fresh mutton.

A few more beats to put herself back in the mists. Wisps of moisture interfered with her vision, but still, she couldn't see DharSii. For a deep-orange dragon marked by black stripes, he could be difficult to see when he chose to move in forested shadow. Was he on foot or on wing?

Wing would be safer, but easier to see from a distance, and Long-fingers might hide. On foot he had a better chance of following the trail so he might spot the troll before it saw him—if that cluster of sensory organs trolls dangled about had eyes as she knew them, that is—

DharSii would probably be on foot, accepting the contest of wits with a troll.

She headed south, in the approximate direction of the troll's track. It knew the ground as well as DharSii, and was crossing the ridge in a jumble of boulders and flats that offered concealment—and a possible easy meal of bird or goat.

Still no sign of DharSii, or the troll. She doubted it

had made the meadows, the sheep and goats there showed no sign of being alarmed or disturbed.

She searched shadows, crevices, high bare trails and thorny hillside tangles. Her mate and the troll had disappeared.

To the winds with the plan!

She narrowed her wings and descended toward the jagged shadows of the ridge.

Wistala flew, more anxious with each wingbeat. She should have met DharSii by now. Visions of her mate, lying broken and half-devoured by the troll, set her imagination running wild to years of empty loneliness without him. No chance at more hatchlings, to raise as their own, no more long conversations, no more uncomfortable throat-clearings when she scored a point . . .

Dust gave them away. Dust and a noise like glacier ice cracking.

She followed the telltale feathers of kicked-up dust to a boulder-littered hummock in the ridge. Here the ridge broke into wind-cut columns of rock like ships' sails, with brush growing wherever soil could find purchase out of the wind.

The dust flung into the air came from DharSii's wings, beating frantically at a monstrous figure riding his back. His whipping tail struck limestone as he turned, sending more flakes and dust into the air.

The troll squatted astride DharSii, as though riding him. It's great arm-legs gripped DharSii's crest at the horns, pulling him in ever-tightening circles.

Wistala's firebladder pulsed at the sight, at the same time feeling her hearts skip a beat in shock.

DharSii—oh, his neck is sure to be broken! The troll is too strong!

Trolls were put together as though by some act of madness by the spirits, to Wistala's mind. Their skin was purplish and veined, like the inner side of a fresh-cut rabbit-skin. Their great arms functioned as legs, tiny legs hung from their triangular torso more to steady the body and to convey items to the orifice that served as both mouth and vent. Great plates covered lungs on the outside, working like bellows to force air across their back, and their joints bent in odd and disturbing directions. Worst of all, they had no face to speak of, just a soggy mass of sense organs on a gruesome orb alternately extended and retracted from the torso like a shy snake darting in and out of a hole.

This troll used its thick, powerful leg-arms grasping the horns of DharSii's crest to wrench her mate's head back and down. Wistala braced herself for the inevitable, terrible snap that must come.

Wistala had killed a troll once before by breathing fire onto its delicate lung tissue. But dragon-flame, a special sulfurous fat collected and strained in the firebladder and then ignited when vomited by a saliva spat from the roof of the mouth, could hurt DharSii just as much as the troll. Dragonscale offered some protection, but DharSii's leathery wing tissue could be burned, or he could inhale the fire, or it might pool and run under his scale.

If she couldn't use her fire, she could still fight with her weight.

She folded her wings and turned into a tight dive, perhaps not as neatly as a falcon but with infinitely more power.

This "Long-fingers" was perhaps as experienced against dragons as she was against trolls. It had Dhar-Sii by a dragon's weakest point, it's long neck.

She swooped around jagged prominences, risking skin of neck, tail, and wing. Heedless of the danger to her wing—a hard enough strike might leave her forever broken and unable to reach the sky again—she flew to DharSii's rescue. This was no longer a simple hunt to exterminate vermin but a death-struggle between dragon and monster.

Pick it up—drop it from a height. Stomp and smash!— warring instincts raged.

Teeth would be next to useless on a creature that size, her neck just didn't have the power to do much more than score its hide. Better to strike with her tail, or there might be two dragons with broken necks. She altered her dive as though trying to reverse directions, so that the force of her swinging tail might send the troll flying right out of the Sadda-Vale.

The troll, showing the uncanny sense of its kind, threw itself sideways just as she struck, rolling DharSii along with its bulk.

"I'm here, my love!" Wistala called.

Wistala missed the troll, lashed DharSii with her tail. It struck, a whip-crack against horseflesh a thousand times louder. She saw scale fly and scatter like startled birds.

Wistala roared, half rage, half despair.

The troll, in avoiding Wistala's blow, put itself in a position so DharSii could anchor his head by hooking horn on rock. The great black-striped dragon twisted his body and struck with his *saa*.

This time, instead of dust being kicked into the air, droplets of dark liquid flew. DharSii's claws came away sticky.

Vaaaaaaa! DharSii roared as the wounded troll pulled him around in a circle as though trying to yank his head off by pure effort.

DharSii suddenly lunged into the troll's pull, digging his horns into the fleshy torso. Now it was the dragon's turn to plant his feet and pull.

The troll used its mighty limbs to push itself off the dragon's crest, tearing skin and ripping open its own veins. DharSii's horns and snout looked as though they'd been dipped in ink.

Wistala banked and by the time she swung around the troll was covering ground in an uneven run, leaving a trail of blue-black blood.

She vomited fire and the troll pulled itself in a new direction with one of its arm-legs. As she passed overhead, claws out and wings high and out of reach, the troll lashed up. Tail and leg-arm struck with a sound like tree-limbs breaking.

An orange flash and this time DharSii was atop the troll. He severed the sense-organ stalk with a sweep of his *sii* and the troll tumbled, righted itself, and ran blindly into a limestone cut.

The troll bounced back and fell, a buzzing beetle-wing noise coming from its lung-plates as the bellows forced air across the vulnerable flesh.

Still, the troll fought, lashing out with leg-arms and arm-legs, but blinded and deaf against two dragons the contest was hopeless.

She and DharSii stood far enough apart that they just might touch wingtips, making a perfectly equal triangle with the wildly swinging troll. They raised their heads in unison, lowered their fan-like *griff* to protect delicate tissue of ear and neck-hearts, and spat, eyes as slits with water-membranes down and nostrils tightly clenched.

The thin streams of oily-smelling flame made a hot, low roar of their own as they met at the troll, painting it in bright hues of blue, red, orange and yellow. Black smoke added a delicate, spiderweb framing to the inferno of sizzling flesh and sputtering flame.

They had it well aflame before it could pick itself up from the stony slope. It still writhed about horribly as the heat consumed muscle.

Big-footed rabbits fled in panic from the heat, which set puddles of water a-sizzle and cracked rock. Birds shot out of the patches of yellow-and-white flowered meadow about the mountainside.

The dragons ignored them, leaning against each other and crossing necks as they caught their breath. Spreading dark smoke seemed to stain the iron-colored clouds above like blood dark against a sword's edge.

The stench of burning troll was as bad as Wistala remembered it. Unpleasant business, but it had to be done if the Sadda-Vale's hatchlings, and dragons, were to eat the herds they and their blighter servants tended.

"You arrived just in time, my gem," DharSii said. "Long-fingers had one more trick behind his ears for me."

"Next time, let me follow the troll-tracks while you watch from the skies."

"Trolls interest me," DharSii said. "Look at them, my jewel. In form and function they're like nothing else in the world."

"Couldn't the same be said of dragons?" Wistala asked.

"Well, there are great birds, as you know, the Rocs. I've seen art in bestiaries of two-limbed dragons, wyverns, though they appear to be incapable of breathing fire, but the record is vague on that matter and there's no way to settle the matter, as they appear to be extinguished from our world."

"I wish the same could be said for trolls."

DharSii panted. Wistala let him breathe, catching his breath as he talked. "The interesting thing about trolls is the ancient hominid books have no record of them. There's plenty on dragons, Rocs, even fanciful creatures like winged lions. Anything that carries off livestock and a hunter here and there is bound to be the subject of some interest. Yet the best dwarf compilers of arcana are mute on trolls, which have huge appetites and are very difficult to corner and kill."

"I know. Mossbell was plagued by one when I was a drakka."

She'd grown up on a gentle elf's lands. Rainfall had been like a father to her after she'd lost her own to war with the Wheel of Fire dwarves.

"Odd that they have no relatives. Think of all the varieties of fish in the sea, they're broadly similar in form. Reptiles, cats big and little. The insects that live in and above the earth, the variety of four-legged herbivores, rodents, two-legged hominids, come in a range of forms. Where are the smaller troll cousins, the heavier ones, the ones adapted to living in the surf, as seals and sea-lions have?"

Wistala found the question interesting but the need for discussing it curious. DharSii was a dragon of strange obsessions, perhaps this was the reason he'd never quite fit in anywhere—the Lavadome, here in the Sadda-Vale, or while serving hominids as a mercenary warrior. She found it charming. In all her travels among the beasts, hominids, and dragons of the earth she'd never found anyone quite like him. Powerful but open and friendly, intelligent but not pompous—well, rarely pompous— well-traveled and experienced but still full of a young drake's wonder.

"Odd, too, that they don't appear to communicate, socialize. I'm not even sure how they mate, or if they do."

"They plant a young in a corpse, something big and meaty. I saw a young one once, in a piece of a whale,"

Wistala said. She'd cleaned out the troll's cave after disposing of the troll. Bad business, killing young, but she'd regretted the necessity, not the result. Without the troll, the lands around Mossbell were prospering.

"What's in its hands?" DharSii sniffed. "My jewel, you didn't tell me you were wounded."

"I wasn't. A bruise or—"

"This is dragonscale, in its claws. Look, there's another at that mouth-vent orifice. Green."

"Green? The only other female here is Aethleethia. You don't suppose—"

"Aethleethia hunt trolls? Not even if our hatchlings were starving. Oh, I'm sorry—"

They had an agreement not to speak of the hatchlings as theirs. Too much pain in that. Better to pretend, like the rest of the Sadda-Vale, that Aethleethia had laid the eggs.

Not that there weren't still issues with their upbringing.

DharSii and AuRon had almost come to blows about having the hatchlings fight. DharSii believed the tradition, being based on instinct, was part of a dragon's natural heritage and should be respected.

Finally her brother RuGaard, crippled in his front *sii* since the hatchling duel with AuRon, pleaded with Aethleethia and her mate NaStirath. NaStirath was a silly dragon who treated everything as a joke and had no opinion, though Wistala would always be grateful to her, but Aethleethia, who'd been taking counsel from DharSii all her life, defied him.

"The more hatchlings, the better for us," she'd said.

Giving up her eggs to Aethleethia rankled. Wistala would have liked nothing better than to care for her own hatchlings, but her own position, and her brothers' as refugees from the Dragon Empire in the Sadda-Vale, demanded her to accept the bitter bargain.

Scabia, with some eggs around her in the great round emptiness at Vesshall at last, could not care less how Wistala spent her time once the eggs came. She could spend all the time she liked with DharSii, even though publicly she was NaStirath's mate.

She even suspected she and DharSii could appear openly as mates, but the suspicion wasn't strong enough for her to engage in what a human might call "rocking the boat." Too much depended on Scabia's goodwill toward her and her brothers.

"So if it didn't come from you, who does this scale belong to?"

"Let's find out," Wistala said. "We followed the troll-tracks in one direction, I think we may go in the other equally easily."

"Happily. The sooner we leave this smell behind, the sooner my neck will recover."

"Poor little drake. Good thing you're so taut, being stiff-necked about everything was good training."

"*Ha-hem*," DharSii grunted.

The trail gave out halfway up the mountain.

"Now what?" Wistala asked.

DharSii answered her by inflating his long lungs

and bellowing. His bellow was loud enough, she tracked echoes even from the other side of the lake.

"That may even bring RuGaard running," Wistala said.

A faint cry answered.

They found the troll-cave, a little quarter-moon cut in the rock. DharSii made it through easily enough, but Wistala had to twist to fit. She had always been a muscular dragon-dame, stronger than either of her brothers.

They found the source of the green scale. She was a dragon familiar to Wistala, her own sister removed by mating through RuGaard. Incredibly, it was Ayafeeia, of the Imperial Line, one of the most devoted-to-duty dragonelles Wistala had ever known. She'd pledged herself hearts-and-spirit to the Firemaids and had led them in battle after battle.

Wistala couldn't imagine what kind of catastrophe would take Ayafeeia from her comrades.

Now she lay pinned by a great boulder put across her neck, trapping her on her side in the cave.

Wistala put her spine under the rock, ready to carefully shift it off her former commander in the Firemaids, when DharSii grunted and pointed with his tail.

A horrible sort of leech clung to Ayafeeia's torn-away skin. It was a newborn troll, or at least that's what Wistala guessed it was, it resembled a full-grown troll about as much as a tadpole resembled a frog.

It looked to be in the process of burrowing under her skin.

"What do we do?" Wistala asked.

"Get it out, please," Ayafeeia said. "I think the troll put it there, I thought it was eating me at first. I can feel it moving."

"Grip it with your teeth, Wistala," DharSii said.

She did so. Ayafeeia screamed in pain.

"It's tearing into me. Biting!"

"This is going to hurt. Prepare yourself," DharSii said, extending his sharpest and most delicate *sii*.

Wistala had to close the eye facing him. She heard more cries from Ayafeeia and the splatter of dragon-blood striking the floor of the cavern.

"If I die, there's a message—" Ayafeeia said.

"Go' eh," DharSii said through locked teeth.

She heard him spit something out and opened the eye facing him. The troll-tadpole lay on the floor, giving a residual twitch now and then.

"And I thought the smell was bad! I shall never get this out of my mouth," DharSii said, spitting *torf*s of flame in an effort to burn out the taste. "They taste like no other flesh."

"That bad?" Ayafeeia managed.

"I'd rather eat poison ants," DharSii said.

Wistala shifted the rock.

"Thank you," Ayafeeia groaned, able to raise her head.

"Wistala, find some dwarfsbeard for this," DharSii said. "I believe I saw some on the downed tree where we first saw the troll tracks. Who knows what kind of filth this thing left in the wound."

"In a moment. What do you need to tell us, Ayafeeia? Why did you come here? What's happened to the Firemaids?"

"Lavadome. Tearing itself . . . apart. Firemaids—broken up," Ayafeeia managed.

Had she gone mad from the pain?

"We can talk later," DharSii said. "Let's see to the wound."

Wistala squeezed herself out of the troll cave and flew downslope.

She, who'd as Queen-Consort once directed the defense of the Lavadome against an invasion, who'd held the Red Mountain pass with a handful of Firemaids against the Ironrider hordes, now waged campaigns against trolls and hurried to find dwarfsbeard to patch a painful but minor wound.

The terrible methodology of war, the chaos and life-and-death decision making, the ceremonies over the dead and the praise to the heroic living . . .

She didn't miss any of it one bit.

She'd so much rather be trading philosophy with DharSii after a good dinner, or watching birds go about their clockwork routines, or trying her voice at poetry.

Alighting at the fallen tree, she searched for the ropy mass of dwarfsbeard. Yes, there it was, a thick tangle like hair run wild on an ancient dwarf. When broken and pulled apart, the thick white glue, like a thicker and stickier dandelion milk, acted on wounds, both cleaning them and speeding healing.

Unlike on her long-ago errands with her father to gather dwarfsbeard, she simply broke off the rooted end of the trunk, thick where water was pooling and rotting out the wood, and flew back holding the piece of tree tight under her chest. They could pluck it off the stump at leisure.

She returned and found Ayafeeia unconscious.

"Just as well," DharSii said. "With that skin missing and torn, it must be painful. She won't have an easy recovery."

"I doubt she'll be able to move," Wistala said. "We'll have to fly some blighters up here to tend to her wounds and sew her up again."

"This is my old warwing Imfamnia's sister, is it not?" DharSii asked.

"Her name's Ayafeeia. Her Firemaids rescued me from the demen."

"Was she part of the conspiracy against RuGaard?" DarSii asked.

"She's never been interested in politics. She's in charge of the Firemaids. Really in charge, I mean, back when I served as Queen-Consort I was their chief by tradition."

"Strange of her to leave them, then, if there's war building," DharSii said.

"I'd heard from more than one dragon that the reason my brother had any success at all in the Lavadome is that he wasn't part of any faction. No one could tell which line of dragons he sprang from, and he favored none, so they accepted his rule. The new Tyr and his Queen must not be quite so acceptable."

"Oooh, glad that's over," a new, high-pitched voice squeaked.

DharSii and Wistala turned and sniffed.

A huge, leathery bat emerged from behind Ayafeeia's ear like a groundhog coming out of its hole.

"Beggin' your pardon, your worship. M'name's Larb, one of Tyr RuGaard's faithful servants. Oooh, I'm chilled, no bat was ever meant to fly so high, I'm frozen from ear-tip to fantail. I'm not askin' too much by supposin' you could—"

"Don't listen to him," the exhausted dragonelle said, opening a bloodshot eye. "He's one of your brother's dragon-blooded bats."

"Then he can leave off begging us and go to work on your wound," Wistala said. "No opening up a fresh vein while you're in there, either, you little flying rat, or I'll toast you with some mushrooms."

"No need for threats, now," Larb said, scuttling behind Ayafeeia's crest for cover. "I'll lick the wound clean, I will. Jes' I'm so stiff and sore from the cold of the airs."

The bat scooted across Ayafeeia's flank and buried its nose in the wound, licking and snipping ragged flesh with sharp little snaggleteeth.

Bat saliva, Wistala had learned, brought a pleasant numbness to minor wounds.

"We'll need to close that up as soon as possible, dwarfsbeard or no," DharSii said. "Perhaps, Ayafeeia, you can make it out into the light. Fresh air and what passes for sunlight around here will help keep it clean until we can get you stitched up. I know your instinct is to retreat to a cave to lick your wounds, but in the interests of hygiene—"

"My love," Wistala interrupted. "Your turn to run for help. Go back to the hall and get some blighters who can stitch wounds, won't you?"

"Of course," DharSii said. "I shall return with help before the sun peaks."

He exited and Wistala listened to the fading beats of his wings before returning to Ayafeeia. She nosed more dwarfsbeard into the trail left by the cleaning bat.

Ayafeeia winced as the bat incautiously planted a wing on raw muscle beneath torn-away skin.

"What brought you such a distance, through cold and winter storm and danger?" Wistala asked, both curious and eager to divert her relative by mating from the bat's not-so-tender ministrations.

Ayafeeia managed to raise her head. "Another civil war's begun. Struggle for power between NiVom and Imfamnia against the twins. Skotl kills Wyrr. Assassin hominids kill protectors in their resorts. It will be the death of all of us."

It all sounded dreadfully familiar.

More war, more deaths, more pain. RuGaard would be in agony of the fate of poor Nilrasha. And AuRon, on his way to one of his secret meetings with Natasatch—what was he flying into?

All that could wait. Once more, she had duty to attend. It wouldn't do to have Ayafeeia fly all this way just to die on their doorstep.

E. E. KNIGHT

DRAGON FATE

BOOK SIX OF THE AGE OF FIRE

Scattered across a continent, three dragon siblings are among the last of a dying breed—the final hope for their species' survival.

After fighting a war that cost each of them kingdoms, friends and family, and their honor and glory, they have removed themselves from the troubles of the world. But the order they fought to establish is falling apart. Ancient sorceries have been awakened. Dragons battle dragons. And men are taking up arms against their winged overlords. Now, the three must unite once more to save dragonkind from extinction, before the chaos and fire of war consumes them all...and the world with them.

R0079